MANOR
ON THE
VIRIDIAN SEA

ELEANOR P. SAM

A Novel

ISALEA
PUBLISHING

Content Warning: Eating disorder, Fat-phobia, racism

This is a work of fiction. Any names, places, organizations and events are used fictitiously. Any resemblance to persons living or dead is a creation of the author's imagination and purely coincidental.

Manor on the Viridian Sea
Copyright @2023 Eleanor P Sam
Published by: Isalea Publishing
Toronto, Ontario, Canada
Cover Design by: Dorian Danielsen

ISBN 978-1-7782538-2-9 (Paperback)
ISBN 978-1-7782538-3-6 (Epub)

First edition

ISALEA
PUBLISHING

Men were instrumental figures in the early years of my life and many continue to be important to me in the most beautiful ways. Their love in the present, and remembered from the past, has guided, sustained, and held me up through this mortal existence and its many storms. They include my father, Daniel, and my godfather, James, who taught me that love has no colour. This story is dedicated to these men, and to Caribbean men like them.

"Sometimes yu go looking fuh gold but yu find diamonds instead" ~ Eleanor P. Sam

ISALEA
PUBLISHING

Chapter 1

Jemma

My fingers tapped a staccato of small sharp sounds on Jack's walnut desk. The rhythm grew faster as my anxiety built. It was 11:30 a.m., and Johannes, the realtor overseeing the bid for our dream manor at auction had promised to be in touch by 11:00. Why hadn't he called; what did it mean?

Tension and excitement galloped like wild horses in my stomach. I paced between the living room and bathroom, my silent cell phone gripped in my sweaty palms. I glanced at the tall windows of the Manhattan penthouse, and the reflection of my five-foot, seven-inch house-coated figure, crowned with dirty blond curls, greeted me.

My mind travelled to the Caribbean Sea and the beachfront manor house on the sunny island of Sierra Majestic, assessed at $3.2 million and placed on auction at

$2.2 million. Our realtor's warning repeated in my head, *Jack and Jemma, you guys should expect a multiple bid scenario. It always happens for homes in these locations listed by Top Tier International Realty.*

In our search for sun and sea locations, I had seen many attractive properties. But there was something special about this one. Time slowed and then stood still as the manor's image filled my desktop screen. Like an old photograph of a forgotten childhood friend, it kindled a sense of familiarity. This was, of course, crazy because I'd never been to the Caribbean.

The high-pitched ring of the phone shattered my daydream, and Jack's transatlantic accent filled the receiver. "Any word yet?"

"No. I would've messaged you had I heard."

"I assumed there was a glitch of some kind, and you couldn't reach me. I'm late for my 4:30, but I'll keep my phone on vibrate." Then he was gone.

Ping. A notification from WhatsApp. Shit, it was Johannes. The message read: Auction underway $2.2M. I hit the waving hand emoji to signify my agreement. Another message: $2.5M. The numbers flashed on my screen in swift succession. Oh crap, this was moving faster than I'd imagined. It had to slow down. Then $3M lit up the screen. I hit the emoji again, and the next message jumped to $3.5M.

My pulse throbbed in my throat. *Stop, Jemma! You've got to stop. You agreed to no more than 3.2 million, and you've gone over.* I heard a gentle voice whisper in my head … *'Go for it, Jemma.'* I closed my eyes and hit the emoji. My final bid: 4.5 million dollars.

A few seconds dragged by, then the clapping hand emoji popped up. It was done! An overpriced luxury manor on the Caribbean Island of Sierra Majestic was ours. But how to break the news to Jack?

I paced around the room, my fisted knuckles bouncing against my mouth. I let a few minutes go by, and then sent him five rapid text messages:

Why aren't you answering?

Where are you?

I'm stopping now.

I refuse to go any further.

Shit, $4.5M.

Finally, after about thirty excruciating seconds, my phone rang.

"Jemma, no. We agreed to stay around $3.2M and nothing more. You know my money is tied up elsewhere."

"Oh crap, Jack, it's done. The clapping emoji from Johannes came up about twenty seconds ago. It's ours, Jack… yours." I caught myself becoming overly confident and hoped he hadn't noticed. Trying for humility, I continued: "I didn't get your messages, honey, there must have been a technological glitch. I'm so sorry."

Silence filled the phone line. *What was he thinking? What was happening? Say something, Jack.* Silence.

"Tell Johannes to call me. I'm still in meetings but will try to reach him as well. Let's see if we can work together to fix this mess." His voice was brittle with stress.

"I will. I'm sorry, sweetheart. I'll get on it right away. Be in touch."

I lay across the bed and imagined Jack sitting in his meeting, tense. He wasn't usually like that. I enjoyed watching him throw his head back, a grin stretching across his face, fists pumped in the air every time he closed a deal. I hoped he would soon see this transaction as a success. This beautiful man in his early sixties was twice my age and in phenomenal shape, his one hundred and eighty-five pounds proportioned on a six-foot two-inch frame. He sported a shock of thick stone-gray hair, that matched his eyes, and wore it combed away from his clean-shaven face: a face that made me think of strength but with a hint of sensitivity in his thin lips and ready smile.

Later that day, Jack reached Johannes, and after intense negotiations with the brokers and auctioneer, they settled on $4.2 million. When I spoke with Jack again, as my contribution, I offered to cover the day-to-day costs of living on the island. After a prolonged silence, he agreed.

I felt relief, closed my eyes, and mulled over how I had gotten to this place.

Ollie's image flooded my thoughts. Her great big grin and the excitement in her voice as she yelled 'Goal!' It's how she would've seen this purchase. I wished I could share the news with her.

Chapter 2

Jemma

About two decades prior, my sister, Olympia, and I had grown up in relative affluence in Toronto's Kingsway neighbourhood. We'd had the benefit of a well-rounded education at Havergal College, the largest private girls' school in the city. With old fashioned gothic ivy-covered walls, it sat on over twenty acres of green space, surrounded by tennis courts and woodland paths. Ollie was my sister's nickname. We attended the liberal arts programme from junior through senior school, and as a lover of the arts, I did well. We had our share of the good life, including international summer travel experiences with our classmates. I fell madly in love with Italy's old-world charm and told my parents I'd move there the first chance I got.

Ollie was tall, slender, and olive complexioned. She hated her thick, dark curly hair and wore it under a baseball cap every chance she got. I was lighter, with porcelain skin, and curvier. My round face and full lips were a contrast to Ollie's angularity and thinness.

A talented hockey player, Ollie was a top line centre on our school team. At an intervarsity game against the Animaada'e Girls Hockey Team from Northern Ontario, my dad and I sat in the best seats in the arena on Bloor Street bundled in dark green bomber jackets and yellow earmuffs. It was -6 Celsius, but with the wind chill, it felt like -15. Ollie had talked this game up so much, we had to come watch her outsmart and outplay the other team and make their new goalie's debut a nightmare by putting many pucks in the net.

"We're going to the provincials," was her daily morning chant over her oatmeal and fruit smoothies. "That was a breakfast of champions," she'd say as she hopped off her stool, grabbed her knapsack, and headed for Dad's car. "Brush your teeth," mother would yell, and our upcoming star would rush to the half bath near the garage door, swish some minty mouthwash in her mouth, and jump into the backseat in under thirty seconds. "Skill and heart always get the job done," she would announce with a giggle as she buckled herself in. Dad would hit the remote, the door would lift, and we'd cruise out of the garage on our way to school and him to work.

This was an important game, as the teams were tied two games apiece. The first period was scoreless, but both teams found the back of the net in the second period. Ollie's speed amped up as she carried the puck across the red line, weaving around the other team's forwards and breaking across the blue line towards the goal. But then, in a blink of an eye, the opposing defence misjudged a full-on body check and sailed into the boards instead of stopping Ollie. The player's helmet flew off, rolling across the ice as she lay crushed against the side of the rink. Cheers rose from fans in the green and gold sections. But when the player lay still for a few seconds and the referees skated over to her, Ollie joined them and almost immediately her shrill voice rang through the arena "Dad, Dad ... get my dad."

A commotion ensued as paramedics rushed in, placed the player onto a board, and escorted her off the field. A shaken Ollie skated over to us and announced that the player was bleeding from her right eye. Dad hurriedly followed the paramedics, and Ollie slowly skated back to the benches, too upset to go back on the ice. The Northern Ontario team won, despite their injured player. Mother picked us up from the arena at the end of the game as Dad rode with the paramedics and player in the ambulance to the hospital.

On our drive home, Ollie was mostly quiet. She hardly touched her dinner and later came into my room and sat on my bed, her face sullied with worry. I told her what had happened had been an accident. But she stared blankly for a while and then got up and quietly paced the hallway between our rooms. When dad pulled into the garage about an hour later, Ollie bolted down the stairs and accosted him in the mud room.

"Is she okay, Dad? Will she go blind? Will she be able—"

"She'll be fine, and the small cut on the side of her temple will heal. I talked to her, and they're keeping her overnight for observation to monitor for concussive symptoms."

The next morning at breakfast, Ollie asked Dad to check on the player's status in the hospital. If she was still admitted, my sister wanted to visit her. I learned something about Ollie during this experience, under her tough 'must win' exterior, she had a sweet, caring soul.

Our dad had inherited property in Cape Town from his parents, and we took frequent trips to this South African port city. My sister, an animal lover, especially treasured our safari summer vacations. During ice skating practice, Ollie liked to compare herself to the African gazelle, gracious and swift. On safari once, she spent hours watching the animals sprinting across the savannah or pronking into the air.

It was during one of these trips that Dad discovered Ollie sprawled across the bathroom floor, face covered in her vomit. By the time he'd found her, she had been gone for a while, and the warmth had left her body—yet he still tried to revive her.

I remember sitting on the couch, the air in the room close and heavy, my mother's face a bloodless mask. The ambulance came and Dad showed the paramedics to the bathroom. Then came muttering sounds and silence followed by metal squeaks and the sight of a gurney with a white shape on it being trundled out the door. Dear God, my sister!

Our parents had been out for dinner and dancing at a local sailing academy fundraiser. As the older sister, I was in charge by proxy. Ollie had gone next door to hang out with our neighbour's kids, and I'd chosen to relax and watch a movie. I fell soundly asleep.

After drinking to excess, Ollie had come home and must have binged on everything in the fridge. She might have attempted to purge and could have choked on her vomit and passed out. I couldn't believe I hadn't heard her – hadn't been there for her when she needed me. God, I hoped she hadn't suffered much. An image of her small frame lying crumpled on the bathroom floor brought hot tears rolling down my cheeks.

The coroner raised questions about undiagnosed bulimia nervosa; our parents realised that the intestinal problems she had complained about to avoid various family commitments had been real and not imagined. But now it was too late.

Ollie was my closest friend, and when she left us, I was devastated and suffered in silence. Our parents had opposing views about the cause of her sudden tragic death, a death that signalled what must have been a long and painful struggle within my sister. Words between them flew like daggers in our home.

"How did you miss this, Jasper? The man who jets around the world giving sight to the blind, misses the signs of desperation and cries for help from his own child."

"So now you're blaming me, after all your sermons on body image and the perils of weight gain, you blame me. Think about it …"

"I don't have to think, you failed to see all the medical signs and symptoms. You were too busy looking elsewhere for problems, and clearly one was right here staring you in the eyes."

"Enough with the eye references. The child is dead because of her apparent obsession with control. Blaming me won't bring her back."

"Just accept it …" Mom screamed and ran from the room.

I lay in bed at night scared they would both accuse me of not looking out for my little sister and angry at Ollie for keeping this secret which took her away from me. How could I spend so much time with her and not know what she was up to? I assumed she could eat whatever she wanted and never gain any weight. But all along, she was taking dangerous risks that had now caused her to lose her life.

Our father had Ollie cremated and brought the urn home for a small private service. A few of our friends and close relatives attended her funeral. I watched my parents put on a show of solidarity. Not having attended a memorial service before, I took cues from the adults. I swallowed my tears, pursed my lips, and clenched my teeth; my face hurt.

Right when my chest was about to explode from holding my breath, I saw her—Ollie's almost twin, only much older. She sat sobbing quietly in a corner, wads of tissues squished in her right palm—wiping her tear-stained face and the snot that ran from her tiny nose. Who was she? And why wasn't anyone comforting her?

I leaned over to Dad. "Who is that woman in the white lace blouse and black pencil skirt?"

He didn't look over to where I had signalled. Instead, he took a deep breath, glanced over at my mother, and exhaled like a deflating balloon.

"Tell her Jasper, or I will," my mother whispered, her bloodshot eyes locked onto dad's.

"Okay, okay," he replied. And, without looking over at me, he whispered, "that's Ramona …"

"Who's Ramona?" I blurted out and searched his face for clues. I found none.

Then he looked directly at me and softly said, "She's Ollie's biological mum."

Time stopped. Did I hear him correctly? My eyes leapt from one parent to the next and my shoulders tensed.

"Ollie's mum! She has another mum; how could that be?"

My face grew hotter than the midday sun in July. The death was already surreal—and I couldn't process this new information.

"My God, Dad …" I began, but Reverend Jenkins tapped Dad's shoulder and interrupted the awkward moment between us.

"Dr Worley, we're ready to begin," he whispered.

I sat through the service vacillating between grief and shock. How could they keep this secret from me? And is it really true? Maybe Ollie knew. I wanted to ask her so badly, so I stared at the urn and spoke to her in my head. *Ollie, is it true that you weren't really my biological sister —that the same blood didn't course through our veins?* Silent tears tracked down my cheeks.

Dad had let me select the urn, and I chose a Danish designed chartreuse vial. That particular shade of green was Ollie's favourite, and the design, an acknowledgement of my mother's ancestral country. My parents chose to adorn it with fresh ivy as a nod to our private school. A photograph of a grinning Ollie decked out in her green and gold hockey uniform sat next to the urn on a small table draped in black.

Mother, Dad, and I wore black with a chartreuse ribbon pinned on our chests. It dawned on me that Ollie's other mum should have had a ribbon too, but only a few were created for immediate family. As we waited for Reverend Jenkins to take the podium, the organist played Brahms Lullaby—a request from Ollie's biological mum, I later learned. I sobbed quietly throughout the scripture readings, the sermon, and the prayers for the dead. I have no memory of the eulogy my dad gave. Apparently, he spoke about the spontaneity of youth and undesired outcomes.

The service concluded, and I stood in place for a moment, then gradually walked over to Ramona. Suddenly, my feet were like cement, arms numb, and lips stuck together like glue. I was immobile with dread. As I unpinned the ribbon from my jacket lapel, a thought raced through my head: *Will she think I was offering her something trivial or would she know the ribbon's special meaning? How could she?* I swallowed hard and held my hand out. Ramona looked up slowly, and Ollie's penetrating dark eyes stared back at me. She took the ribbon, and I nodded, and scurried away. Another moment in her presence, and I would've completely lost it.

That night after all our visitors had left, I lay in bed, eyes closed and wet with tears, floating on waves of sadness. Ollie's face and voice returned to me over and over, our times together replaying in my imagination. The sister who was not a sister and more than a sister, a friend who was more than a friend, my other half, my lost one, lost twice: once through a lie and then again through death.

Later, dad came to my room. He sat at the edge of my bed, shoulders jittery, hands grasping and ungrasping each other. His customary smile was missing, and his five-foot-nine-inch frame slouched like Rodin's *The Thinker*.

"We didn't want you growing up alone," he whispered, his eyes glassy. I watched his Adam's apple move up and down as he swallowed.

"From the moment we saw your sister, we loved her, and your mum chose to adopt her. Are you okay, Jem?"

I was in anguish from losing my sister. "*I'm not okay,*" I screamed inside.

"It would have been nice to know before now; everything's a bloody mess, Dad!" I pulled the duvet up to my neck.

He sat quietly for a few more minutes, eyes fixed on the floor, as though searching the polished wood for a solution to the issue at hand. Then he turned, looked at me, and whispered, "I'm sorry." Soon after, he eased himself up and left my room.

A disturbing idea snuck into my head: was I also adopted? What if I was? I pushed the speculation away; it would be dangerous to feed it. I shifted my thinking back to Ollie. Had she known or even suspected that she was somebody else's kid? If she knew, how had it shaped her?

Doubt crept back in, and frightening questions filled my head. What if I'm not who I think I am, how could I find out? And would Dad be honest with me—now that he no longer had Ollie. It was why she and I looked so different; we weren't related. It made sense. Dear God, maybe we were both adopted. But how could I know for sure?

My sister always wanted to please our mother and never rebelled. Maybe she knew that she wasn't her biological mother and was scared she'd be sent back to her other family. At times though, Ollie taunted me endlessly and did things she wouldn't let mother see. She was, after all, the good kid.

Yet, at times, Ollie was that annoying young sibling who when she couldn't find her hair bands, leggings, or socks, snuck across the hall into my room and helped herself to my stuff. She never cared that they were my last clean pair of socks. She stole my lip balm innumerable times when hers was finished.

Ollie wore nothing larger than a size one, though zero was her target. I learned early that I couldn't compete, and a size six or eight was an okay goal to maintain. Mother's friends referred to me as the plump one. My dad however told me that I had a womanly figure, and curves were a good thing. Bless his heart.

On one of our trips to the Muskoka cottage country with my mother, when I was ten and Ollie eight, we received an unforgettable lesson. We'd wanted her to stop at Weber's for burgers and ice cream, not because we were hungry, but because our dad always stopped.

"How far till Weber's, Mum?" Ollie began the chant.

"Can't be far. We've already passed Barrie," I chimed in. From my window I'd seen the gas station where Dad always filled up.

"Girls, we're not stopping for burgers. We're going straight to Port Carling for a healthy lunch."

"But, Mum… please? Dad always—"

"I'm not Dad, and burgers are fatty, and fat is unhealthy and ugly. To be pretty, healthy, and have your choice of boys when you grow up, you girls must learn to eat small portions, exercise each day, and weigh yourselves every other day. Fat is a curse."

We gave up our burger quest; we'd lost the battle before it began. And our mother nattered on.

"Let me tell you girls a story. I grew up in the country, and we all ate great food fresh from the farm: milk, eggs, butter, chicken, lots of meat, beef, and pork. My mother even made her own bacon. We ate some vegetables, and a whole lot of pies—apple, strawberry, and rhubarb. Can't say we wanted for anything, and our diet showed in our sizes. Everybody was chunky.

"When I moved to Toronto for university, I had a strange awakening. All the girls in my classes looked like the rakes in my father's barn: skinny, pale, and tall. But I noticed they all had boyfriends. No one acknowledged me until my second year at school, and ninety pounds had slid off my frame. Soon I became quite popular with the other students, and it stayed that way throughout the rest of my university years. I've remained slim and never looked back. So yes, fat is a curse, girls. Stay slim, stay healthy, stay beautiful."

I looked out the window as the car cruised by Weber's and towards healthier options. I still loved Weber's, and at ten years old, I was already ninety pounds. Too late for me, but still time for Ollie.

That night I had the first of what became a recurring dream that saturated my sleep. In bed at our cottage on Lake Rosseau, I see myself prostrate on the living room floor, my eyes squeezed shut, I feel the oppressive weight of the soles of my mother's feet move across my back, then along my spine to my neck, and the top of my head. Pinned down, I am immobile, my breath suspended, waiting, waiting. My blood thumps loudly in my head. I'm flooded with shame as I shrink to make myself smaller. My body melts into a tiny version of me, and I breathe again, slowly… but then I wake up and find all of me still intact.

Upon reflection, that summer trip to Muskoka began my path to self loathing, although friends at school and in our neighbourhood, plus television and magazines did reinforce the slim-girl image. I felt shame about my body. But I only came to the realization of how destructive and unhealthy this emotion was, after I had moved away from one of its major sources—my mother.

After Ollie's death, friends at school, either kept their distance or asked questions about the type of drug that caused her passing. There were no illicit drugs involved, just alcohol. But gossip was so much more delicious than finding out the truth about what really happened.

Days turned into weeks, turned into months, and the pain of Ollie's loss loomed like a dark shadow in our home and our school halls. But why was I remembering all of this now? Because Ollie would be the first person with whom I would have shared the purchase of Seaview. *Now she was gone. God how I missed her.*

Chapter 3

Jemma

My thoughts returned to Jack. About a year and a half before, I met him at a party on Lake Como, just off Bellagio. It was at an event where you're invited to meet the "who's who" and where the wealthy came together to make deals. I'd planned to meet an old acquaintance there, but he hadn't shown up.

Jack watched, and then flirted with me from the minute I entered the rear deck of the million-dollar yacht, as though daring me to look over. And I did, with what I hoped was a shy, girlish smile. So began the play between us. Later that evening, this handsome stranger dressed in a light-blue linen shirt tucked under a navy Armani blazer, a pair of light brown trousers, and matching Santoni penny loafers—a vision of striking elegance and confidence—strode over to me. Lips pursed, I raised my eyes to meet his.

"Please let me see more of that sultry part of you," were his first words. "It's beautiful, don't hide it."

"Thanks, but that's a lame pickup line, not one a refined woman would fall for," I replied.

"Who says it's a line? Pouty and luscious are just two of the words I'd use to describe your lips." He took two steps back and swept me up in his gaze. A warmth rose in my cheeks. Without rising, I returned his scrutiny.

"You see," he continued, "I love old Hollywood, not just the cinema but the lifestyle, and in you I see a mix of June Wilkinson and Sophia Loren." I wasn't sure who June Wilkinson was but was all ears by this point.

"Let me sit close and drink in your loveliness."

Flattered, I indulged his wish and moved my handbag from the nearby barstool to make room for him.

"This might just cost you," I said, flirting back.

"And it might just be quite rewarding," he replied, with a smirk. "I'm Jack."

"Let me think on it," I replied. "Jemma."

Up close, this man was stunning. His eyes, soft yet piercing, sent a quiver down my spine. We sat next to each other, sipping our drinks saying nothing, but having a full conversation with only our eyes. His gaze moved from my lips to my breasts, which were tucked tightly into a white knit blouse, my nipples slightly raised beneath. Occasionally our eyes met, and I slowly began to melt from the inside out. With legs crossed and arms fidgeting, I tried desperately to maintain composure, but I was quickly losing ground.

Our playful exchange lasted for about ten minutes, then his thigh brushed up against mine, and his hand landed on my knee. I scanned the room quickly from left to right, hoping no one was paying attention to us. Everyone was occupied, and I looked back at my suitor with a reassuring smile. He quickly chugged down his drink, and taking my hand in his, we left the bar in silence. We made our way along small, carpeted corridors and past portholes, and with a quick scan of a card, we entered cabin number five.

The sudden light revealed a room filled with rich furnishings and the smell of leather, polished wood, and brocade fabrics. We fell into an embrace, our mouths hungrily seeking each other's, his palm cupping and fondling my breasts, my fingers kneading his firm backside. Our clothing swiftly discarded, we slid onto a king-sized bed draped in luxurious bedding and spent the rest of the night in unbridled pleasure as Lake Como slowly rose and fell beneath us.

Our first real conversation happened over a room-service breakfast.

"I hope you enjoyed your sleepover, dear lady," Jack said, leaning in and kissing me.

"I did, and how about you?" I traced his lips with my index finger and returned his kiss.

"I surely did. I'm surprised such a beautiful woman is unattached." He peered over the rim of his glasses. "Are you?"

"Currently, I am." I hoped he'd say he was too. He didn't.

"Wonderful news! Would you like to join me for drinks and a bite later tonight? I do like your company and hope you like mine."

"As it turns out, I am free," I responded as casually as I could, though, perhaps, a bit too quickly to sound that preoccupied.

He smiled. "What do you say we seal our liking for each other with a kiss?"

He didn't wait for my answer, passionately kissing me. We left the cabin and agreed to meet later at Enoteca Bianchi, one of Jack's favourite spots.

That evening, I walked along cobblestone streets, the small shops and balconied house fronts hung with flowers, all overlooking the lake. Finally, I reached the stone staircase and found the doorway with a giant corkscrew he'd told me to look for. A small iron trellis laden with green plastic grapes served as a canopy for the secluded wine bar. The room inside was moody, set with a handful of cosy tables – a shelved display of its wines slotted into the back wall.

"So how do you spend your time on Bellagio?" I asked, after we'd settled in.

"Usually in consultation meetings, overseeing designs and renovations for a plethora of construction projects across Northern Italy. I'm an architectural engineer. And how about you?" He tilted his head and waited for my answer. My day-to-day existence had no such importance, except for the occasional meeting with one or two of my customers, but I felt the need to make them sound just as important.

"I attend runway events to stay abreast with the latest fashion and lifestyle trends. It keeps my boutiques across North America timely."

"Oh, how many of these do you own?" he asked, honing in on the proprietary aspect of my response.

"I don't own them, Jack, though that would be wonderful. I'm a fashion supplier. I provide the latest and the best merchandise to specialty stores."

"I see, like a buyer."

At almost thirty years old, I ran a small online fashion business supplying intricate Italian silks and leather items to modest start-up fashion houses in New York, Montreal, and Los Angeles.

"Are you American?" he continued. "I'm trying to place your accent."

"I'm Canadian, born and raised in Toronto, and I didn't know I had an accent." I smiled.

"So, how did you get to—"

"I moved to Italy for school," I said, interrupting him. "College in Genoa." It was all I was willing to share, and Jack seemed content with my minimal disclosure. He smiled and nodded.

"How about you?"

"I'm British; I was born just outside London and emigrated to the US as a teenager with my parents."

Before he went on to tell me his life story, I cut to the chase. "Is there a woman in your life?" I asked abruptly. "I hate to be so direct, but…"

"You can be direct, and no, there isn't. My wife, Maggie, passed away just over a year ago after a short illness."

"Oh, I'm sorry," I whispered.

"Thank you," he replied.

"Do you have children?"

"No, there weren't any children; it was a mutual decision."

"Was Maggie English, American or …"

"She was American. Or as she would say, an American Hippie."

"How so?"

"Maggie grew up in Haight-Ashbury, a neighbourhood in the San Francisco area that embraced the Hippie culture."

"She must have been fun."

"She was."

"So, what do you do for fun now?" My boldness was paying off, and I liked it.

"Since Maggie passed, I've been fully immersed in my work and hardly come out to socialise."

"Well, I'm glad you did last night," I teased.

"Me too," he replied, sipping his Barolo.

Over a bottle of the full-bodied wine and an antipasto platter, I learned a bit more about Jack and liked what I heard. He was someone I could enjoy having in my life, especially his extravagant means—the kind of excess I'd fantasised about during the years I'd spent in boarding school. Not to mention Jack's contacts and financial backing could catapult my small business into a successful, upscale fashion house. My line boasted items from Italy's most distinctive cities, including Rome, Florence, Milan, Venice, and Capri.

I slept with Jack every night after our first meeting, so apart from work, he had time for only me. After only a few weeks, I'd moved into his flat on Bellagio and catered to his every need. And mine.

"Work's taking me to New York City for an extended period," he mentioned one evening at dinner.

"How long is extended?"

"I could be there for eight months to a year. Would you like to come and stay with me for a while?" We'd been together six months, and it was, in my mind, an appropriate next step.

"I'd be delighted to join you there. Who doesn't love New York?"

"I agree. Do you ever go back to Canada? You'll be close enough for trips over the border."

A lump caught in my throat.

"Canada isn't on my radar right now, but we'll see," I replied, eager to shift the conversation. "So, when do we leave?"

"I leave next week, but you can join me later."

New York is exciting, but troublingly close to Toronto— too close to my parents.

"I'll have to sublet, so will need a few weeks." I wasn't ready to run into my mother in the theatre district or browsing along Fifth Avenue; two of her favourite pastimes.

Less than twenty-four hours after our conversation, I found a new tenant for my apartment but waited a few days before telling Jack. I wanted to give the appearance that it required some effort to free myself from the rental.

Flying to New York on his tab meant business-class travel, civilised. My parents always travelled this way, and my first experience in economy on a flight from Toronto to Rome was horrifying. I recalled the cramped leg room, the snoring passenger in the seat ahead of me who reclined almost into my lap, and the passenger next to me who coughed and sneezed half the flight. I vowed never to repeat the sickening experience; I deserved better.

Two weeks after Jack left, I joined him on the Upper West Side of The Big Apple.

I was now a fixture in Jack's life, and his desire for me morphed into an emotional attachment, or at least that's how it seemed at the time. He sent me exquisite bouquets of yellow or white roses at least once a month, and on a few occasions, bought me luxurious pieces from Greenwich St. Jewelers. Jack became more affectionate, and foreplay between us was no longer rushed, but slow and prolonged.

While I brought my wants and love of adventure to the relationship, Jack taught me a lot. One night, walking home from dinner, I suggested some spontaneous skinny dipping in Central Park Lake, a tad too edgy for Jack.

"Jemma are you out of your mind?" he exclaimed, half kidding, half serious. "This is New York. Central Park? Hundreds of people are in and out at all hours. You can't go skinny dipping in there."

"Of course, we can …"

"We'll end up in jail for public nudity or what have you." The pitch of his voice rose with anxiety.

"My dear Jack," I said, trying to suppress a giggle. "Be vulnerable. Just think of the rush you'll get from taking the risk. You have to try it—come on."

I watched panic consume him and his face flush at the thought of showing his body in public.

"Look at me, I'm sweating." He mopped his forehead with the back of his hand.

I felt a rush of adrenaline as I peeled my clothes off right down to my underwear; the fall wind whispered across my buttocks and thighs, and my nipples hardened from the sudden chill. It was late October, and the leaves had begun to fall; a carpet of yellow, orange, and red blanketed the path leading towards the water. I took a few steps forward without him, and when I turned around, he was standing there without a stitch of clothing.

"Yes, Jack! Let's go, there's no turning back now!" I cheered, dipped my toes in, and then glided into the cool invigorating lake. He followed me cautiously, his head swivelling from left to right.

"It's crazy. I can't believe I'm doing this."

"But it's good though, isn't it? It's forbidden and we're doing it Jack, do you feel the high?"

"I feel a shiver; let's get out of here," he said with a nervous snicker.

I took his hand, and we waded back to dry land.

"Wasn't that exhilarating?" I said as I kissed him on the cheek.

"It was, but promise we'll keep this excitement to the bedroom? I don't know how much of it my heart could take," he held his chest and stifled a laugh.

Yes, Jack and I had lots of fun, and it had now led to an imminent move to a newly purchased property in the Caribbean. When he arrived in the United States from his overseas trip a few days later, Jack was less frustrated and more conciliatory about the purchase. He agreed to travel to the Caribbean in a few weeks to sign the final papers and take possession of the property. I showed my delight by taking us out to a luxurious dinner at Oceana on West 49th to celebrate our seaside purchase.

Chapter 4

Jemma

Two weeks later, we flew to the Caribbean by private jet. Javier, Jack's business partner and close friend, had given him access to his aircraft so we could get to Majestic and back over the weekend.

"I need to be back in New York to sign off on a major deal we've worked on for two years," Jack said.

It was my first time flying by private jet, and I was thrilled. "I bet it's going to be a classy aircraft."

"That it is. Javier has just upgraded from the Bombardier Challenger 300 to the 350."

"So, it's Canadian then? One of my dad's friends worked for them."

"Yes, Canadian engineered."

"This Javier must be loaded; and to be so generous?"

"It's business, mostly, with a bit of pleasure thrown in for good measure. Javier is much wealthier than I am, and yes, he's a very generous partner."

"Well, I'm happy to enjoy his generosity. Count me in."

He grinned. "Consider yourself in."

A slim medium-sized aircraft, much smaller than a Boeing 737, but larger than the sea plane that Dad and I had flown in over Garibaldi Provincial Park, sat on the runway. Its sleek gunmetal and white body shone against the sunrise of a fall morning in New York.

I climbed up the five steps and entered the passenger cabin. A warmth radiated throughout my body as I scrutinized my surroundings. Soothing earth tones wrapped the space. The sleek leather seats looked comforting, and large windows lit each side of the aisle.

The flight crew of three welcomed us on board with smiling faces, arms reaching to relieve us of jackets and valise, and a young attendant immediately took our drink orders as we settled into seats like recliner chairs. We both requested coffee and mimosas. I breathed in the luxury, entertaining myself with fantasies of wealth and privilege, hoping that one day we would also own one of these jets.

Amid a steady flow of meals, drinks, and online entertainment, the jet glided on its five-hour trip to the sunny isles. I dozed off and then awoke as the plane descended slowly through stacks of clouds to reveal an emerald island spreading out below, encircled by a blue-green sea so intense it almost hurt my eyes. The ground grew and expanded, dotted with colours and the shapes of trees and villages as we circled the airport. The runway appeared in the window and then disappeared from sight as the jet settled into a smooth descent, with a soft lurch and squeaking wheels signalling we were earthbound once again.

Coming to a stop after taxiing along the airstrip to the small terminal, the flight attendant's cheerful banter was lost as the door opened and the warm, heady breath of tropical air, full of fruit and floral smells, surged into the cabin. Welcome to Sierra Majestic!

A Volvo sport utility vehicle with Top Tier's imprint on its front door was parked near the hangar. A young male driver greeted us outside the terminal, and soon we headed up the steep streets out of town, the sail-flecked harbour far below as the vehicle climbed into the green hills of Majestic.

I was taken aback by the beauty of the island. The road cut through foliage that leaned over us on either side with red and yellow hibiscus, and orange, pink and purple bougainvillea. When we reached the manor, my heart melted. It was magnificent! The property had a sweeping 180-degree view of the Caribbean Sea, with the manor set back from terraced cliffs that stepped down to an expanse of beach where waves licked at yellow ribbons of sand. The sky, streaked here and there with clouds, was a blue dome above a restless sea, dotted with hints of white that danced and faded towards the remote horizon.

The garden needed attention. A combination of neglect, sun, and water had created clumps of dark green beach cabbage growing thick and weedlike in large sections. Yet, hopeful starlike pops of red and sometimes yellow or pink peered out from under the massive overgrowth. I later learned that these were the West Indian jasmine. And the clustered tongues of yellow and red poking out from large green leaves was the bromeliad. But all were smothered by coarse invaders. A rescue was in order.

There was a soothing breeze and melodic birdsong everywhere. Not even on the beaches of Cape Town, like Platboom with its soft white sand, rock pools, ostriches, and other exotic sea birds, had I experienced such a feast for the senses—a captivating blend of sights and sounds. I paused and inhaled deeply. I'd made the right decision for us. I knew it in my gut.

The first islanders we met were the Whittles, who welcomed us to the property.

Amanda Whittle's family had owned the manor for decades, and according to the brokers, this was the first sale outside their holdings on Sierra Majestic.

"You must be Jack Generson; we're Amanda and Sebastian," the petite blonde said, gazing at Jack and completely ignoring me.

Despite a perfect complexion, her face was unattractive; eyes like dark buttons set too close together, and a thin-lipped pursed mouth.

"Yeah, I'm Jack, and this is Jemma."

"Are you a fam... I mean, is this it, for your family?" she probed.

"Jemma is a friend, and we plan to spend a lot of time here." Jack smiled politely and nodded my way.

"Oh, forgive me. I didn't mean..." She appeared ruffled by his response.

It was apparent that at least a twenty-year age gap existed between us. Though significantly older, Jack looked at least ten years younger.

"Well, we welcome you both to Majestic." She batted her eyes and finally looked directly at me.

"Thank you," I replied. She was rude and bold, which I disliked.

"Will you join us for drinks and a bite at the club after you've wrapped up the final papers?" Sebastian struck an apologetic tone, as if to make up for Amanda's rudeness. "It would be a nice way to officially welcome you."

"We'd be delighted to," Jack replied. "Our hotel is—"

"The *L'Orangerie*," Amanda, said, cutting him off.

"This is a small island, Jack. We know everything," she said jokingly.

"Ah, of course it is."

"How about we meet back at your hotel at six? And we can answer any questions that arise on your tour of the manor."

"That's very generous of you. We'll see you at six," Jack confirmed.

Amanda instructed us to wait for the brokers at Seaview Manor—the name of our new island home. And with a quick wave, the couple hopped into their Audi Q5 and headed down the driveway. A few minutes later the brokers arrived, and together we did a walk-through.

The front door opened into a circular vestibule dotted with entrances to rooms on either side. Cream-coloured walls—spread with sunlight from floor-to-ceiling windows—contrasted with dark floors that extended in all directions. A glimpse of ceramic tile and stainless steel on one side hinted at a modern kitchen, and on the other side a gallery of doors identified a row of ensuites. A staircase sat in the center of the room and ascended to the primary bedroom level. The sea and sky were everywhere, filling the windowed wall and detectable even in the background sounds of wind, gulls, and waves.

Satisfied with our purchase, Jack handed over the final

cheque to the broker, received a copy of the deed, and we were officially island homeowners. Well, Jack was, and vicariously, I as well.

The Whittles arrived promptly at 5:45. The club was located about five miles away and overlooked a sprawling field where rich, mostly white, islanders played polo. The triangular foyer of the club house was decorated with long-handled wooden mallets and balls previously used by celebrity players, which included those from a royal bloodline, such as the Duke of Windsor.

Dinner began with an appetizer of seafood bisque, followed by a main course of lobster creole with seasoned dirty rice: a perfect combination of the sea and the island. Both Amanda and Sebastian drank gin with a twist of lemon. Jack and I had aged rum on the rocks, and we discussed the island's history, its inhabitants, and local politics.

"Is it your great-grandfather who owned the property?" Jack enquired of Amanda.

"Correct. My fourth great-grandfather removed; Colonel R.A. Browning of the British Marines purchased the property after he was medically discharged from duty." She braced her shoulders, tilted her head back as she spoke, an air of arrogance in her tone.

"His love for the sea brought him to Sierra Majestic, and

he acquired the plantation with his severance. So began our history here."

"Were the island's first European settlers the French or Portuguese explorers?" Jack asked.

"The Portuguese came before the French, but the English captured it in the end. It was originally called Tureygua, a Taino word that means "celestial," but was later renamed in honour of her majesty Queen Victoria."

"Fitting!" Jack interjected with a nod.

Amanda sounded like a history professor giving a treatise on The Discovery of The New World, and Jack's agreement spurred her on.

"It is quite a mountainous little island. Although the Aboriginals lived here way back, it was the Europeans who brought civilization to these parts." She took a breather, and then asked,   "What are your backgrounds?"

I'd been quiet throughout, and like an eager child finally given permission to speak, I piped up. "I'm Canadian, but my parents are of European descent."

She glanced over at Jack. "I'm American, originally British," he responded.

"Oh! Sebastian and I were born and educated in Britain. My parents lived here, so I spent a lot of my summer and Christmas holidays on Majestic. I moved permanently after completing my studies."

"Nice getaway from the cold and damp of British

weather, I'd say," Jack mused.

"I suppose. Sebastian made the move after we married five years ago."

"Are there kids in your household?" I asked, hoping to connect as women of childbearing age.

"Oh, dear no! And we don't plan on having any." She rolled her eyes in disgust and continued. "All the little critters do is nibble at your ankles and poop and pee all day—*not* our idea of bliss. How about you … are marriage and kids on your radar?" She forced a smile and finished her second drink. I let Jack take this one.

"We're not kid friendly either, so that would be a no." He grinned and lifted his glass in a toast.

Amanda and Sebastian appeared pleased by Jack's comment; they exchanged quick glances and joined him in the toast. My stomach lurched at the remark, and I kept my glass lowered.

"But seriously though," Jack hurriedly added, "we're not the parenting types. We like our freedom, so kids won't be a part of the equation." I stifled a scream.

I was appalled to hear Jack so emphatically state that I, too, didn't want kids. We'd never had the conversation, and I was annoyed he'd made that claim so publicly. To shift my discomfort, I asked Amanda about the history of the house.

"How long has the manor stood on the hill?"

"It's been there for about two hundred years, though not

in its current form." She glanced over at Jack as she spoke.

"Our family owned Plantation Emerald Hill on that very spot and employed generations of islanders over the years." Her sharing of this information reminded me how little I knew about my own family history.

"Two hundred years, wow! The stories that must be part of its history!" I interjected, reasserting my position in the conversation.

"There are legends alright—like the one that says on a moonless night, if you lean out the east window, you can hear the moaning of the slave woman Octavia."

"A slave woman?" Her response baffled me, and it must have shown on my face.

"No worries, Jemma, it's just a made-up story." Amanda chuckled and winked at me.

This time it was Sebastian who raised his glass. "Here's to Octavia."

We all joined him and shared a bit of laughter.

"Excuse my curiosity, but why are you selling this prime piece of property in such an idyllic location?" Jack picked up the questioning.

"Some venture capital requires a lot for start-up. We've kept our other property on the north side of the island—that's about twenty years old." Amanda batted her eyes and flipped her hair from her face.

"It's great that you've kept the property in the family and

have links with the local community. It shouldn't be difficult to find hired help on the island, correct?" I questioned, moving the conversation forward from her vague response about the reason for selling.

"Not at all. What did you have in mind?"

"A helper and a groundsman would be perfect, at least for the beginning months."

"The house is fairly large, but with just the two of you, that might be sufficient. I'll get the word out."

"Thank you." I smiled at her.

"We should head back soon, as a storm is expected to roll in." Amanda scanned the large eastern window as she spoke.

Sebastian rose, paid for our meals, and we followed them to their car and headed back to the hotel.

I quietly focused on the bends and curves along the road as Jack made light banter about the beauty of the island. I couldn't get his earlier comments about parenthood out of my head.

When we arrived, Amanda said, with an annoying chirp in her voice, "Please stay in touch and have a good flight back to New York." We hopped out of the vehicle, waved, and made our way into the opulence of L'Orangerie's lobby.

"They seemed like a nice couple." Jack looked over at me as we walked to our suite.

"Not my impression; especially her. I'd say she was

obnoxious." The snap in my voice surprised me.

"I would say she was nosey; obnoxious is a tad strong."

I was miffed that he hadn't experienced the interaction with Amanda the way I had, so I threw out the question that had been plaguing me. I inhaled deeply and turned to Jack. "Why are you so sure that I don't want kids?" The words rolled off my tongue, slow and precise.

"Jemma, I'm not privy to your thinking on the subject. I was merely sharing my perspective."

We entered the suite and, to hide my frustration, I walked into the bathroom and began taking off my makeup. "But Jack, that's *your* perspective, not mine." I twisted the lid on the jar of cleanser, glancing into the bedroom to ensure I had his attention.

He stuck his head through the bathroom door. "Hey, if being a mother is part of your plan, you're sleeping with the wrong man. I had a vasectomy over thirty-five years ago."

Another crushing blow: first he denounced my desire for motherhood, now he killed any hope I had of changing his mind. I leaned forward and splashed water on my face to cool the flush of hurt rushing through my body. How to react? I swallowed hard.

"I simply assumed we weren't yet at that point in our relationship. Thanks for the heads up." I steadied my voice, so the disappointment wasn't apparent. I'd imagined that Jack not taking precaution when we slept together showed his openness to becoming a parent. I was saddened to learn that his confidence was a result of his fail-safe procedure.

When he reached for me in bed that night, my body responded, though my mind was miles away. I'd never known before tonight how much I wanted children.

We flew back to New York midmorning the following day. I spent most of the flight wearing earphones and engrossed in movies, while Jack discussed strategy with Javier. That afternoon, they met at Javier's office on Fifth Avenue to sign off on the restoration project. Jack didn't return to the penthouse until well after daybreak, the next day. I drank too much that night, wallowing in my quiet hurt. I now knew that I'd have to settle for no kids if I wanted this man and the cushy lifestyle I desired. I was stuck.

For the next six weeks I kept busy preparing for our move to Majestic. Amanda kept her promise and found a helper that could begin work as soon as I arrived. The groundsman came—recommended by an acquaintance—and since he was male, Amanda wanted my stamp of approval prior to hiring him. The final decision would be mine.

Jack was in Europe for three of the six weeks before my move to the Caribbean; he spent two in France and one in Spain. We agreed that I would travel to Majestic ahead of him to set up our new home, and he would join me a couple of weeks later. Meanwhile, Raul, my part-time assistant and

I, visited auction houses across the city to find appropriate furnishings for the manor.

One cold January morning, I left the New York City penthouse, for what I hoped would be a fairy-tale life on Majestic.

Chapter 5

Jemma

I sat in the lounge at the John F. Kennedy airport in New York. My flight had been delayed because of a wicked winter storm. One of the travel assistants on duty reminded me of Maya, and her image filled my head. I wished she was with me on this trip. Mother would never approve of our friendship, but Maya and I had been close for a while now.

We'd met at a party on Lake Como, off Bellagio. I noticed her right away, the only Black woman on the luxury yacht. She looked out of place, though seemingly self-assured. Tall and stunning, with a firm butt and long shapely legs. Our eyes met and she smiled.

For much of the evening, I observed her play the deck, men 'accidently' brushing her ass. Once, a brazen man placed his hand against her thigh, and with a half smile, she gently guided it back to his side. Maya radiated a smooth sophistication that fascinated me. I wanted to make her my first Black friend. I hadn't grown up around Black people. There were only White kids in my classes at school, and in my neighbourhood, except for a few Asian kids.

We ran into each other at a few more events, but we really hit it off one evening during our stay at *The Savoy* in London during The Renaissance Architecture and Urbanism Conference. I had accompanied Jack, as his business partner had to take care of family commitments in Seville and couldn't attend.

One evening after a day of shopping, I walked into the hotel's bar. Maya sat alone, and I asked if I could join her. She waved me over and we exchanged pleasantries. I told her that I'd spent much of the day checking out shops on Bond Street and was now simply parched. I ordered a martini and offered to buy her a drink, which she accepted.

I remember admiring and commenting on the polished black and white stone floors with columns rising to gilded capitals, the woodwork, art deco, and accent vases everywhere. After a few drinks, we relaxed into girlish chat, though I did a lot of the talking. I had assumed that, like me, Maya was with one of the other conference attendees and was surprised to discover that she was a conference attendee herself, seeking clients and new business. I felt kin to her, as I had been in the same position until I met Jack. At least, that's what I thought.

Our conversation crisscrossed the countries we'd travelled, lived, and played in. We even talked fashion for a while, and I learned that she was American, born and raised in middle-class comfort in the South, and had lost her parents in a hit and run accident. She and her siblings had been fostered out across the country, and she'd been sent to Athens, Georgia to live with Ms Bea, a kind relative with no children of her own. She reminisced about the poverty she'd faced through those years in Georgia, and her first job at the Piggly Wiggly supermarket, when she was old enough to work. I remember stifling a giggle at the name of the store, but Maya was too caught up in her story to notice. She shared how hard she had worked to keep her grades up, going to bed many nights on an empty stomach, unless she got day-old bread from the bakery, or slightly bruised fruit from the produce section for doing extra shop chores. Despite these challenges, Maya graduated from high school at the top of her class and won a scholarship to college in New York. She delayed it for a year until she'd saved up enough for room and board. I was appalled at her story, and clearly remember thinking … 'thank goodness I never had to do poverty.'

I shared a bit about my Canadian childhood and that I'd moved to Genoa to finish high school and then college. Maya and I chatted well into the night.

I must have felt relaxed enough with her, or by then had had too many martinis to care, because I leaned over the table and, with a smug smile, asked her which of the men at the conference she had been with and if she'd been successful in meeting her goals. That was when her congenial tone flattened, her eyes widened, and she said something to the effect of "Wait, you think I'm a whore? You think I'm here to pick up men? Do you have any idea what a fucking insult that is?"

Her eyes had locked onto mine and I distinctly remember feeling the blood drain from my head and my ears start to burn. And then I felt her words twisting into my chest, cold, slow and precise. "I'm a Stanford and Fordham University trained Intellectual Property and Real Estate attorney. My clients are, largely, architects and real estate developers. I charge for my legal advice not my body."

This bit of information came a tad late, and I'd already put my foot in my mouth. There was no way out other than profusely apologizing, which I did, while trying to dampen my intention.

"I'm sorry ... but 'whore' is such a strong word," I said. "I simply assumed that *you* would be like me, a woman who uses her natural talents to secure the things she desires. There's nothing wrong with taking advantage of our physical assets to get ahead, you know. It gives us one up on men, who usually have the power." I winked at her to break the tension building between us but failed miserably.

Her voice was hard as iron and her eyes cold and piercing. I remember her reproach clearly: "Jemma, you just don't get it, do you? Those words should have never crossed your lips."

I recalled thinking '*Why is she so hot under the collar?*' To me, she was overblowing my comment. Instead of acknowledging her hurt, I dug in, and a verbal tussle ensued. I told her that I had played the game, and it wasn't that bad, and she claimed to be highly offended and super sensitive to being thought of as a sexual object. She underscored that historically, sexual abuse of Black women, especially by White men endured during and post slavery—a history that was often borne out even today. I realized that in my case, it was my choice to play the game—but for her and other Black women, especially during slavery, that choice didn't exist.

Upon reflection, I felt like a complete jackass. There was so much I didn't know about what she had shared. And it had surprised me that she didn't stay angry for long. Though her voice was still firm, her eyes no longer sent daggers into mine. We've been friends since.

The American Airlines flight left later that morning and arrived at Baptiste International Airport just in time for me to clear Customs and catch the midafternoon ferry to Majestic. A quick trip across the short stretch of water brought us to the island's ferry terminal. I flagged down a taxi and arrived at the manor house in less than fifteen minutes.

A tall, willowy woman waited at the front entrance of the curved driveway, her skin smooth and dark as obsidian, without a crease, dimples gracing each cheek. Her thick eyebrows arched above wide-set eyes that lit up when she smiled, and her hair was in a simple ponytail that lay midway down her back. Her shoulders squared as though readying herself for inspection, an apron draped over her right arm.

"Hello," the woman said, a lilt in her voice, as I climbed out of the taxi.

"Hello," I responded.

"My name is Primrose. Ms Whittle told me you need a housekeeper."

"I do, Primrose, and you can call me Ms Jemma. Thanks for meeting me here. Would you help me with the luggage?"

"Yes, yes, ma'am, Ms Jemma." I watched her assist the taxi driver move the bags to the front door.

Two large woven baskets spilling over with what I assumed were local fruits, along with bread, still warm, from the local bakery, cheeses, and jars of spices sat outside the door. Beside them lay a case of Dominio de Pingus, and taped to it, a note on vellum signed by the brokers under the heading "In appreciation and welcome."

I put the key in the lock and let us in, then strutted around like the lady of the manor and paused to observe the great room. Something was different.

"Ms Whittle let me in the house last week so I could clean it before you come to the island. I hope it's okay," Primrose said haltingly, as if unsure.

"Oh, that's lovely. I'll get to the seaport tomorrow and arrange the delivery of items I sent from New York. In the interim, there are new linens in the larger suitcase. You may use those for the beds. I'll just open it for you." She stood quietly and observed me; I handed her the linens, and she left the room.

For the next hour, I went through the lists from the real estate broker and made calls to ensure all the utilities were connected. Thankfully, water, electricity, and Wi-Fi were already operational. I entered the kitchen where Primrose was wiping down shelves.

"How far away do you live?" I asked.

She paused and looked over at me. "About two hours away by bus, on the west side of the island, ma'am… Ms Jemma."

"So, then it's okay that you live here, at the manor? I did make that clear to Mrs Whittle."

"Yes, Ms Jemma, I will live here, but if it's okay, I like to go back to my cottage once a month, stay there three days, come back, and start all over again. That's how Myrna, Ms Whittle's housekeeper do."

"Let's see how it goes. We can adjust as we go along. Do you have a family?"

"No, ma'am, is just me. My mother and grandmother gone over to the great beyond a little while back."

"Oh, I'm sorry. So, you're not married, or have a partner? If I'm being too—"

A half smile flickered across her face. "No, ma'am, is just me."

"Okay, then you'll take the housekeeper's room at the far end of the house on the left. I'm not too fussy about meals, but I hope you can cook, somewhat. Mr Jack enjoys simple meals, but we both like seafood and are not big meat eaters."

"And Mr Jack, ma'am—he's here on the island?"

"No, he won't be for two weeks, so it'll give you a chance to practise on me." I grinned. "I'll go online and put a grocery order together. Let me know if there's anything special you require."

"Okay, Ms Jemma, I will."

"Oh, and by the way, I like to sleep in. I will let you know when I want my meals." The memory of my mother making that exact statement to Teresita, our housekeeper in Toronto, floated into my head. Not a great parent to emulate, but she must have made an impression on me.

"Yes, ma'am."

I had a feeling about Primrose. She could be good for the manor.

I tried reaching Jack at least four times that afternoon without luck. After a light fare of cheese, prosciutto, olives, and half a bottle of wine from Top Tier's welcome hamper, I fell asleep.

Chapter 6

Jemma

The next morning, I woke to my cell phone ringing. Jack's face lit up the screen.

He was calling to check on my arrival and first night alone on the island. I assured him that all was well, and that Primrose was here to keep me company and get the house in order. He'd bought some type of a sport cruiser boat and shipped it to the island, and I promised to let him know when I was notified by Customs of its arrival. Jack thanked me and hung up. I needed coffee.

I wandered into the kitchen to find Primrose busy at the stove. She'd already brewed coffee and was awaiting my instructions.

"Morning, Ms Jemma. Will you have toast with marmalade or jam?"

"Toast with marmalade, and I'll have it in the conservatory."

"Okay, ma'am. It will be ready in a few minutes. And how do you like your coffee.?"

"Black, please. I like it black and strong."

I had a further flashback to Toronto and my dad making the very comment to Teresita the first morning she plunked a mug of creamy sludge on the kitchen island in front of him and said: "Here's your coffee, Dr Worley." The mix of repulsion and astonishment on his face was priceless. He calmly looked up at her from his favourite bar stool and replied: "Thank you, but I like it black and strong and without sugar."

Primrose's coffee and toast were perfect, and she included segments of a sun-ripened orange from the welcome hamper.

As I swallowed the last drops of my coffee, she stuck her head through the door. "There's a man here to see you, Ms Jemma. He says Ms Whittle send him." Primrose's voice again had a quality of uncertainty.

"Yes, it's the groundsman. Tell him to wait, and I'll see him in a few minutes."

"Alright, ma'am."

I went back to the bedroom, removed my robe, got dressed, and walked into the kitchen. Standing at the doorway was a tall, muscular man, about five feet, eleven inches in height, and somewhere in his mid-forties. He was dressed in a black T-shirt tucked into baggy, dark brown drawstring pants, his feet in cotton sandals with rubber soles. Coils of dreadlocks cascaded down his back, and his skin was a mix of bronze and toffee. As I entered the room, he turned to face me.

"Hello," I said, and was greeted by the broadest smile.

"Hello, I'm Zeke. Ms Amanda say you need someone to take care of de grounds."

"Yes, I do, Zeke. Do you have any experience with landscaping?"

"Been working de land all mi grown-up years, and travelling to different islands selling mi trade, though sometimes giving it to de natural cause."

"Natural cause?" What was he talking about? He must have seen the tentative look on my face and quickly clarified his statement.

"I mean taking care of Mother Earth without worldly payment."

"I see. I need someone full-time. Are you interested in the job?"

"It depends, madam."

Sweetening the offer seemed appropriate. "I can start you off at two hundred dollars a week, and I'd expect you to be here Monday to Friday."

He stood, legs astride and listened without committing.

"Weekends would be yours unless something major requires your help. How does that arrangement work for you?"

His response was slow and cautious. "I can do some days, madam. How 'bout if I start off with three days a week and move to four if de job require it?"

I was hesitant; I wanted the job completed quickly, and his proposal slowed it down before it even began.

"I suggest we begin with four days and move to three if the job doesn't require it," I replied.

A few seconds elapsed before he responded. "Okay, we see how it work for now. I have some tools, but you will have to supply de rest."

"And how soon can you begin work? The landscaping needs immediate attention."

"I can start tomorrow."

Surprised, but pleased, I continued. "Do you live far from here?"

"Not really, bout two miles down de beach."

"This is great, Zeke. I'll see you tomorrow then."

"You didn't tell me your name, ma'am. What you want me to call you?"

"Jemma, it's Jemma, but you can call me Ms Jemma. Ma'am is alright too," I said cheerfully, delighted that the exterior work would begin almost immediately.

I searched his face, and his steady gaze and soft brown eyes promised kindness and intelligence. Missing was any trace of the menace my mother had warned was present in Black men.

"See you tomorrow, ma'am," he said, nodding as he exited the back door.

I watched him leave and returned to my computer to begin work on my merchandising platform. I paused for a moment and reflected on a conversation Ollie, and I had had with our mother. She had scolded Ollie for smiling at a Black boy in The Bay Department store on Queen Street. He had been practising the Michael Jackson moonwalk as he appeared to be waiting for his mother to return packages at the service desk. Ollie was fascinated and couldn't take her eyes off him.

"He's really good, Jem … isn't he?" she crooned, wide-eyed.

"Ollie," Mother leaned in and growled with impatience. "Stop staring. Avoid him and anyone who looks like him at all costs."

When we got home, my little sister was not about to let our mother off that easily, and as we relaxed in the living room after dinner, she piped up. "Why should I avoid the dancing boy and anyone that looks like him? Is it because he's a dancer or because he's Black?"

"So, there are many reasons why, but I'm going to tell you about my first experience…"

"Sure, Mum, tell us." Always ready for a story, Ollie sat on the living room rug at Mum's feet, and I listened from the loveseat on the other side of the room.

"When I was growing up, there was a little enclave of about half a dozen or so small cabins a few miles from our farm. Locals called it Coonsville, because Black people lived there. It was said that they were descendants of enslaved Africans, and White people from our area didn't mix with them. One Christmas Eve when I was around seven years old, my mum took me to the early church service. Just before it began, two dark figures entered and sat in the first empty pew closest to the back door. When they removed their winter hoods, I saw the faces of a young boy and an older woman, who could have been his mother. Grown-ups slowly shifted seats to leave a clear divide between them and the two visitors, or as Mum said later, correcting me, 'They were intruders, Eileen, no one invited them.'

"When the service ended, a church deacon walked over to the woman and child as they prepared to leave and said in a loud voice, 'There are negro churches in Dresden. It's where your kind belongs.' As though to shield me from some type of contamination, Mum held my hand and led me out the front door, far away from the two coons making their way out the back door."

"Were there churches for White people and Black people back then?" Ollie's face bore a frown of confusion.

"Society has created specific places for specific people ... it's just how it is." A thick silence fell across the room. And then, as if to drive home her point, our mother continued.

"When school was back in session two weeks later, my friends MJ and Larissa who were at the Christmas Eve service, couldn't wait to discuss the shocking incident. It was big news, and I remember Larissa questioning us about what the strangers had done to cause such a commotion.

"We arrived late, so we missed it," she chirped in her high-pitched voice, glancing from me to MJ.

"They should not have been there. My parents were horrified that coons had made it into the church," MJ whispered. My mum said that coons are animal-like; it's in their blood. They are evil, loud, and can't be trusted. It's a trait they can't change.'

"How do you mean evil?" Larissa leaned in, lowered her voice, and squinted.

"Mum said Black men and boys are the worst threat to White women and girls. They will harm you and do awful things to you if you let them come close." MJ's eyes were wide like saucers. She dragged her words out as she made her case: words that were like puncture wounds in my chest.

"But how does she know this?" I quietly probed.

"Because she's a Sunday School teacher, that's how. They know everything." MJ's voice dropped an octave or two as she drummed this fact into our heads. I realized then that she was right.

Black people were evil, loud, and can't be trusted, and Black boys will hurt you if you let them near you. "Those sentiments stayed with me, and I've kept far away from coons ever since."

"And how is that different from White people Mum …" Ollie began but was halted in her tracks.

Mother snarled at her "Don't you ever ask that again."

Neither Ollie nor I questioned our mother further.

Now, Black people were increasingly becoming a part of my world; first Maya, then Primrose, and now Zeke.

After reading and sending a few e-mails, I sent Maya a note and a selfie I'd taken from the conservatory, holding the phone up high so the turquoise Caribbean Sea was visible in the background. Hopefully, Zeke would bring the messy garden back to order soon.

By evening, things were falling into place. Sometimes I'd reflect on Jack's bombshell on our initial visit to Majestic and whether I was doing the right thing—giving up motherhood for him. I imagined two kids, a girl and boy, keeping me busy around the house, on the grounds, and taking walks along the beach. Seaview could be the perfect place to raise a beautiful little family. I still had time, and maybe, just maybe, Jack might consider a vasectomy reversal.

Chapter 7

Jemma

The next morning, Zeke and I sat under the pergola with stripes of sun and shade everywhere, looking at flower and plant images on my laptop. "Is this the croton? The orange and pink in its hue reminds me of the colours of sunrise." I'd seen versions of the plant before in the indoor tropical section of our local plant nursery in Toronto. Mother had told Dad that it was the plant of change. How appropriate for my new garden.

"It is ma'am." Zeke answered.

The aroma of sweet almond and kiwi fruit emanated from his buffed body. The longer we chatted, the more I enjoyed his invigorating scent. Today he wore beige shorts with a mustard-coloured tank top that showed off his well-formed biceps.

The sound of a horn interrupted our dialogue. I scanned the horizon and saw the outline of a ship. A second short blast made me focus more sharply on its intruding presence.

"Does that happen often?" I frowned at Zeke in dismay.

"No, ma'am. Dat's a warning to leisure boats getting in de cargo ship way. No recreation craft allowed past *Nearly Dere Island*—de small cay way over yonder." He pointed in a southerly direction, and I followed his gesture to the cay off to the side.

"That's a peculiar name for a cay."

"Well, locals been calling it dat since de hundred and twenty souls drown after de slaver dey been in hit a shoal and tear de bottom out of de ship. De ones dat could swim try to reach de cay, but de sea was too rough, and it swallow dem up. Dat is how de cay got de name hundreds of years ago."

"Wow, that's tragic, Zeke, if it's a true story; sounds more like folklore though." I glanced up at him with a wink. His face was expressionless.

We ended our conversation, and Zeke walked over to the garden shed to store the tools he'd brought. By midafternoon he'd begun hoeing and preparing the grounds for fertilizing.

My vision of a Caribbean paradise further unfolded. Over the next few days, I imagined myself connecting, hanging out with, and hosting celebrities at Seaview Manor. The perfect life!

Jack arrived early one afternoon on Majestic, two weeks to the day I moved into the manor. I picked him up in the new Peugeot RCZ Roadster we had shipped from New York. He immediately noticed the touches of luxury I'd added to the place.

"I like your decorating flare, the varying shades of blue and pops of chartreuse, the gold and terracotta accents too. It is tranquillity broken by excitement and mirrors the environment: the sea, the lush surroundings, and the sun."

I was delighted that he liked the colours I'd chosen, especially the chartreuse—a secret nod to my sister sharing in my new adventure. Every time I looked at the rich green pillows on the sofas, I pictured Ollie sitting there as part of the living room.

"Thank you, Jack. I was going for serenity," I said with a smile.

Just then, Primrose walked into the living room.

"Jack, this is Primrose—our housekeeper and cook extraordinaire. Primrose, this is Mr Generson. He'll be here for a little while. How long will you be home this trip, honey?" I asked with the sweetest disposition. Jack responded in similar fashion.

"Only for a few days, dear; duty calls in Barcelona. But it's good to meet you, Primrose. I look forward to trying your fare." Jack smiled widely, and she nodded and smiled in return.

I didn't like that he had to leave that quickly; maybe I could charm him into staying a bit longer.

Sensing my displeasure at his plan for an early departure, Jack coaxed, "How about we go try out the new boat later?"

"Sounds wonderful," I replied.

We went down to the marina later that afternoon to check out his new Mastercraft 300. The boat was a slick white aluminum with pale blue stripes, about thirty-feet long and eleven-feet wide, roomy, and great for speed or relaxed cruising. We took The Javson out on the open sea and around the island for an inaugural cruise. Turbocharged, it started immediately, and propelled us out of the marina and over the open water, carving a white trough through the blue waves. A peace came over me like the one I'd experienced cross country skiing on the trails of Algonquin Park in the dead of a Canadian winter. I wondered about the boat's peculiar name, but let it go without questioning Jack.

That evening, Primrose turned out a fancy dinner of seared lobster in garlic butter with a disc of saffron rice, served in two heart-shaped warmers. Her attempt to strike the element of romance didn't escape either of us, and we glanced at each other and smiled as she left the room. A bottle of chardonnay completed our meal, and we passed on dessert. Then we took an evening stroll along the beach.

Warm sand crept up between my toes, and I took Jack's hand and admired the moon's silvery reflection on the water. I easily fell into a daydream about how magical it would be to share walks with him on evenings after supper. I imagined it being part of our alone time, when we relaxed, enjoyed nature, and each other, and planned the rest of our lives together. Keeping my thoughts private, I paused, kissed his cheek, and fondled his ass. Our Central Park Lake night crawl flashed before me. But Jack chuckled, reciprocated, and raised the topic of work.

"How are things with your business? It must be challenging to place online orders without being able to see and touch the physical products?"

"It is, but I'm learning to adapt and trust my suppliers. We have a good partnership, and they know my taste. It's kinda like us in some ways; we're in sync." I kissed him again, this time more passionately. I brushed up against him, reaching my hand into his drawstring linen pants. I hoped the beach would inspire some spontaneity under the stars.

"I'm glad it's all working for you." Jack's lips brushed my forehead. I reckoned any beach nooky would have to wait for another time, so I backed off and resumed the conversation.

"The tricky part is keeping an eye on trends and how they're worn by European women. You can't get the full experience by reading fashion blogs and magazines. It's just not the same."

"You'll have to find a better solution."

"I'm working on it. How about you?" As co-owner of one of New York's top architectural agencies, Jack did major restoration work on projects around the world.

"Currently, things are a tad unsettled. I hope I've convinced Javier to walk away from a deal that's not working for us."

"What's happening?"

"Our perceptions of an arrangement differ, so we're experiencing some agitation."

"Why, pray tell?"

"The problem is with two newly contracted Spaniards who believe they're like Gaudí, a renowned architect who shied away from drawings. Javier invited them into our lives, thinking they would bring in a strong understanding of Spanish architecture."

I peered over at him. "What's the problem?"

"These folks show up to project meetings without detailed plans and with decks of playing cards stacking them up as architectural models. Then they make ridiculous inferences about how restorative changes to heritage properties should be made."

"And that's a central part of your work, the restoration of historic and heritage buildings, yes?"

"It is, but their conceptual approach is utterly ineffective. You need actual plans to efficiently refurbish and retrofit these historic gems. It's an utter waste of time and money and will cause more harm to the structures."

"Have you reasoned with them? Explained your concerns?"

"The pompous asses wouldn't listen. Where do they get off telling me, an accomplished architect, how to restore heritage sites? Jemma, it's infuriating!"

I reached over and rubbed the middle of his back.

"I hear your frustration, Jack; maybe it's time to have a serious chat with Javier."

"I've had a few chats with him and, though if done well it could be lucrative, I believe our only solution now is to walk away. I hate losing money, and the disorganization is outrageous. These folks are wealthy, but I'm not sure they could differentiate between French Provincial and Georgian architecture."

"Well, I hate to burst your bubble, but most people can't. I know a bit about the varying architectural styles, because growing up, our neighbourhood was sprinkled with many kinds of houses, and my dad talked about the people based on the kinds of homes they lived in."

"Really? I thought your dad's an eye surgeon?" He looked over at me with raised eyebrows.

"He is, but architecture is one of his hobbies. For example, he made a point of telling us that the Smiths and Gormleys lived in a Tudor revival, the McMillians in a Georgian, and the Powells and Rottenbergs lived in Arts and Crafts homes. He never really commented on the more contemporary steel and glass looks like Seaview."

I paused, scooped up a handful of sand and let it run through my fingers as I spoke. "The Kingsway, where I grew up, is beautiful, but in a stylised, man-made way. Here on Majestic, things are raw, more natural, less altered by human hands. Look at that bright moon; you would never see that in the big city." We leaned into each other for a few moments and admired the silver seascape.

"Tell me more about this place called The Kingsway—you've piqued my interest."

"Well, a predominant style in the neighbourhood is the Tudor revival with its two-toned half-timber detailing, arched entryways, and brick chimneys."

"British indeed."

"Dad often pointed out that the Georgians, like ours, were also popular, with their neoclassical touches, white columns, capitals, and porticoes." I felt smart and had his attention, so I flaunted my knowledge.

"French Provincials with shutters and steep roofs are also big. Dad used to say: 'that house shouts 'England!' and that one 'France!' I guess it was someone's idea of England and France."

"Doesn't sound like a neighbourhood of middle-class families, I would say." Jack's eyes had an approving twinkle.

"It's more upper, than middle. My mother, who took great pride in our neighbourhood, called it 'a gallery of mansions, set back from the common road on expanses of perfect grass.'"

"Sounds rather stately." Jack rubbed his chin as the image marinated in his head.

I told him about the way mother described our neighbourhood to a friend at our Cape Town vacation home. "She'd claimed Kingsway homes, and I'm paraphrasing, had controlled bands of flowers bordering their walkways, all shaded by columns of mature maples and oaks, that rise to support the dappled canopy of sky, sun, and green overhead."

"Nice image. She's quite poetic."

"She can be. But to me, one of her most memorable statements was, 'The Kingsway is like a cathedral of wealth: beautiful, safe, and closed to anyone who does not belong.'" I felt like a performer on stage in a Shakespeare production and batted my eyes to imitate my mother's gloating persona.

"Well said." Jack beamed.

"If I hadn't already lived there, I would want to. She should have worked in sales," I added.

"Sounds like a very charming area. Our new partners can benefit from a lesson in architectural styles from you." He winked at me and we both grinned.

We made it back to the house and headed to our bedroom.

"I've noticed the gardener has begun work, but I haven't seen him on the grounds," Jack said.

"He is sourcing fertilizer from Baptiste Island. You'll meet him tomorrow."

Once inside, he didn't waste a second, leaning against the bedroom door and closing it. His strong fingers expertly massaged my ass and we rolled onto the bed, our kisses passionate, filling a hunger for each other. Jack's mouth travelled from my lips to my breast, and continued down to my belly button, along my hips, and ended with feathery kisses, up and down my inner thighs. His persistent teasing and steady progression reignited an excitement I had missed and longed for desperately. But I had to remind him of my prowess, so I flipped over, draped my thighs over his legs and with the lips he'd always admired, worked my way up in reverse, caressing every inch of his manhood. Jack hummed with pleasure and his body flexed in response.

That night I slept soundly in his arms and woke up to his warm breath on my neck, his chest rising and falling against my upper back, arms wrapped around my body. My heart beat joyfully in response to his embrace.

Zeke was already busy when we ventured outside for breakfast on the lanai.

I introduced the men and noticed Jack checking Zeke over when he wasn't looking directly at him; I hoped this beautifully chiseled human would spark some jealousy in

Jack and make him want to be home on the island more often. After all, Zeke was ripped.

"So, what are your plans to relocate and telework?" I asked casually over breakfast.

Jack bit into a scone, chewed for a moment, then patted his mouth with his napkin.

"The company needs me to be out and about to maintain our competitive edge. It's beautiful here, Jemma, but it's more a place of leisure than a place of work. There are too many distractions," he said, and squeezed my thigh.

"I thought you enjoyed this distraction, unless I'm losing my edge," I pouted playfully.

"Your womanly edge is ever-present, and that's a distraction I can't resist." He grinned, leaned in, and kissed me with verve. Zeke must have really struck a nerve.

"Well, my expectation is that you'd slowly begin to run your business from Majestic, just like I'm doing. It gets really lonely here without you, especially at night. Please say you'll think about my suggestion and move at least half of your office here, and soon."

"But my business partners are based between New York, Seville, and Rome. It's not practical to have half of my office here. You know that Wi-Fi can be sketchy in the Caribbean; especially during hurricane season." His response was quick, as though he'd previously thought about it.

"Honey, I'm sure other celebrities and businesspeople

in this part of the world do it; please try to find a way. I need you here with me." It was like he'd already made up his mind. I got up, walked over, sat in his lap, and rested my head on his chest.

Jack hugged me gently and kissed my face. "Jemma, I can't promise anything except that I'll talk to Javier and the junior partner on one of our Italian projects that's going full steam right now. If it can be accomplished, I'll consider doing some more work from Majestic. It won't be an office relocation though."

My heart skipped a beat. "I'm glad to hear you're going to at least explore the idea. Let me remind you of the joy you'll be gaining with this move," I said, and then began to unbutton his favourite blue Tommy Bahama shirt.

"We left the bedroom less than an hour ago." He chuckled and glanced over his shoulders.

"Are you complaining?" I joked.

"I'm not, but on the lanai? Let's move your reminder to our room." We walked upstairs, undressing along the way.

Later, Primrose served lunch in the conservatory after which we headed back to our room for a siesta. A sense of relaxation flooded over me as I lay in Jack's arms; everything felt right. But three days later, when he left for New York, emptiness crept in. From the library, I listened to Primrose humming away as she stripped the linens from our bed. I wondered about her cheerfulness—she was alone and yet lighthearted. I bet her story was intriguing.

Chapter 8

Primrose

Primrose is my real name, the one I was christen with on August 8, 1964. It says so on my baptismal certificate from Joshua Seventh Day Adventist Church down in the valley. Some people on the island call me Rose, but I like Primrose much better. If you writing to me by mail, you have to put the full name, so that no mix-up happen with Rosemond or Rosemary, the twins from up the hill.

I'm happy to have a job again so I can stay on Majestic and live a good life. I never ask for much. And it's not that I wasn't ambitious; sometimes you just get what you get, and you have to do the best with it.

I grow up on Majestic but left for Baptiste to attend high school. I did well, but my mama had some medical expenses and couldn't afford the university fees plus room and board when I finish. Though she wanted to help, my grandmother Gertrude Gray old age pension couldn't stretch far enough to help cover them expenses. So I did the next best thing persons do; I look for jobs on Baptiste. I found a few at hotels but never in the restaurants where you serve tourists and get tips, or in housekeeping where guests sometimes leave you two dollars for each night they stay. Most of the jobs I got were in the kitchen, where you work hard in the heat and get no tips because nobody can see you behind them hot kitchen walls. Although, I did get a different type of tips. I used to watch Chef Pasqual from Anguilla and Pepe from Haiti create lots of fancy dishes for the patrons, and I had a good sense of how to repeat them. After two years of looking for better positions, I give up. And six months before Granny Gertrude, or GG, went home to be with Jesus, I come back to Majestic to live with her and Mama.

My mama must have missed GG a whole lot; one year later, she died from an aneurysm.

Although I was much closer with GG, when Mama pass, I couldn't catch myself for a long time. When GG went, I was sad, but I comfort myself in the fact that she had a long life and was ready to meet her maker, and I still had Mama.

Me and Mama got close, and she even begin to show interest in my plant brews. One night I was doing the washing up after dinner, and she ask about some new plantings I had collect that day.

"Rosie, how you know how much of each scent to put in a vial?"

"I just guess, or as GG used to say, I *guesstimate* the quantity," I said with a chuckle.

"So, you really don't know what the end result will be then?"

"No, Mama. I use a little bit of this and a little bit of that, just like GG used to do when she cooking. And it usually work out. After a while you learn to eyeball the correct amount. Smell this one and tell me what you think." I hand her a vile of a new fragrance I was trying to perfect.

I watch her close her eyes and inhale. Immediately her countenance change. She squish up her face and turn up her mouth as if she suck a lemon, and then she scream, hold her nose, and run to the toilet. She heave for a few seconds and then she said, "My God, child, that scent remind me of flowers from Island Breeze Haven funeral home, sprinkle with peppermint oil and smelling salts served up at an Adventist funeral procession."

The two of us laugh so hard, my eyes start to water, which was followed by the hiccups. I walk outside and empty the brew; I was making scents for the living, not the dead.

After Mama pass, I inherit the two-bedroom cottage we shared and live on the little money she left, and whatever I manage to save from my hotel jobs. So I was happy to get the message from Mama's friend Myrna, the Whittles' housekeeper, that a couple moving to Majestic was looking for a housekeeper. I was never one before, but just finding work on Majestic was a relief.

Before I get the call, I was making homemade oils and skin creams from the different fruits and flowers on the island, but I still had a secret wish: to train to become a chemist at the university.

My two favourite blends were a night cream with avocado, almond, passion fruit and hibiscus oils; and a mint-avocado balm that I use to remove dead cells from my feet. I would massage it into my soles and instep and then let the cool sea wash away any stress of the day, like when I use to stand on my feet all day at the bakery.

Working with Ms Jemma also end any job-hunting ideas on Baptiste. Though it had been many, many years, God knows my pain from that place was still raw. I never did heal, or maybe it was just shame—my shame.

At Fern Valley High School, the students call me 'whitey' and 'uppity.' Light skin or pretentious I wasn't, I was just quiet and didn't fit into their world. Coming from Majestic, my experience growing up didn't include plaiting maypole, watching Guy Fawkes bonfires, or going to the market on Saturdays. Church was the only thing we had in common: me on a Sabbath, them on a Sunday. The churches on

Baptiste were Catholic, Anglican, or Methodist, and no one else from my school attend the only Sabbath one on the island.

"Primrose Mortley, you're always present in class."

That's what Ms Burrows my science teacher use to say. I spent a lot of time in the biology and chemistry labs with beakers and Bunsen burners. Most of the other girls skip and either went into town five minutes away or were meeting boyfriends in the park. I learn to extract oils from frangipani, rose, hibiscus, and lavender plants. I also pull oils from lemon and mint leaves and use them as a base for balms, since I couldn't afford the skincare creams in the local shops. The oils kept my skin smooth and supple in the Caribbean heat.

It was during those school days that I meet Clarence Brandt. I can still remember our first conversation.

"Which do you prefer—Rose or Primrose?" A soft confident voice trail behind me. I turn around and the tall, dimple-face lad who play netball on the beach was standing there.

After the initial shock, a croaky voice escape my throat. "I, you can... Primrose, it's Primrose."

"Well, Ms Primrose, they call me Clarence. Why you keep to yourself? We're not good enough for you?" His eyebrows drawn close together, his head slightly tilted, he wait for me to answer.

A sudden heat fill my face, and I fumble to dismiss his accusation. "I… no, I'm not like that – I don't know…"

Clarence move into my space, reach out, and place his right hand over my mouth "*Shhhhh … you don't have to explain.*"

That touch break something in me. Shivers ripple down my spine like a splash of ice-cold water against my back on a hot and humid day. Until then, I never realize how much I missed the closeness of another human being. I was on Baptiste almost a full school year without any, and the loneliness consume me. I scream on the inside. *Yes, let me explain; I'm hurting, please, somebody help.* Yet my external stance said *No, don't come close and please don't touch me.*

I think back on why I kept to myself. Fear, total fear and embarrassment that someone might find out what I had experience earlier, my second week on Baptiste.

He was Mama's friend and would bring food and gifts from the big island to our house on Majestic. Sometimes he would sit for hours and chat with GG, and I trust him because GG trust him.

"Ms Gray, I'll check in on Primrose when she come to Baptiste, make sure she settle in okay. Don't you worry."

"Thank you, Maynard. Thank you," GG had gratefully reply.

Maynard lost the key to his house in my second week on the island, and his landlord offer to bring a spare by so he could get in. It rain heavy that afternoon, and he had come by my room to wait for his landlord. I began my homework while he sat reading the newspaper he brought over with him. I was so focus on my trigonometry, that it catch me off guard when Maynard throw one arm around my neck, jerk my head back, force his tongue into my mouth, and start to fondle my breast. At first, the act and the speed at which it happen scare the 'bejesus' out of me, but, I recover real quick and put up a fight. I lash out, scratch and punch him, then wiggle out of his grip and run from the room.

For about an hour I hide in the stairwell, shaking like a leaf in a rainstorm. Then I hear his landlord arrive and Maynard leave with him. I tiptoe back to my room, lock the door, and push the chest of drawers behind it. I crawl onto my bed, still trembling, and lean my back against the wall, scared, upset, and embarrass. I couldn't find tears, only confusion. Every time I drift off to sleep, I jump up startled. I didn't sleep properly for the next two weeks, worry that Maynard would come back to finish off the attack; he only lived two streets away.

That betrayal rock me to my core and all I could think was, *I can't tell nobody what happen. GG and mama are so proud that I got a scholarship here, I can't let them down. I can't tell them what Maynard did. It would spoil everything. I could hear GG say, 'Come home, baby girl, come home.' Lord, it would be too shameful. And what if he deny it? It would be my word against his. GG would believe me, but I don't know about Mama. It's too risky; no, I have to keep it to myself.* So, Clarence, it's not what you think, not what you think at all.

For the next month, at the end of the school day, Clarence and I walk on a quiet path in the shade of large almond trees that led to the sea. We only exchange glances on school premises, and no one else knew we had become friends.

We shared stories about growing up; both of us had strict grandmothers we adored. Mine live on Majestic all her life, his move to Long Island in New York. One afternoon while lying on our backs against a tree trunk, chatting, he roll over and plant a kiss on my open mouth, mid-sentence. It catch me by surprise, but it was my response that terrify me. It was like Clarence turn into Maynard, and the old fear come over me. My arm fly up at lightning speed and sent a slap across his face so hard, his head jerk in the opposite direction.

Clarence let out a scream like a banshee, jump up and back away while holding his face.

"Sorry, sorry," he whimpered, "I thought you like me."

Rage grew in me, and I shake like a steaming kettle.

"Sorry, Primrose, I didn't mean to." He sink to his knees and plead for forgiveness.

"Why you did that Clarence? You mustn't do things to me without asking me first."

"You not suppose to ask the girl," he interrupted. "The man suppose to take charge." He stare at me, rocking back and forth and rubbing his cheek.

I face him head-on and take a deep breath.

"No, you can't just take anything." The words left my mouth slow and deliberate." You can't take what is not yours. My body belong to me, Clarence, not you; you have to ask." I grab my schoolbag and start to walk away, and Clarence call out to me in a whisper.

"Primrose, please, I learn my lesson. Can I still walk home with you?"

The Maynard experience flare up in my head again.

"Maynard … I mean Clarence, is okay. I will walk by myself. See you tomorrow." I left the beach, my knees wobbly with every stride.

Clarence and I remain friends, but we didn't spend time at the beach after school like before. I continue to help him with his biology and math homework, and he shower me with funny stories that slowly endear him to me again.

A few months after the kissing incident, Clarence come up to me in the hallway near the cafeteria. I was surprise since we were at school.

"Primrose, I have something to tell you. Can you wait for me this afternoon, and we can walk home together?"

"Straight home?" I clarify.

"Yes, straight home," he answer, rolling his eyes.

He took much longer than usual getting to our meeting spot, and when he arrive, he was quiet and serious.

'You okay, Clarence?"

"I'm fine. I just had to wrap up some stuff with Ms Carey."

We slowly walk along the main street towards my boarding house, but Clarence suddenly stop and look at me.

"I wanted to…" he began. "I'm leaving tomorrow for New York, and I'm not coming back." The words roll off his tongue like when paper bag bottom rip and rice spill out.

"You … y-you leaving?"

"Yes, I just… my mum just told me. I'm going to miss you, Primrose. Miss you and me."

"But how?" I become tongue-tied and can't find words.

Shock, then sadness come over me. I would be alone again. I trusted this boy. Despite his mistake, he was the only person that befriend me at school, and now he was leaving. A sudden fear grip me. I couldn't tell Clarence this, but unbeknownst to him, he had become my protector. Maynard only lived a few streets over, and I knew Clarence would rescue me if that creep did ever come back. This idea, though pure fantasy, make me feel safe.

When Clarence walk away that afternoon, there were no goodbyes or promises to write. "See ya" were his last words.

For the rest of the school year, I bury myself in my books. I got good grades on all my science and math exams and score well on my other subjects too. I missed Clarence and secretly wished he would hate Long Island and come back to Baptiste. That didn't happen.

When I move back home after high school, GG and Mama became test cases for my scent experiments. Mama tried all the different scents, especially if she was going on a Sunday evening date. She didn't go out on worknights and never on the Sabbath.

Mama used to say she was looking for the right man; a man who would love her with all her faults. I was one of her faults. She got pregnant with me at fifteen, and my father, who I never meet, was a much older married man with a family on St Kitts. Mama never tell me about him, but one time when I was about six years old and she and GG had a falling out, I hear GG say, "They tell you they love you, and you believe them. Then they hand you a pickney and disappear. Is when you gon learn? I hear this one just like the others, wutliss! You go on. Wah sweeten goat mouth does hurt he belly."

After that conversation, I use to worry that Mama wish she didn't have me, so I stay out of her way. Maybe if she didn't have me, she would have enough money to buy a big house. She might even own horses like the White people who live by the sea. After all, she was a customs officer at the airport. Instead, she had to care for me and GG, who was too old to work.

To GG, my torment was so clear that she used to say, "Girl, you gon rub them hands together till you see bone. Sitting there bouncing your foot and looking at the clock. You mother ain't coming home yet, why you so nervous?"

I never answer GG, but I believe it was around that time I start talking to myself in my head. I use to close my eyes and think about how when I grow up, I gon start a business and bring in lots of money and buy Mama a big house by the sea. Then she won't feel like I was a fault. She would be glad she had me even though the man did vanish.

Well, now I have a job and live in a big house by the sea. *Keep dreaming Primrose, and maybe the rest will come.*

Chapter 9

Jemma

One of the greatest joys at Seaview was waking in the luxury of my king-sized bed and opening my eyes to the blue vista of sea and sky, framed by the room's floor-to-ceiling glass doors. I could also see the violet wisteria and yellow morning glory cascading down the slope. But it was the sea, the sea that always held my gaze as it stretched out like a new land, endless and forgiving.

It had been three and a half months since Jack's last trip to the island. Negotiating a multi-million-dollar contract with several engineers and architects spanning the globe was his most recent project. Though we tried to connect every day, time differences made that effort fall by the wayside. He was spending an inordinate amount of time in Europe, instead of in our new sunny Caribbean paradise.

With so much time on my hands, I'd been doing more marketing and outreach, and it was paying off. My month-end sales figures had tripled since my move to Majestic. I was thrilled.

I often worked from the chaise beneath the mahogany pergola and enjoyed the sloped view below. Peach bougainvillea, burgundy and yellow hibiscus, tri-colour crotons, and shady palm bushes blanketed this part of the surrounding terrace. All were immaculately cared for by Zeke's powerful hands.

"De garden must be contained, and not be invasive," Zeke had said, when I wanted him to add another bit of shrubbery I liked from an online image. "I can add some here and dere, ma'am, but you have to be careful, because *Jacobs Coat* will spread quick," he cautioned.

He worked on this portion of the property early afternoon when the sun had shifted overhead. I loved to watch the rows of his kinky dreadlocks spilling down the middle of his back, his bare shoulders glistening with sweat as he sheared and shaped the flora with cylindrical precision.

I'd often wondered what lay behind his beautiful smile, gentle eyes, and quiet demeanour. For the first time in my life I was drawn to a Black man. Could this be happening to fill the void of Jack's absence? But why couldn't I be attracted to Zeke for his own sake. Because it wasn't supposed to

happen according to the script I had been read at home—
that's why. But, it was happening anyway.

Crotons were a favourite of mine. They reminded me of
being left to my own devices in Mr Jameson's high school
art class. He had encouraged us to use our instruments
to express our momentary thoughts: brushes on canvass,
pen and ink, or charcoal on paper. I leaned into whatever
medium was available. Shapes and colour spoke to my
mood during these times of creative expression. Exuberant
colouration of bright yellows, vibrant oranges, iridescent
pinks, and greens swirls were my go-to choices when I was
happiest. They gave me a sense of overcoming and leaping
over life's hurdles.

So as I watched Zeke mulch this particular croton with
its twisty corkscrew shape and brightly coloured cascading
leaves of red, orange, yellow, green and bronze, I recalled
an earlier conversation with him. I'd asked the name of this
croton, and he had answered "Dreadlocks, ma'am. Dey call
it dreadlocks."

I'd glanced up at him to ensure that he knew I was
talking about the plant, and he smiled at me and nodded.
"Dreadlocks."

I asked him to plant it in several sections of the
grounds. And I knew why. On my late afternoon strolls,
when no one was watching, I could reach in and twirl my

fingers through its leaves and imagine it being his beautiful hair. *Get ahold of yourself Jemma; he's a man, but he's a Black man. You just shouldn't go there.*

As the days went by, a kind of magnetism continued to pull me toward Zeke, so I went there in my musings. As I watched him from my favourite chaise, I found myself wondering if sleeping with him would ruin our employer-employee relationship. I could imagine his strong arms around me, especially since Jack had been gone for many months. It would only be temporary until Jack's stays on Majestic increased. Yet, I didn't want Zeke to perceive me as a loose woman; he had met Jack, so he knew there was a man in my life—though a mostly absent one. But would Zeke even be open to a tryst with me? We were so culturally different.

Like the chemistry Jack and I shared, I fantasized about a similar connection with Zeke. Though with Jack, I wanted a family, with Zeke, I wanted a physical stop gap. A flutter of excitement grew in my belly, followed by a twinge of nervousness. Maybe I could broach the topic with Maya and seek her input. But for now, I had to be content to gawk from afar, behind my Prada sunglasses.

I refreshed my second glass of gin, a slice of lemon hung from the rim. Pearls of cool water trickled down and formed at the base. I smiled as the lyrics of one of Primrose's favourite songs popped into my head: something about drinking gin and sinning. And I focused on Zeke, my eyes following his every movement, as if reading music.

Early one afternoon the following week, I ventured into the kitchen for a chat with Primrose. A packet of organic sunflower seeds like the ones I'd purchased online, lay on the kitchen island. I'd asked Zeke to plant similar ones just off my bedroom window. They hadn't germinated, and I assumed their location had caused the delay.

"Primrose, are these sunflower seeds yours?" I asked.

"Yes, ma'am. They were in the garden trash. I will plant them at my cottage when I go home."

"Well Zeke might have dropped them by mistake. I'll check with him."

I'd purchased a specific gold variety, a poignant reminder of the ones in the poster of Van Gogh's painting that hung in Ollie's bedroom, next to the one of his Yellow House. I ventured over to the garden to chat with my landscaper.

"Zeke, did you lose a packet of seeds? Primrose found these in the trash." I held my hand out and offered him the envelope. He peered at my hand and did not respond.

"These were part of the gardening items I gave you, correct?" I continued.

"Could be, ma'am," he said, then turned away without taking the packet. "Sunflowers are very special to me. I'm surprised you didn't plant them like I asked. Why is that?" I breathed in as normally as I could so he wouldn't sense my displeasure. *How dare he?*

"Ma'am, sunflowers don't grow well here. Dey will just die." Zeke kept his back to me as he spoke.

"That's ridiculous, Zeke. Look at me. How could they not? It's the Caribbean, it's sunny." I forced my hands into the pockets of my white denim dress to contain my annoyance. He turned and faced me, his eyes focused, but not on me. Something in the distance had captured his attention and I spun around but saw only the picturesque landscape. I turned back to an alarming sight. Zeke's eyes were squeezed shut, deep lines etched on his forehead, his teeth bared and clenched.

For a split second I imagined he needed medical attention. "Zeke, are you okay?" I asked, while keeping my distance and awaiting his response. But almost immediately, he turned around, dropped to his knees in the dirt, and began uprooting weeds.

Confused by this odd display and not seeing the logic in his behaviour, I slid the seeds to the ground, and left the garden. He had gone silent.

For the rest of the afternoon, I remained in the manor, glancing out to the garden ever so often, trying to read Zeke's mood, which appeared calmer. Was it anger that I'd seen earlier, or stubbornness? Did he believe I was trying to tell him how to do his job? Whatever it was, his behaviour was off-putting. I needed to find out what had caused his disturbed state.

The next day Zeke was in a much better mood, and I asked him to have a conversation. I told him that I had done some online research and confirmed that the sunflower does grow well in the Caribbean.

"Is it that you don't like this particular flower, Zeke?"

"It's not dat I don't like sunflower, it is a personal matter. If you don't mind, ma'am, I don't want to talk 'bout it."

What's so personal about a sunflower that he couldn't share? Don't push it Jemma, you'll get it out of him sometime, just not now.

"That's okay. I will bring sunflowers into my life in a different way. Yellow hibiscus looks just as pretty anyway." I'd hoped to lighten the mood.

He thanked me and returned to mulching the crotons.

Days after the incident with Zeke, my chat with Maya was still pending. But the uncomfortable feeling I'd had after our exchange about sunflowers was fading. It didn't make sense, but I must have touched an old bruise that hadn't healed. Maybe if I got to know him better, I would understand. With that thought, warmth spread across my body.

Over the next few weeks, colourful new blooms filled the terraced slopes, reminding me of my visit to the Bodnant

Garden in Wales. Back then, their multi-coloured roses, hot pink and white camellia with stunning evergreen foliage, and Himalayan blue poppies had put me in a happy mood. These new blooms at Seaview had a similar effect.

I thought back to Northern Italy and how I'd searched for someone to fill my emptiness—there had been a few relationships. Younger men came and left quickly, and my one older lover stayed much longer. Before Jack, I was never fulfilled, though. Relationships were like bits of refreshment—there for that moment to satisfy a need. And when they ended, I looked for the next adventure.

There was Armando, a gentleman from the South, a good lover who serenaded me with poetry and love songs but hadn't a penny to his name. He taught me to make pizza and a tasty marinara sauce. He hung around for five months and stood me up in a cafe when it was his turn to pay for dinner. I got home and he had moved out.

Étienne, my Frenchman, was charming and treated me well. He also treated every other woman in my apartment building just as well. Coming home from classes or part-time work, I would find him painting nudes or tippling wine with them. He eventually painted his way into apartment number three with the six-foot, two-hundred-pound redhead, who wore high top leather boots and matching handbags even as she walked her poodle. My stint with him lasted close to three months.

For about six months or so after Étienne, I dated occasionally, until Mr Verrazano, who'd been my art teacher years earlier in college. I called him Zany, and our affair lasted on and off for fifteen months. Because he was a married father of two adult children, we met at my apartment or at his country house when his wife was in Paris. He was safe, kind, gentle, and good looking in an odd sort of way. He loved the renaissance and baroque periods like I did, and we visited many museums across Europe. Initially, we did so under the pretence of sharing in our passion for the period but fell into bed on the second night of our first trip. We might have continued the affair if his wife hadn't found his credit card receipt for the flowers he'd sent me for my birthday. A few weeks later, I met Jack.

That night in bed I decided to forgo the chat with Maya and go after this alluring man and slake my thirst for new physical pleasure.

I had a wickedly pleasant dream, and the following morning, I opened my eyes to a little surprise: Jack, in our bed, watching me, his face soft and close. I had mixed emotions: a warm happiness that he was home but then a sharp regret that my game plan would have to be placed on hold. "Good morning, sunshine. It's been too long," he said as he cupped, kissed, and then massaged my breasts.

"To what do I owe this surprise visit?" I asked, a wisp of resentment in my voice as I forced myself not to pull away from him.

"We recently completed two major projects, so I came to the next best place I'd rather be —with you. For your patience, there's a small package waiting on your night table."

I looked over and saw a tiny robin-egg-blue box tied with a silky white ribbon—a gift from Tiffany & Co.

"You know how to win me over," I said as I unwrapped the package. Inside lay a delicate silver necklace with a blue sapphire encircled by diamond chips.

"Oh, Jack, thank you," I murmured and kissed his cheek. He placed the necklace around my neck, kissed me back, and returned his attention to my body, fondling my breasts. My resistance melted into longing. Jack's lips slowly travelled to my neck, his warm tongue crisscrossed my back and along my spine, tracing slow circles of excitement. His teasing brought me to ecstasy. Had I forgotten how good he was at this?

I learned something surprising about myself during Jack's stay. Though we spent every night together, I continued to fantasize about Zeke. I found this confusing at first but figured it was because my fantasy had been interrupted. In fact, one night I almost called out for Zeke during a most intimate moment with Jack. That had been *too close,* so the following day I had a chat with my landscaper.

"Zeke, you've done a marvellous job with the landscaping in just a few months. We'd agreed on a work schedule of four days as a start, but you've worked five days most weeks. I'll keep my end of the deal; how about you take the rest of the week off and two extra days next week."

Zeke stared at me blankly for a moment, and then asked, "You don't like de work, ma'am?"

"Oh, please know you're being rewarded for your good work, and this is not a reprimand."

A wide smile filled his face, and he left the premises in less than fifteen minutes.

I breathed a sigh of relief and fully focused my days and nights on Jack.

"You seem more relaxed now, Jemma. I should come back more often if it will take you this much time to adjust to me being around," Jack said, peering over his purple-framed Burberry glasses.

"A girl's got to get used to switching from inanimate to animate. I hope I didn't disappoint you," I joked.

"Inanimate is fine just as long as they don't replace me," he teasingly scolded. "It's always great with you, Jemma; it took you some time to get into sync, but I've been gone for a long time," he said and turned back to his laptop.

Phew, I guess it did. I had to make up for the half-assed performance before he left for his meeting in Luxembourg. I had seven days.

Over the next week, though Jack spent time in online meetings and on international business calls, we made up for lost time. Primrose served meals in the conservatory or sometimes in our bedroom. By day five, Jack was pleading for more rest in between our lovemaking. I was pleased.

During his stay, Jack raised many topics about the island, except when he would move some of his work here, so I broached the subject.

"How soon can I expect to spend this kind of glorious time with you—permanently? Your departure is approaching, and I'm already missing you." I looked directly into his eyes.

"I'm still working it out, Jemma. New projects have come our way, and now is the time for me to be more hands on. Its best for our bottom line. You're a businesswoman, you understand, right?" Jack pleaded.

"I understand that finances are important; it feeds our lifestyle. But when you're in North America and Europe for months on end, it is difficult for me."

"I appreciate that, and all I can promise is to do my best to work it out, but it's a delicate balance."

Jack left that afternoon for Rome. I hoped he would return soon. But then, there was always Zeke.

Chapter 10

Zeke

I grow up in a cottage by de sea. At de end of a school day, I used to spend lots of time climbing mango and guava trees, flying kites, or collecting corals and shells. Pon Sundays or holidays, I would go wid de men out to sea to haul in swordspine snook and silver belly fish. I was a regular boy's boy and liked to watch mi father light a wood fire and fry up de catch right dere pon de beach. It was de only time Mama eat dinner wid out cooking it, and she suck dem fish head dry, dry.

Eating never happen, though, until after Pappa break de seal of de rum bottle and pour three cap full and toss one to de east, one to de west, and the last one to de south, calling pon de ancestors—de ones dat live beneath de sea." I didn't understand dis ritual, so I stay quiet and watch from de corner of mi eyes.

I did rememba him doing a similar act of pouring rum, though not calling on any beings, when he was helping de men in de village dig de last resting place of Old Smithers, Pappa's good friend. Just after he poured de liquor dat day, a large branch of de hundred-year-old peepal tree in de cemetry break off and come crashing down in de path nearby. Grown men scatter like bees in flight. I figure den dat dis practise was someting to fear.

So after one of dese beach fry-fish sessions, mi curiosity went full tilt, and I turn to Pappa and say "Wha is an ancestor, and why you wasting de rum so?"

He look out to sea, and in his low, deep voice he said, "Is not wasting de rum, boy. Is call a libation. I calling pon de fathers and mothers, brothers and sisters, uncles and aunties—our people who went to de nether side and sometimes come back to bless and guide us in dis life."

"You mean jumbies, Pappa?"

"Dey not jumbies, boy. Dem is ancestors dat live in de spirit world, and de rum is an offering to let dem know we rememba and to thank dem for dey sacrifice."

Pappa slowly turn, and wid squinted eyes, he added, "Look at me boy ... dey can hear we."

The skin pon de back of mi neck tingle and mi shoulders rise up to mi ears. I didn't want to raise no jumbie from de grave, so I didn't ask him no more bout de libation. Just like de jumbies, I let it rest. But Pappa never stop asking de ancestors to bless de fish food we pull in from de sea before we eat it.

I liked to listen to Pappa's stories bout his ancestors. He say dat his people originally come from Essequibo. And, when de trading of enslaved people was happening back in de 1820s, Colonel Browning buy his entire family of eight from an Essequibo plantation owner to work on his estate. So Pappa say he is first an Essequibian—and dat's why I adopted de Guyanese nationality. I call miself a Majestic Guyanese!

Mi Daddy used to grow vegetables for sale at de weekend market, and mi Pappa, mi brother Stan and me, would help on Saturdays. Daddy use to say dat plants grow well pon Majestic, but de farmer must work hard to get de best results. De soil good, but it need a lot of assistance to get decent crops. He praised cow manure as one of de finest farming aids, but to get it pon Majestic required nuff work.

One of Pappa's sayings was, "Yuh ever see de White man play polo wid a cow? He gon eat de meat and drink de milk, but he want nutten else to do wid de beast. Dat's why Majestic don't have cows—any cow manure would have to come in from Baptiste or odda islands." He used to think de image of a man pon a cow wid a stick, chasing a ball, was comical, so he used dat image to talk about farming, again and again. Even now, dat picture brings a smile to mi face.

Polo players were plentiful pon Majestic, and so was horse manure, rich in organic matter. But Pappa said horses don't digest food as well as cows. And farmers had little choice but to use horse manure to fertilise de land and run into a common problem: de undigested seeds and weeds would remain in de horse manure, spring up, and cause more weeds and unwanted crops to compete wid de plants dey were trying to grow. But it was all dat dey had. So just like Daddy and Pappa, I gather and store horse dung to fertilise de garden.

Now, as a grown man, I continue on dis path. Each day I rise from bed, greet Mother Earth, and all de sentient beings dat surround her. I ask for her blessings for de day, den I brush mi teeth, wash mi face, and lift some free weights. I run long de beach punching de air to get mi muscles in motion, do some laps in de refreshing sea—all in all—bout an hour. After dat, I walk back to de homestead, cook some cornmeal porridge, and enjoy a cup of soursop leaf tea. If it muggy, I crack open two coconut and quench mi thirst. And by seven o'clock, I'm fully energised and ready to take on de day.

Today was a heavy Saturday: weeding, hoeing, fertilising, and planting new cabbage, cucumber, green beans, and squash seeds. De parsley, thyme, rosemary, and chives only needed watering, and de ganja was bountiful inside de big patch.

Breakfast dat morning was hefty: yella yam, breadfruit, fresh green okro, and bright yella pumpkin in a coconut milk oil down, with thyme, sweet and lemon basil, and wiri wiri pepper to bring out de right flava.

As mi daddy use to say, "Nevva look pon nobody fi throw rice in yuh pot. Yuh must do it yuhself." And boy, was he right! It is very satisfying to eat food from your own land, 'specially if you farm every morsel from de ground and watch it come up.

All day I work in de heat, with short breaks in between and cool down in de shade. And just before sundown, I stand back and inspect de rows of newly planted crops; mi daddy would be proud.

At sundown, I sit down in a shady corner of de beach, swallow de last drop of fish head soup, and watch de sun fall into de sea. Right across from me, nature is unfolding. A mama crane is flying back and forth between de brown sargassum patch, and a branch of de big almond tree. She is carrying pieces of matter from de seaweed in her beak and placing it in de mouths of her babies nesting in de tree. I watch her repeat de fetching motion over and over, and it remind me how much lil ones depend pon parents for life.

De need to honour de ancestors creep up pon me after mi successful day of gardening. Although I learn bout de practise of pouring libation from Pappa, I became less scared and slowly embraced de custom after I see de beautiful Asabi, mi lady friend, mix a blend of fermented homemade wine in a calabash wid sea water and pour it by the shoreline, while calling on African deities and her parents for guidance. She explained dat it was paying homage and nothing was sinister bout it. It was den I realise dat de act of libation was indeed truly sacred. So, I pour some rum, close mi eyes, and feel de wind pick up and mi body sway. I listen to de waves crash 'gainst de coastline and roll back out to sea ... swish... de surf taking mi thoughts wid it.

All of a sudden, a strange ting happen; I hear a loud slapping sound, like a barracuda get catch in a net and trying to free itself. I open mi eyes to a head slowly rising from inside de sargassum, a body following. Dressed in a long grey robe, de image was dripping water like streamers. "Ahhhhh ... ahhhhh" I scream and start to back away. Mi heart pound in mi chest, and mi pulse race. *Lawd, was it a jumbie?* It stare me down wid big glassy eyes. I stare it back. And it talk.

"I am Sule." A deep voice come out of dis jumbie man, trailing seaweed and floating just above de waves. "I'm son of Chief Mustapha Samba, but I've lived for centuries in the sea far away from my home. I have come with a message, so listen with care." I hold mi breath while keeping mi eyes pon dis creature.

"Long ago, the White men of empire came up with a scheme to make themselves rich. They pillaged our land, carried us across the seas in slavers to what they called the new world to work us to death and build their wealth. But sometimes the sea held the ships in the thick of the Saragossa, and the trade winds died and the sails went slack. Many perished and many were sickened in the stinking ships."

De words continue to pour out of dis jumbie man, his body shifting wid de breeze. Mi knees begin to shake, and I curl mi toes in de sand and brace for traction. All de while Mr Jumbie talking.

"The men of empire threw both the dead and the sick, no longer useful, into the sea. But, my dear brother, know this: obiara ntumi nku me, gye Nyame. In the White man's language, it means nobody can kill *me* except God. I am, and we are, timeless as eternity, and the sea has become our new home. Our flesh and bones became part of the sargassum—a life-giving source that stimulates growth and abundance. This happened while our spirits slept. Now the men of empire have bought Mother Earth in her entirety and are killing her to boost their riches. Our spirits have awoken to protect the land and sea and to renew the lost generations of our people living in her."

I blink and shake mi head. Dis jumbie man carrying on like he giving a sermon at mi mama's church. But maybe I smoke too much weed, and now I seeing and hearing tings. So, I butt in. "Wha … what …?" Mi tongue tie up. "You mean you live like de fish in de seaweed? Mi eyes and ears must be playing tricks pon me."

I blink and shake mi head again. Mi thoughts foggy, mi legs shaking like a tree branch in a hundred-mile windstorm, and I struggle to stay upright. De jumbie carries on.

"Here is my message for you. We know that you love and respect the land and sea. Use the sargassum and give new life to the land through us in the sea and to new life from the womb."

De whole ting sound like mumbo jumbo, so I interrupt him again: "But how?" He lift his finger to his mouth to quiet me, so I stop talking.

"You are a father to the change that is coming, my brother. You will bring new life to the land and people to the world, people that carry us inside them. They will learn to protect the earth and sea so that the world recovers as we recover and return inside them. Use your body, your mind, and all you have to help us. The men of empire will be changed from within by our people. This is my message, and now I must leave."

I watch him sink back into de seaweed and poof, he disappear.

I pace back and forth, kicking de sand and shaking mi head like water trap in mi ears. As mi pappa used to say, "None a dat mek no sense."

How he live in de sargassum? But he come up from de weed and go back in... de whole ting was confusing. And what he mean dat I will bring new people to de world? *Blouse an skirt—clear yuh head, Zeke, clear yuh head.*

I drag pon a spliff till it finish, and den walk back to mi cottage, glancing over mi shoulder to see if de jumbie man surface again. He nevah come back up.

After meeting Sule, I begin to add de sargassum seaweed mix to one section of mi garden and only horse manure to de odda. Both sections do well, but de seaweed section always look healthier and give more blooms, fruit, and vegetables.

I bring Sule secret to de manor, and just like he promise, de landscape was soon lush with flora. Now I pour libations to Sule, mi daddy, Pappa, Asabi, and all de ancestors dat guide mi path every day. I feel dem watching over me and helping mi gardening from de odda side. I see it as de ancestors giving to de land and de land giving back to me.

Chapter 11

Zeke

Word in de neighbourhood is dat I, Zeke, is a loner. In some respeck is true. But it wasn't always so. Several years ago, I live pon Grenada wid Asabi, de woman I hoped one day would be mi wife. She was de most beautiful being I ever lay eyes pon. I remember one night, mi lady cook de best vegetarian oil down stew I ever tasted, chock full of green fig, sweet potato, dasheen, dumplings, and callaloo, wid nuff fresh green seasoning, and hot guinea pepper, in a coconut milk sauce. I turn to Asabi, rub mi belly and say, "Best meal ever. Dis bredrin just find himself a wife."

She lean back, look at me wid a big smile, and say, "Zeke, if you looking for a wife to cook for you and take care of you, hear this: you ain't looking at her—not this person. I like my independence, see. I don't want to be responsible for nobody else but me, but if you looking for a partner, I can think 'bout it."

Her reply stump me. Growing up, I use to hear de men say all women want to be considered wife material. What mi father would say bout Asabi is dat "Dis woman got balls, and she would go head-to-head wid you to show you she equal. You either accept it or you run like hell."

Sabi sensed mi surprise and drove her point home.

"I been a caretaker for my young sister since I was seven, when my mother and father up and died suddenly. Even now, we don't know what really happened, but rumours say they were killed for their politics. So, we went to live with my mother's sick auntie, and little me had to run the house, even though I could barely reach the stovetop. I look after my sister till she was fifteen and could care for herself. I ain't 'bout to go back to being a sitter again. Nah!"

After she rejected mi partial marriage proposal, I begin to see Asabi differently. Mi ego took a bruising, so I figure some good lovemaking might win her over. A few weeks later, I buy her a green, gold, and black tie-dye scarf she been eying at a stall in de market for a while, and I give it to her at dinner. She acknowledge wid a nod and was about to walk away, and I pull her back, and sit her pon mi lap. I start loving pon her, kissing and caressing her breast, and surprisingly, she kiss me back wid no excuses.

Sabi was a woman of order and never fool around if de kitchen untidy, but mi lady follow me to de bedroom, and we enjoyed a night of sweet passion. She was in charge and told me what pleased her, and I gave mi queen de pleasure she deserved. We wake to de sun beaming through de window and me feeling like I still riding de waves.

"What time is breakfast, honey?" I stretched, yawned, and hugged mi woman.

Asabi didn't reply. Feeling dat she was drifting back to sleep, I ask de question different and louder. "Baby, you gon make you man a meal soon?"

But Asabi prove me wrong again. Dis woman showed me dat she know herself and didn't let sex tie up her mind or throw her off her path. She slowly rolled over and look me square in mi eyes.

"Well, if my man want to eat, he can make his own meal, and make one for his woman too." A beautiful smile fill her face, and she pull de sheet up around her neck.

The game of lawn tennis flash through mi mind and it was mi turn to serve. So I send back mi facts to her. "But, de woman is de chief of de kitchen. Dat's what my father always say."

She chuckled, her dry sense of humour shining through "Why? Because the end of the word kitchen is 'hen' so is a place for females? Well, consider the beginning, 'kitch.' It mean tacky. In other words, it is tacky to think that a female's place is in the kitchen. I learn that from my mother. And I will add that the word female ends with 'male,' so you better show up 'cause it's your space too." She tilted her head, the smile still present. She was winning de match and knew it.

Her words sailed over and hit me smack between mi eyes. I had to find a way to redeem miself. "No, no, no, Sabi, dat's not what I mean. Mi mother is a great cook, and mi father always ask her when de next masterpiece hitting de table. I can't cook, but I happy to help out."

"Okay, my dear man, we'll go to the kitchen together, but remember—you not helping out, you ... taking ... care ... of ... you, feeding yourself. That's important!" Her words were slow and packed a punch.

On dat day, she gave me a lesson in making pot bake and fish soup.

Asabi became mi teacher in many ways. She said caring for miself in mi small world, would help me care for de world I want to live in—de bigger world—in which my little world fit. She said, "My parents tried to take care of the bigger world before taking care of themselves first, and that was why I lost them."

Mi love for Asabi grew more deeply each day, and I still refer to her as mi queen. It wasn't until she was brutally ripped away from me, dat I experience true, gut-wrenching pain. It was de ill-fated day de Americans invade de Isle of Spice.

Shortly after 5:00 a.m. dat morning in October, we wake to what would be a shameful day in dat island's history.

Sabi always rise early, and well before de sun come up, she went out to de garden shed to collect manure and sunflower seeds to plant in de front yard. Bout five minutes after she left de bedroom, a thunderous rumble cause de floor to shake and a *crump-crump*-like noise break de quiet of de new day. Someting was destroying de peace and tranquillity of de morning.

A pounding sound fill mi ears, throat, and stomach and punch through de hut we used to call home. I run to de window and scream for Sabi, but I couldn't see her because blinding balls of fire light up de sky. I run outside, still calling her name, dodging bright flashes as de ground heaved, and strange-smelling smoke drifted into de yard. She wasn't in front of de house or in de garden shed.

Suddenly, everyting stopped. De neighbours come rushing outside to check de damage. A few minutes later we find Sabi's body, cut by metal shrapnel from an explosion. She was full of dark, leaking holes, toss like a rag doll against de garden fence. I held her close, she was still warm, but widout breath. I often wonder if she would be alive if she hadn't gone outside to get dem sunflower seeds. Dat day was de anniversary of her parents' death, and de sunflower was her mother's favourite. It was de symbol she chose to honour dem, but instead de honour she gave was her life, and now she wid dem in eternity.

I was twenty-two years old, numb and in a daze for months after I lost Sabi. She was twenty-four when we find her body, mangled and twisted up against de fence. It was close to de sacks of seeds she had collected for de reforestation project. I saw dis as an omen, and a way to keep her wid me, a way to hold on to her.

So, I joined The Green Belt Volunteer Movement and restored forests, planting tousands of trees in South America and de Caribbean. It was where I hone mi planting and growing skills from de Wai-Wai people in Konashen, pon de Essequibo River in Guyana. I had some basic skills, but I learned 'bout many species of plants and types of soil. And now, I'm taking care of mi small world and giving back to de larger world.

Many days I long for Sabi. Sometimes de air is ripe wid de scent of coconut oil in her hair, de coco butter smell of her skin, and I sense her close to me. I swear I could reach out and touch her. For a very long time, de pain was unbearable, especially at night, but I never ever wear mi anguish pon de outside. What only me and she knew was dat when Sabi left, not only did she take mi heart, but she also take mi child; tuck snugly in her belly.

Chapter 12

Jemma

It had been just over seven months since my move to Majestic. I'd begun a daily exercise regimen which took me on brisk walks around the manor's vicinity. This morning, I headed down the gravel path that led to the back of the property. I glanced behind at the double doors and noticed the profusion of pale pink roses that climbed the trellis on each side. Zeke's skills were clearly visible in the tasteful floral accents and plantings. The sun spread gold over the horizon and bounced off a stone structure in the distance. It resembled a castle turret that I'd noticed before and wondered what it was.

As I came to the fork in the path, something drew me left along the unpaved and less travelled route leading to the turret. I'd never had the urge to explore this unmanicured and rugged part of the property.

I hopped across thick purple ground cover and made my way to a nutmeg tree with large protruding limbs. I paused, glanced behind me and then ahead to gauge how far I had come. I'd heard that tropical snakes were common in these parts, so I picked my way forward carefully and listened for any hissing sounds.

Minutes later, I crested the rise to find the building dead ahead. Suddenly, a coldness rippled down my spine. I stood in place for a few moments and then gradually the chill was replaced by a strange sadness—strange because it felt more like a memory of sadness than sadness itself. Puzzled, I nevertheless continued until the stone structure completely blocked the glorious morning sunshine and cast a grey shadow over the surroundings. The peculiar feeling remained and was somehow connected to this tower. I became teary-eyed, as if someone I loved had died. I had no reason to feel this way. What was the matter with me?

I stood there for a few minutes to regain my composure, and a strong urge to back away came over me. The tower was like a living presence, and I turned and headed back, down the uneven path, focussing on something trivial for comfort. *Zeke has to clean up this pathway*, I told myself, *a person could acquire wood ticks wading through this grass.* I had no idea if these insects were common to the Caribbean.

Finally, back at the manor house, I fumbled with the unlocked door, shuffled into the safety of the kitchen, and leaned against the refrigerator; I needed something to lift my spirits, but the icebox was empty of alcohol. I wanted to scream and cry at the same time but instead, slumped onto one of the stools and buried my face in my hands. What the hell had happened back on the path, and why had such an odd sadness come over me?

I poured myself a snifter of brandy from the bottle on the counter and guzzled it, letting the alcohol push the uncanny experience away.

Primrose entered the kitchen in her quiet way and interrupted my thoughts. "You need something, Ms Jemma?"

"No, I'm okay."

That night, I lay in bed and replayed the earlier eerie experience. I surmised it was because I'd been missing Jack. True, as the weeks dragged on, I'd longed for his comforting arms. Jack had filled a lot of the emptiness in me; the void left by an absent father, an inebriated and distant mother, and a dead sister.

After I found out that Ollie was adopted, I'd wondered why my parents had never had other children; why they chose adoption instead of pregnancy. The question of whether I was biologically theirs lingered. One day on a ride to school, I broached the topic with my dad.

"Couldn't you guys have more kids … is that why you adopted Ollie?" I stared at the traffic light—red and

counted down in my head until it turned green. *Answer,
Dad, answer.* Minutes went by, and then he did.

"Your mum had a difficult pregnancy with you. I remember
her playing a song that Bryan Adams had just released. It was
his big 1983 hit "Cuts like a Knife." She had that song play
on repeat as her labour progressed. I guess that's how she
processed the pain. We decided together we wouldn't — well,
your mum felt pregnancy had violated her body."

"Violated how, Dad? Women get pregnant all the time,
so how was I to blame?"

"Jemma, you weren't to blame for any of it. The dark
stretch marks across her stomach and the weight around
her middle that wouldn't go away, were her two biggest
challenges. It was mostly vanity."

"Is that why she wanted Ollie and me to be like she is,
willowy or svelte, as she likes to say?"

"It's part of the reason. A key struggle for her was not
being able to wear bikinis by the pool or on the beach."

"But looks aren't—"

"I know, but it was important for her. She dieted, worked
out seven days a week, and bleached her stomach for two
years to regain her pre-pregnancy look."

His words merged with the engine sounds and blaring
horns as city dwellers made their way through a grey wintery
morning to their day's business. Giant snowflakes covered
the windshield, melting into shapes like tears to be wiped

away by the swish of rubber blades. If only grief could be removed with such efficiency. Meanwhile, the throb and pulse of the frantic city carried on unconcerned.

Dad did his best to make something incomprehensible sound reasonable. All I heard, though, was '*In giving life to you, the beauty of your mother's body was destroyed. You're to blame, Jemma, it's your fault*'—a message that rang through my head for the rest of the day like a church bell tolling for the dead. My mother saw me as the source of an ugliness that had threatened her perfect body. And my figure, which inclined to a voluptuous fullness rather than fashionable slimness, was always a reminder of what she had lost and fought to regain. Me, in my size-six frame compared to my sister's size zero.

Throughout the rest of that school day, I drifted from classroom to classroom, in a haze, feeling unwanted.

After that incident, I spent many evenings in my room, eating, watching television, or the odd time, going shopping. My life at home unravelled gradually, as if a ball of yarn had rolled off a sofa in slow motion and become smaller and smaller with each tumble across the floor.

So, Jack's admiration of my body, ridiculed and rejected by the women in my family, won me over instantly.

Sleep eventually came, and I quickly lapsed into a dream. I found myself in a field of tall grasses that waved well above my head, moving in some strange, persistent rhythm. Voices were coming through the swaying green wall, but the language was incoherent, like an unknown dialect of some kind. While I couldn't see or find the source of this muttering, I sensed that it came from somewhere in the sea of giant grass. Then I looked around and saw a long blade lying on the ground near me.

The disturbing sight jolted me awake. I sat up, shaken, and with the urgent need to pee. I lurched out of bed to the bathroom, squatted over the toilet and enjoyed the sensation of familiar relief.

From my hunched position, I raised my eyes towards the full-length mirror across from me and instantly froze. There in the mirror was the field of tall sweeping grass, swaying slowly in the breeze, and with the same strange rhythm it had in my dream. Now it resembled corn stalks.

My heart raced. I closed my eyes and shook my head to clear my vision, but the picture in the mirror remained. I stared at it. What was happening? The ocean of reeds with thick segmented stems about halfway down their shaft wavered in place. I squeezed my eyes shut again. When I opened them, I saw my own slack-jawed face staring back at me.

I sat for a few minutes vacillating: *I must have imagined the whole experience; maybe I'm sleepwalking, and this is still a dream; but what if it's not?* The weird overgrown grass was perplexing, and why had it shown up in both the dream and mirror? A plausible explanation eluded me.

I eased myself off the toilet, switched on the overhead light, and fully illuminated the en-suite. I peered and poked the mirror, but it stood still, no reeds in sight. I cautiously walked back into the bedroom and sat at the bottom of the bed, the light still shining brightly in the bathroom. I waited and watched, but the stalks didn't reappear. Eventually, I threw myself across the bed. A few things had been puzzling this day. I closed my eyes and willed myself to sleep, hopeful that clarity would come in the morning.

At sunrise, I combed through the internet to find plants that looked like corn stalks and found nothing close to what I'd seen.

Later that day, I tested Zeke's botanical knowledge about grasses endemic to Majestic. As he prepared to prune some of the palm bushes, I stepped into the walkway. "The bushes grow so quickly! I could swear you only did this last week," I called out.

"Morning, ma'am. We been getting lots of rain and good sun, so you feed dem, and dey grow quickly. It must be four weeks since I trim dis section."

Zeke smiled and stepped back to admire his handy work.

"What kind of palm shrub is this one?" I asked.

"It's a dwarf palmetto, ma'am. Dey develop well in de tropics."

"You do know a lot about plant life on the island. Do you know about grasses too?"

"De island ain't got too much different grasses unless Europeans import special seed types. But usually, dey only live a short while and die off."

"Have you ever seen tall, corn-like grasses on the island?

"Corn-like?"

"Yes, tall, about six feet in height, with the bottoms in segments, like joints … is the best way I can describe it."

Zeke twisted a lock of his hair with the thumb and index finger of his right hand. He tilted his head back and squinted in the morning sunlight, as though expecting a suggestion to fly in on the Caribbean breeze.

"You mean cane, like sugar cane?" Zeke asked, looking at me quizzically.

"Sugar cane? What does it look like? You mean … is there a plant called sugarcane?"

Zeke gawked at me for a moment. He appeared confused. Then, explaining in simple sentence structure as one would to a child, he slowly and methodically replied: "Yes, ma'am. Majestic use to have sugar plantations, way back in de day. Dey use to grow sugarcane here, and dat's a tall grass."

He paused and waited for me to snap out of my bewilderment. To hide my ignorance, I shrugged, casually threw both hands into the air, and proclaimed: "Sugar comes in a packet where I'm from." I forced humour into the situation, but Zeke didn't seem to get it, or chose to ignore it.

"De building at de back end of de property use to be where they produce sugar," he continued. "It's called a sugar mill. Enslaved Africans would cut de cane from de fields with a machete and deliver it to de mill to be turned into molasses, then sugar."

"Wait — so there really was slavery in the Caribbean?

"Yes ma'am, dere was slavery in dese parts.

"Wow, I thought that was a Southern U.S. thing"

"No ma'am, only a small fraction of de many many millions of enslaved people went to de U.S. Dey scatter de rest cross de Caribbean and South America and work dem to death. Some right here pon Majestic."

"I had no idea."

My head was spinning with this new knowledge. *Plantation Emerald Hill—Amanda's family—could they have owned slaves? My God, I hope not!*

I thanked Zeke and headed back to the house, my temples throbbing.

I pulled up the words 'sugarcane plant' in Google Images on my iPad, and the page lit up with pictures of the tall stalks just as I'd seen in the dream and mirror the night before. I also looked for an image of a machete, and sure enough hundreds of images that looked like the knife lying on the ground in my dream filled the page. What the hell was happening?

I didn't know much about slavery, except that it was a terrible thing done to Black people a long time ago. Ollie and I had watched the tail end of the miniseries *Roots* with our Dad as we waited for mother to come home from a theatre show. Dad had remarked that 'human beings owning other human beings is just wrong.' I will never forget the picture of Kunte Kinte struggling across the fields with his injured foot, cruelly mangled by slave catchers. Both Ollie and I had nightmares about it.

A hollowness hovered in the pit of my stomach. I had to talk to someone about my experiences… but whom? In my world of confidants, there were very few with whom I could share this information. Maya? *Of course*, she's the one.

Chapter 13

Jemma

Jack had added a Viennese palace restoration to his portfolio, and projects in Italy and Spain were ongoing. This meant he was often gone longer than usual. My loneliness intensified, and my longing for Zeke resurfaced.

Any earlier discomfort about his race had dissipated, yet I could hear mother's voice in my head. "Don't look at them or speak, just get the hell away." Ollie asked why, and mother responded matter-of-factly: "They are not the same as us, they are primitive and dangerous."

I grew up being told to avoid Black men, with every mug shot of a dark-skinned suspect on the late news or morning paper pointed out to me. I had never met any Black boys—my mother made sure of that. But since I'd left home, I had come into contact with Black men, and had no negative experience or any other kind of experience with them, or Black people in general. However, I must admit that the intensity of my mother's abhorrence also fed my curiosity. So, there was a mix of allure and fear of the unknown whenever I thought about getting close to Zeke. But the allure was getting stronger.

I cogitated for a minute. Did I want to be with this man to prove my mother wrong, or to experience the prohibited? I'd only slept with White men until that point, and sleeping with Zeke would be very different, wouldn't it?

And what if he was already in a relationship? Odd that it had never crossed my mind before. Though not ideal, it wouldn't be my first time. How could I find out if he was with someone without showing obvious interest? Would Primrose know?

I paced the floor of my bedroom, tippling gin and bitter lemon, cubes of ice tinkling in my glass like a soundtrack of my nerves. I had to find out.

It had been a full week of scanty sleep, the sounds of the sea no longer effective in sending me off to dreamland. At night I was adrift in the bed, my arms and legs searching and stretching to capture Jack's form and the combination of safety and desire it had always provided: the knowledge that I was wanted, replaced by emptiness. I was alone.

That afternoon, I followed Zeke. He'd said he lived about two miles down the beach. I would find his cottage and pretend to have stumbled across it during my stroll.

I watched him clean and prepare his work tools for the next day and place them in the garden shed. I waited until he passed below my window and headed down the path towards the beach. Then, I slid out the front door, avoiding Primrose, who I'd heard moving around and vacuuming in one of the guest rooms.

I scurried along the driveway and took the path to the right down to the beach. I saw no sign of Zeke, so I quickened my pace and reached the open stretch of sand. Walking at a steady stride, he was now about one hundred yards ahead of me.

I pulled on my floppy straw hat and sunglasses and waited behind some shrubs for about two minutes, then began to slowly follow him. By now he was at least three hundred yards away, far enough that if he turned around, he wouldn't immediately recognise me.

I passed an older woman and a gaggle of kids picking sea grapes along the way, and two young women sunbathing on the sand. After about twenty minutes, Zeke angled left and disappeared. I continued walking at the same speed, kicking sand up into my Birkenstocks. In a few minutes I would get to the area where he'd veered off, and I needed a plan in case I came face-to-face with him. But I had no plan and couldn't come up with one except that '*I needed a walk and chose this end of the beach.*' It sounded lame, but maybe then he would invite me in to see his place or… *God, this is stupid… what the hell am I doing?*

I'd reached the area and, on my left, sat a tiny yellow cottage, with a lush garden of vegetables and herbs on one side and a beautifully manicured yellow and white frangipani bush on the other. It reminded me of something out of a fairy tale, and I stared at it in awe. Could this be where Zeke lived? Van Gogh also lived in a yellow house, but probably three times the size of Zeke's. I wished I could take a picture and share it with Ollie, so I closed my eyes and sent it telepathically.

As I looked around, I saw movement from the corner of my eye. Before I could duck out of sight, a shirtless Zeke appeared in the path leading up to the cottage. For a moment we just gazed at each other: me from behind my dark glasses, my messy blond hair hidden under the floppy hat. It took him a while to figure out that it was me, and the lapse in time allowed me a good, close-up look at his bare chest and chiselled stomach, strong firm shoulders, and powerful arms.

"Ms Jemma? Ma'am, is dat you?" Zeke eventually said, as he squinted and peered to confirm that it was really me.

"It is me, Zeke. I needed a walk, and—" I began my rehearsed explanation, but he interrupted.

"Oh good," he said with a sigh. "So, everyting okay at de house?"

"Yes, it is," I said, changing the subject. "Is this where you and your family live?"

"Well, yes and no," he began. "De place is mine, and I live here. It used to belong to mi family, but now is only me here."

"Oh, did your wife ...?'

"No, ma'am, I don't have a wife. Never marry, and by family, I mean mi mother and father, mi siblings, all of dem in America. But me, I like it here, so I live at de old homestead."

My heart skipped a beat and my face flushed. I hoped that my excitement didn't stick out like a glow light. "I've never been this far down the beach before; I should probably get back."

"I gonna brew some tea; you like to stay for a cup? We can have it in de cottage or pon de beach," he offered.

I looked deep into Zeke's brown eyes and saw warmth and gentleness, similar to what I'd seen in my father's dove-grey eyes.

"I'd love that," I said. It was as if Zeke read my mind. "And either place would be fine."

"Okay, I will put de kettle on; it is a nightly ritual to relax me. You can come in while it brewing."

"So why didn't you go to North America like your other family members?" I probed.

"I choose to stay right here in de sunshine, farming mi land with de sea in mi front yard—at lease for de next lil while. People suffer too much in North America—especially Black people. And everybody can't have de smarts of politicians like Shirley Chisholm, or celebrities like Sidney Poitier, Maya Angelou, or Harry Belafonte. Dem is just a few of de people with Caribbean roots dat become famous in America," he said flippantly. "I'm de king of mi castle right here pon Majestic."

I smiled, since the names in his pronouncement meant nothing to me.

Zeke's face glowed with a mischievous grin, and he added, "Plus people like you and Mr Jack come to share in de sun and sea; North America can't be dat great if you here. People here say dat as soon as it get cold, folks from North America and Europe rush down to de Caribbean like breeding penguins pon an Argentinean beach."

An image of penguins huddled together on Boulder beach in the Cape floated through my head, and I chuckled in return. "You said 'a little while,' how long is a little while, I mean, that you plan to stay on Majestic?"

"My plan was to stay for one year catching my hand here on de island or on Baptiste."

"Well, we're coming up on a year since you've been working for us at Seaview. How have your plans shifted? Do you plan on leaving anytime soon?"

"Renting out de cottage is something I think bout sometime, but dat plan is in mi back pocket. Right now, I like de easy walk to de job," he said with a grin.

"Well, I'll just have to keep you around and busy for your ease and mine; the manor is a large property and needs your expert attention," I said, grinning in return.

A son of the soil, I thought as we entered the cottage. A pleasant mingle of cinnamon, clove and nutmeg filled the room, and a hint of citrus floated in the air. I sat in a baby-blue wicker chair in the neat living room, and through the shuttered windows, the lulling waves washed against the shoreline. He lit the stove and offered me options of guinea hen, cerasee, or ginger tea. The first two were ominous, so I played it safe and chose ginger.

Zeke excused himself and disappeared into the bedroom. In a few seconds he came back wearing a blue T-shirt.

The kettle boiled, and we chatted about plants as the tea steeped.

"You know, we drink a lot of herb tea in de Caribbean, and cerasee and guinea hen are two of de popular ones. Dey cure a lot of ailments, and dey high in vitamins, too."

"What type of ailments are they used for?" I asked, trying to keep him talking so I could admire his firm backside. I didn't really care about his answers; I drooled with lust.

"Cerasee is a good herb to purge de blood and prevent hypertension. Guinea hen help lower blood sugar—also good for fever and treating infection. Many island people turn to dese herbs before seeing de doctor." Zeke just knew so much about plant life.

"Growing up, I heard about the benefits of ginger for colds, especially in the wintry months. Folks drank mint tea or ginger and lemon tea, so I'm familiar with those." He handed me a small curved blue mug that resembled Denby stoneware while he drank from a yellow one.

We left the cottage and walked along the beach for a few minutes, then sat on the warm sand behind a large boulder.

As we sipped tea, Zeke told me about his love for all things natural, including the way he farmed and ate from the land and how he abstained from alcohol. He likened working the land to "Caring for she who gave him food." He also told me of his love for the sea and everything within it. I found his philosophy and way of life profound.

Zeke's consideration showed when he asked if it would be okay to smoke in my presence. I said it was fine. He pulled out the longest and fattest spliff I'd ever seen, from the pocket of his trousers, lit it, and inhaled. His face and locks disappeared for a moment behind a wall of thick light blue smoke when he exhaled.

Then he offered me the spliff. At first, I hesitated, but I didn't want to reject his hospitality, so I took it and inhaled so hard that I went into a coughing fit. He reached over and gently patted my back, urging me to drink more tea.

By the time we finished our tea, I'd caught my breath, and everything was more mellow, crisper... the air, the sea, the sand... and Zeke. I'd come to fill my empty yearning for flesh against flesh, and I was ready.

I leaned forward, softly touched his face and traced my index finger across his mouth. He looked at me and smiled. Then, he took a few more puffs on the spliff and offered it to me. This time I closed my eyes and inhaled slowly and deeply. I opened them to see Zeke's T-shirt slide over his head and land on the sand. I was sitting less than a foot away from him, breathing in his scent, and lost in the warmth of his incredible eyes. I tried to radiate my desire for him without completely losing my composure. He drew closer, looked me in the eyes, and asked, "Are you sure?"

"Yes, I'm sure," I said.

I was as light as a feather; Zeke tapped my shoulder and I fell backward against the sand. His first kiss was gentle and light, as if he was uncertain, but my aching for him was so intense, I kissed him hungrily. His hands travelled along my breasts and belly, gradually moving between my thighs, then he suddenly stiffened and rolled away.

"Don't stop" I said."

"But Mr Jack..."

"Jack isn't here, we are. And I don't know when he's coming back."

"Okay," he whispered.

"Take me, Zeke, please take me…" I closed my eyes. I wanted him, needed him, and I sensed that he wanted me too.

Zeke's dreadlocks brushed my chest as he leaned in, kissing and caressing me. His hands cradled my ass, as my legs encircled his body. I pushed up with my pelvis to create a seal between us. Soon I fell into sync with his slow rhythmic flow, and a pleasure gradually built, stoking the fire of our excitement as it burned through our bodies and ground to an explosive climax. We lay on the beach naked, exposed to the salty air, and then at Zeke's suggestion we waded into the sea.

Later we went back to his cottage and turned on the lights before walking back to the manor. As we did, the setting sun slashed bronze over the undulating Caribbean.

"Even the sea is doing a happy dance!" I smiled at Zeke.

He looked at me with a twinkle in his auburn eyes.

"Yes, And I hope Sule and de ancestors approve," he whispered in my ear.

I was too giddy with joy to question who Sule was, so I smiled and let it go.

We stole kisses and walked along the secluded strip of beach, mostly in silence. I asked Zeke to leave me close to the path near the house; I couldn't let Primrose see us together.

"Our secret," he said, and kissed me on the cheek.

I walked up the path, and he headed back to his cottage. As soon as he was out of sight, I skipped like a little girl the rest of the way. Primrose met me at the back door.

"Dinner is long ready, ma'am. I was keeping it warm and looking for you," she said.

"Thanks. I needed a walk to clear my mind. I'll eat on the lanai."

"Mr Jack here; he gone down to the marina. Should I wait supper for him too?"

My heart thudded a sudden drumbeat in my chest "Is he? When ...um ..."

"Mr Jack arrive about two hours now, ma'am."

"Of course, of course, we'll wait until he gets back," I said as I hurried into the bathroom to get washed and dressed. About ten minutes later, Jack walked into the bedroom.

"Surprise!" he said and threw his arms in the air.

"Indeed, a surprise. Why didn't you tell me?" I forced a smile.

"I'm only here for a few days. I had a last-minute trip to Puerto Rico to see an old client of Jav's; he's wrapping up a larger project in Seville so couldn't be there. I had the pilot file a flight plan for Baptiste and fly me here to see you. Where were you?"

"I took a long walk along the beach and swam in the sea, which I may do again. Proud of me? I met a few young women and stayed for a small picnic with them." My fib odometer was full tilt, and my stomach muscles clenched.

"Good. And how are you doing, and may I have a hug?" he asked.

"Yes, you may," I smiled, leaned in, and hugged him as a sudden giddiness came over me. I had dodged a bullet—maybe.

Primrose served light pasta with shrimp in a crème sauce. Jack and I devoured it over a few glasses of wine. We turned into bed and our coming together was gentle and easy, no fireworks. Our bodies moved together in familiar rhythm.

"I've missed being with you, Jemma. I'll have to visit Majestic more often."

"I'm glad to hear that, Jack. Will you let me know ahead of time so Primrose can prepare for your visit? Hopefully you'll stay a lot longer too."

"That's a promise."

We spent most of the morning in bed, and I kept replaying the previous evening with Zeke. Was that a mistake? But how could it have been? It was so freeing, so beautiful. I hoped that Jack hadn't caught on or that Zeke wouldn't give it away. He had promised to keep it our secret.

I was a bloody mess. I had to be the consummate actress, or I could lose everything.

Chapter 14

Zeke

Zeke, was dat a smart ting to do? What if it mess up your employment... what if Mr Jack come back and find out... and what if she cry rape? Dis lil yappy voice was jabbering in mi head.

Ahhhh, stop it, stop it! She can't cry rape. I double check; I ask her if she was sure, and she say yes. *Consensual*, dat's what Sabi use to say. She like dat word 'consensual,' no guessing—yes or no. But sometimes yes can turn into no, but she say 'Take me Zeke, please take me,' and though I had doubts, I did, and she take me too, Yappy, so be quiet. *Consensual it was.*

But what if Yappy right? De woman is Babylon—de cause of a lot of evil in dis world—so I really got to be careful. She can be one of dem 'African at heart': pink on de outside, yet righteous on de inside. Only time gon tell.

It could be tricky at de job. Wonder how she gon be tomorrow. She might ignore me and act like none a dis happen. Like it was de ganja and not something she would consider oddawise. Yes, I did offer her de ganja, but she didn't have to take it. She's a grown woman, she can say no. Wonder if she would look me in de eye if she fire me?

I roll a spliff, pop in a Peter Tosh CD, and inhale deep to de song "African." De croon of Peter voice lull Mr Yappy to sleep, and I settle down and continue to tink back to de experience pon de beach. I did enjoy being with a woman again, and though I got me principles, sometime a lil consensual coming together can be okay.

Mi eyelids close, and before I know it, morning break. I look at mi reflection in de mirror, a smile cross mi face. I brush mi teeth and credit dis joy to de experience from de night before. But slowly, Mr Yappy wake up and doubt creep in again.

Throughout mi sunrise exercise, Yappy prattle on and on, and mi worry 'bout Jemma deepen. I decide to just go to de job and wait for her to make de first move. Dis way, I get de lay of de land, and I don't have to guess.

I reach de manor compound bout 7:30 a.m., mi usual clock-in time. Everyting is quiet except for de chirping warblers and wrens, and de lapping sea at high tide. I collect mi tools from de shed and position miself down from de conservatory, where she usually come out for her morning coffee and swim.

Almost three hours go by, sweat pouring down mi face in de warm morning sun. *When will dis woman show up?* I empty mi water flask out of uneasiness, and de door of de conservatory open. I glance over and she walk out looking serious—not like de night before. Dis behaviour throw me off, but I decide dat if she want to act like nuting happen, so be it. Two can play dat game. A few minutes later, I figure out why she was acting funny. Mr Jack walk out de house and join her by de pool. He must have come from foreign lands sometime in de night. *Lawd, I wonder if he did see me walk her back to de bottom of de path. I hope he ain't find out where she been earlier?*

Too much was racing round mi brain and mi sweating intensify. I decide to keep mi head down and do mi job, quiet as a church mouse. I mulch and trim de same bush a few times before realising dat I had to change location. And Yappy did not stop. '*Maybe he know, maybe she in trouble, maybe you break de rule.*' Oh shut up, Yappy. Shut the hell up.

Around two o'clock, de madam come and sit under de pergola with her computer, and shortly after I hear a splash. I look over and see Mr Jack in de pool. I glance over at her, and she give me a half smile. I take dat signal to mean dat everyting was alright between us.

For de next couple of days, I come and go, more certain everyday dat what happen between me and de missus was our lil secret.

One morning, about four days later, I see Mr Jack put his bags in de cyar. I let out a big sigh, start spreading heaps of seaweed fertilizer, and humming to Bob Marley's "Three Little Birds." Minutes later, as if to shake me out of mi new comfort level, Babylon was standing over me.

"I've not had a chance to tell you, but your work on the property is impeccable, Zeke."

"Thank you, Mr Jack. I take much delight in gardening. Will do what I can to keep de grounds in tip-top shape sir." I didn't like dat he was towering over me. I stand up and step back, so we can see eye to eye.

"It's apparent; the joy is reflected in your work. Carry on," he say with a nod, as he scan round de garden. A few seconds later, he turn and walk back toward de house where de missus is waiting by de cyar in de driveway. She hand him de key and slide in de passenger side. As soon as he get in de driver seat, she reach over and kiss him long and hard. I watch dem from behind de palm bush and can't help wondering if dat show is for me or Mr Jack.

De whole of de next week, de missus stay mostly in de house and barely come out to de pool. I figure she no longer got interest in me, so I keep to miself, only going to de house on

Fridays to pick up me pay, which she was now leaving with
Primrose. I only see her de odd time, and from far.

One Friday, bout a month after Mr Jack went back to
foreign, I go up to de house for mi pay. Primrose asked me
to come back later, as Ms Jemma didn't leave it with her. De
cyar wasn't at de house, so I figure she could be at de bank.
I promise to return and start walking to mi cottage. Just
before I turn in mi yard, I see de madam leaning gainst de
south wall in a yella dress, looking like sunshine self. I greet
her first.

"Hello, what a surprise," I say, trying to sound relax,
all de time me head churning. Why she come here; what
she want?

"Forgive me Zeke, I ... I'm not sure why ..."

I wait for her to finish.

"May I come inside?" Up close, I see dat sweat is dripping
down her face like a leaking tap, so I open de front door.

"Yes, please come in." We hadn't really talked in five
weeks, so I decide to hear her out.

"Here is your pay. I should've spoken with you before
now, but I didn't know what to say."

"Thank you," I say, and wait for her to continue. "Please
have a seat. Would you like a cold drink or some tea?" I was
playing it cool, and mi mother did teach me manners.

"That would be nice," she say, but she don't choose

a drink.

"How 'bout some lemon iced tea?"

"Yes, thank you, please."

I walk over to de fridge, and she continue to chat: "It's complicated. You see I'm in a relationship with Jack and I ... well, sleeping with you might have been a mistake, but to be honest, I can't get that night out of mi head."

I bring her de ice tea and sit down pon de wicker chair across from her.

"How do you feel about it, I mean about that night?" she continue.

Zeke, don't fall into no trap. She don't know what she want. Yappy start to jabber again. *Shush, shush!* I say in mi head, but he won't shut up.

"I put it behind me. I think is what you want, so don't worry." Mi eyes and she own meet, and she look down.

"Well, it wasn't a mistake after all; I know that now and wonder if ..."

"Go on ... what you wondering?" *Protect yuhself Zeke* is what I tell miself.

"I might need some weed to relax my nerves. Do you have any?"

"Might be some," I say, but I ain't move one inch.

"Zeke, I really need a hit, please."

I study her for a few seconds, get up, walk to de bedroom,

and come back with a spliff. I light it, and she take a long slow drag and pass it back to me.

I watch as she wiggle her hips, pull up her skirt, and ease her legs apart. I figure the heat was causing her clothing to stick to her body. But de madam look up at me, and eased open her legs some more. "I came here for a reason—and he's sitting in front of me," she say, between short puffs, as coils of smoke swirl across de living room."

"But … how I know you sure … how I know you wouldn't ….?"

"What I do know is that I want what we shared on the beach. Do you?"

"We share a few tings dat night; tea, ganja, emmmm…" *Don't elp her, Zeke, let de woman name her wants.* I look up in de roof pretending to figure out what else we shared.

"I mean you, Zeke. There I said it."

I move over and sit down next to her, and the madam get up, straddle me, and wrap her legs 'round me. I start nibbling pon her breasts, and she throw her head back, and whisper, 'Oh Zeke.'

A few minutes later we move to de bedroom. And for de next little while, we melt into each odda.

"I see you're enjoying this just as much as I am," she murmur in mi ear.

"Yes ma'am." A smile cross mi face.

"Call me Jemma; ma'am is for work,' she sigh.

"What does Mr Jack call you?"

"Jemma, why?"

"I don't want you get mix up, and I like Jem, better," I say with a grin.

"Jem is okay, just as long as you promise to keep these meetings our secret." This time her tone is serious.

"So, Mr Jack didn't ask you where you been dat last time?"

"No worries, Zeke. I handled it."

After a few more puffs of ganja, we continue to enjoy each odda, and soon we fall asleep.

Chapter 15

Jemma

The next morning, I lay in bed and thought about Maya. She had kept secrets I'd shared with her, mostly about my sleeping around days, and now I had something new to add. I chuckled quietly. One of those buried truths was about the time I left home for good. I was almost eighteen. I had walked into a shocking image of my dad in a disquieting position with another person. My mother was in the house, present in body but absent in spirit. I'd become overwhelmed, hurried to my room, and threw some of my possessions into a duffel bag. Then I grabbed a stack of bills from my dad's special stash in their bedroom safe, scribbled a note, tossed it onto the coffee table, and ran out the front door.

I'd been gone for three months before I contacted my folks. My money had run out, and I had no other source of funds. It infuriated me that I had to call them, but I needed food and somewhere to sleep, so I picked up the phone and dialled home.

My mother answered. I could tell by the familiar slurred speech that she'd been drinking. I hung up and called my dad's cell phone. Our conversation was short and direct.

"Dad, it's Jemma. Before you say anything, know that I walked in on you *in flagrante* with a girl around my age in our movie theatre. You were so caught up in the rapture of the moment that you didn't see me enter while mother was passed out drunk upstairs on the living room sofa. I'll finish my schooling in Northern Italy, and I need you to wire me enough for six months living expenses. Then I'll get a part-time job and take care of myself."

Silence filled the line for about twenty seconds. Was he waiting for more or thinking about a response? Another ten seconds elapsed.

"How much do you need?"

He surprised me, and didn't come up with excuses, but I'd rehearsed this spiel over and over, so my answer was crisp. "Twenty-thousand euros," I said calmly, feeling like an extortionist.

"That's a lot of money."

"Not for my silence or my mental health. Do you realise how traumatic it was for me to see you in that position, and in our home?"

Again, the pause was deafening. My hands became clammy, and I feared I would drop the telephone.

"I'm sorry for what you saw. I'll send you ten thousand and your airfare to get you there and settled in. I'll wire the rest later after I receive your particulars."

"I'm at the Sutton Place," I said, and he let out a small sigh of relief. A few days later I received the money transfer and a note that read "Love mum and dad."

I purchased my ticket for Genoa the next day, and the rest is history. I never contacted my mother again and dealt only with my father through e-mails: sending my new address and banking information to receive the balance of the promised money, and the occasional holiday or birthday greeting.

I spent most of the day working online, watching runway shows, and placing orders in Milan and Florence. Eventually I took a dip in the pool. It was Zeke's day off, and as I swam, his beautifully buffed body waded into my consciousness. I figured visiting him once a week could be the right balance, if he was amenable.

Later, I sent Maya a WhatsApp message that read: "Hey Maya Kingsley, where in the world r u and r u ready to visit me in this sun-kissed paradise? I need company."

While I waited for her response, I strolled down the hall and entered the conservatory. Primrose had set up the small table for dinner, so I sat and contemplated recent events; my two-timing with Zeke was top of mind. I watched the sea begin to swallow the sun, leaving an orange residue on the waves. A familiar ping pulled me out of my musing. It was Maya. The text began with a grinning emoji.

Maya: I'm in Paris tonight—just walked in from a very late working dinner. Sun and beach sounds wonderful.

Jemma: That's great!

Maya: And we should talk. I ran into Jack today at a business function.

Jemma: He's in Paris? How did Luxembourg become Paris?

Maya: That you must ask him. I can talk tomorrow early afternoon after I wrap-up my morning meetings. My calendar is open after that. Chat then?

Jemma: K.

Then she went offline.

Had Jack mentioned Paris? Why don't I remember Paris in the mix of the places he would be visiting for business? I must have missed it.

Primrose entered the conservatory with a tray, and a mouth-watering aroma filled the room. "I made baked snapper with greens and a small salad. Hope you enjoy it, ma'am."

"Thank you," I said apathetically, replaying Jack's itinerary in my head.

I remembered him saying Luxembourg for a week, London for two, and Vienna for one week. I had written it down in Notes on my iPad. There wasn't a Parisian connection in there. Maybe something new had come up and he'd fill me in later.

I straightened my chair and placed the white linen napkin on my lap. Primrose's cooking was exceptional. Amanda had said "Women don't cook in the Caribbean," and I had misinterpreted the statement. I understood her to mean that customarily, men did the cooking, like some house boys did in Cape Town. It took me a while to figure out that she meant rich white women in the Caribbean hired out their cooking, like they did everything else. And women of colour made the most delectable dishes with minimal ingredients, and usually without recipes. Primrose was a recipe-free woman. The fish was succulent: seasoned with fresh thyme, onions, locally grown garlic, and set in breadcrumbs. The side was baby bok choy, stewed tomatoes, and steamed and lightly buttered long beans. A shredded cabbage and carrot salad perfectly drizzled with lemon and olive oil completed the meal.

I savoured two fruity glasses of Gewurztraminer imported from a vintner near Strasbourg. Jack and I had visited his old friend Armand in nearby Kaysersberg a few times, and so began a tradition of him sending us wines from the region twice a year. By the end of dinner, the bottle contained less than a full glass. I made it to bed and fell asleep listening to Mozart on my iPad.

I woke to the distant cry of gulls and pushed the black sleeping mask up to reveal the morning sun streaming through the window. The air was still, and the sea soundless far below.

After lying in for a few more minutes, I rolled out of bed, slid into a pink satin robe, poured a mimosa, donned my Burberry sunglasses, and sat out by the pool.

Zeke was already working, moving slowly, smooth, brown arms pushing in and out of earth and plants. I watched him for a while, but my conversation with Maya the evening before resurfaced. It was now early afternoon in Paris, and I looked forward to our chat in a few minutes.

"Calling ..." her text said. My phone rang thirty seconds later.

"How are things in the City of Love?" I began on a high note.

"Just depends on who's loving who."

"Seems like you have something to tell me—do you?" I took a sip of my drink and waited.

"I might, but it's the sort of thing girls talk about in person. As it turns out, I have the next six days off. One of my clients settled earlier than expected. So, I can come to Majestic for some downtime."

"Amazing! I'd love to see you. How soon can you come?"

"Does the day after tomorrow work for you?"

"Message me with the particulars, and I'll pick you up at the ferry docks."

"Perfect. I'll see you in forty-eight hours."

Chapter 16

Primrose

"Primpuss" is what Amanda Whittle call me. At first, I ignore her, but recently I just say, "My name is Primrose, Ms Whittle. It's *Primrose!*"

I never did like Amanda Whittle. My old boss, Madame Manon Fournier, or Madame F, was a classy lady who always treat me well and dress real fancy. She like frilly blouses and simple skirts, and always had nice nails. She was the first person I ever see with blue nail polish. She said it match the ocean and the sky. I used to think it match her gentle eyes perfectly. Ms Whittle, on the other hand, was always in white tennis skirts, sleeveless shirts, and tennis shoes, and her face always screw up like when tiger suck sour plum. There was nothing special about her, not even her pixie haircut.

Madame F and her husband, Monsieur Pierre, ran the best bakery on the island, Patisserie Paradis. It is where I bring my Caribbean know how and she her European skills to make magic. People say we work together like plait bread, one braid overlapping the other to make the perfect loaf.

I cook with my granny from the age of six years. At first, she used to send me to collect kindling for the fire from the park across the way. It made me feel important.

"My First Rose, is time to feed the fire so we can feed our tummies and grow," she would say almost every day. Or sometimes she'd say "FR time to FF."

Anyone not a part of our household would be baffled by the strange command, but it was special between GG and me. The old wood stove would need feeding, and I was the one task with feeding her, until my mother got a nice, two-burner kerosene stove.

At a very early age, I learn to mix cornmeal dumplings for eddoe and split pea soup. By the age of eight, and under GG's supervision, I was turning out a full course meal for GG, Mama, and me. GG used to say, "FR got photo memory and learn well." Except for the time that I sneak and put extra cured pig tail in the soup without boiling out the salt first. I figure I would end up with a few more pieces in my bowl, but the meal turn into a pot of brine, and even GG couldn't eat it. She didn't throw it away, though, and use it instead as the base to make two more pots of soup.

I grasped a new lesson. Never add ingredients to any meal without GG's direction.

One time I watch her open a newspaper packet of grouper Mama bring home, place it on a cutting board, and with a sharp skinny knife, remove the scales. Then she pour rain water from a galvanize bucket into a bowl and wash the fish. Right after that, she walk outside the house to our small garden, pick a few sprigs of fresh thyme, green onion, a couple of wiri wiri peppers, and a clipping of married-man-pork. She pluck a fresh lime from the dwarf tree near the kitchen window, cut and squeeze the juice on the fish, and let it soak in the water. Next, she rinse all the seasonings, grab a few fegs of garlic and a dash of salt, place then in the small mortar and pestle, and crush the daylight out of them. The room immediately come alive with a fresh lemony, minty smell, with the thyme and married-man-pork competing for top spot. I close my eyes, inhale and let my nose suck up every inch of this captivating aroma; one I hadn't experienced before. GG voice pull me out of my odor trance. "Wake up, child, there's work to be done." Then she turn her attention back to the fish.

She take it from the bowl, wrap it in a sheet of gauze—the kind that Christmas ham come in—to absorb the excess water. When she remove the fish from the gauze, she nicked shallow slits on both sides, rub the crushed seasoning into the openings, and divide it into three even pieces. She dust the fish in a flour and cornmeal mixture and drop it into a dash of hot oil in the old blackened frying pan, and with quick flips of her wrists, I watch as both sides of the fish take on a golden colour. To finish off her masterpiece, she add a dolop of margarine, some coconut milk, and slices of tomato to the pan and let it simmer. Peeling ground provisions and boiling them in coconut milk was her next chore; she especially like eddoe and plantain. Served up together, it was the big meal of the week, and me and mama looked out for it every Friday night.

If no one was watching me do the dishes, I run my index finger over all the plates and lick any drippings, before putting them through the dishwater.

Now, at Seaview, I prepare fish for Ms Jemma the same way GG did back then, but I bake rather than fry it. This way, the aroma stays in the oven and don't spread throughout the house. And I only make salads or steamed vegetables to go with the fish; I don't know if her stomach could handle heavy provision like we can.

GG was all about improvising. If we didn't have cassava for pone, she used sweet potato instead, and a new recipe was born. And if she ran out of split pea for the Sunday soup, she would use pigeon pea instead. When we were low on cooking oil to fry her famous float bakes, she introduced pot bakes. And don't ever ask her about a recipe. She would say, "You just add a pinch of this and a pinch of that, not too much fuss."

When things didn't work like she wanted it to, GG never complain. She would say, "Sometimes God put you in a difficult position so you can find another way, because he knows you smart enough to do it."

So, I learn to adapt and create new things very early in life. And after Madame F left, I use sour cherry jam for pie filler instead of raspberry and condense milk instead of cream for sweet tarts. I guess that made me smart.

I blame Amanda Whittle for me losing my job at the patisserie. There I was near the end of my day pushing the swing door into the baker's room to set up ingredients for puff pastry. Right in front of me, on either side of the pastry table, were two white legs dangling. And at the other end, Mr Pierre was hovering over two small mounds of breast, dripping chocolate sauce on them, and then licking it off as though he was enjoying an ice cream cone. Then the body with white legs raised its head and became Ms. Amanda herself. She stare at me with them steely dark eyes, and I wanted to laugh and vomit at the same time. But I just turn around and left the fornication scene.

Monsieur Pierre, too involve in his chocolate detailing, didn't notice my entrance or exit, and she likely found my intrusion an annoyance, rather than an embarrassment.

Madame F had been on a trip to Colmar, France, to see her ailing mother, and this man was carrying on behind her back. As I replay the incident, I wish I would have walk over and thump his head and make him choke pon a mouth full of chocolate bubby. But it wasn't my business, so I walk home and didn't breathe a word to no one except, of course, GG, who said that I was put in that position to learn something new. Then she added: "But you must stay out of things that don't concern you and remember to never take your drawers off in public places." If GG only knew that I had to fight to keep my drawers on—though it wasn't in public.

Working in the pastry room about three weeks later, I hear the Fourniers having a bitter argument in their bedroom one floor above. A week after that, they closed the bakery for good and left for France. The French sous chef from the bistro down the lane had a lot to say to anyone who would listen about the Fourniers' sudden departure.

"Madame found out about her husband and Ms Amanda. Elle a trouvé ses sous-vêtements de bikini en dentelle fourrés dans le tiroir de la table à patisserie."

"Quoi ? Le vilain clochard!" Someone yelled.

"Oui… Madame a demandé le divorce en France."

Because I'd picked up some of the language from high school and Madame F, I smiled. What I didn't know was that Ms Amanda had stuffed her lacy bikini underwear in the pastry table drawer so Madame F would find it. Now Madam had file for a divorce from Monsieur Pierre.

From then on, Amanda call me a puss, 'Primpuss,' in reference to my light, catlike footsteps. But the name wasn't belittling enough and didn't stick, as she is the only person that calls me that to my face.

So, you could imagine my surprise when I learn that Ms Amanda recommend me for the job with Ms Jemma. But I find out later from Myrna, her maid, that Ms. Amanda did want to make a good impression on Mr Jack who she had her eyes on. She had come back from meeting him and Ms Jemma and couldn't stop talking about how tall and handsome the man was. He could have been her next target if he gave her a chance.

And she know I had good cooking skills and that Madame F always praise my work. She would say, "Primrose est un naturel." I was such a natural that she started a line of pastries I develop and call it French Caribbean Delights.

Now, being at Seaview Manor, and with access to many of the fancier ingredients, I take every chance and showcase my skills to Ms Jemma and Mr Jack, whenever he visit.

Chapter 17

Jemma

The ferry arrived at 6:20 in the evening, right on time. Passengers came ashore and filled the dock with chatter. Maya stood out, alone and scrutinising the many greeters dockside. As soon as she spotted me, her face lit up, and she inched her way over to where I'd been waiting.

"Look at you, Ms Sun Goddess! You're almost as dark as I am," she said, reaching out and hugging me.

"You and I are like coffee with and without milk!" I joked. "And there's lots of milk in my case. I'm glad you're here."

"I've been working in London a lot recently, and the sun appears to be doubly mad at the British this year. The grey days are even greyer, if there can be such a comparison."

"So, you *do* need the sun!" I exclaimed as I looked her up and down. "How long will you stay?"

"Oh, I'll be soaking up every drop of sunshine for the next four days."

"Four days… Nice, but why not a week? You said you have six days off."

"I do, but two of them are partial travel days. You're not in New York, you know," she said, and grinned at me.

"We'd better put down the top of the car and begin your sun worshipping," I said, walking over to the Peugeot. "Hop in and let the wind whip through your hair my friend." I threw her light luggage into the trunk, and we sped off.

We drove up the hill, greenery looming heavily on both sides, interrupted by six-foot concrete walls carpeted with bougainvillea that marked property lines.

"How do you like it here? Must be at least a year since you've been in the islands?"

"It's been eleven months for me, but Jack's only been here a total of four times. The longest he's stayed was three weeks, and that was at the beginning. I'd hoped he'd work from here more often."

"Did you talk with him about working from here?"

"I have, but he thinks making money is contingent on him travelling and building connections. Even at sixty-one, a slower pace isn't on his radar."

"What made you believe he'd want a slower pace?"

I glanced over at her and then back at the road. "I just assumed that we'd purchased this place, so we…

he... wanted the same thing I did—a slower and more relaxed lifestyle."

Despite Maya's presence, desolation crept over me, and I longed for Jack to be with us at Seaview, so that as a couple, we would entertain our guest.

We rode in silence for a few seconds and then I added: "I'm ashamed to tell you— there's a gaping hole in my life. It gets lonely in that big rambling house, and though I've made some acquaintances, socialising is mostly to kill time."

Maya smiled. "Ahh! So shallow mixing, huh? That won't build solid relationships."

"Most of the women on the island have significant others, and it gets tiring being the brave partner-less girl showing up at these paired gatherings."

"Doesn't sound like fun."

"No, it isn't," I replied.

A gallery of cabbage palms welcomed us at the foot of the driveway, and we cruised toward the manor set like a great jewel in the ring of gardens at the end.

"And here we are! Seaview Manor, my dear friend. Welcome!"

"Lady Jemma! It's stunning. You've outdone yourself. And such a spectacular garden. My, my!"

We parked in the carport, walked up the driveway and through the front door where Primrose greeted us.

"This is Primrose. She takes care of the house."

"That's an unusual name, and I like it," Maya said with a grin.

"Thank you. It means 'first rose,' ma'am, but there is not a second." Primrose giggled. "My mother only had me."

"And a sense of humour too!" Maya smiled broadly.

"And," Primrose added, "my middle name is Sapphire."

"Well, well! And would that be Black Star Sapphire? That's a rare gem, you know."

I was pleased by the easy banter between Maya and Primrose.

"I don't know, ma'am," Primrose said, laughing.

"I'll go back to the kitchen and finish the meal. Is there anyone else joining you, Ms Jemma?"

"No, it'll just be us."

"This is magnificent," Maya said as her eyes moved from the interior of the manor to the azure expanse of sea that filled the wall of windows. A Paul Klee canvas, *Ad Parnassum*, hung in the entrance hall above a large ivory camelback sofa. Two armchairs stood on either side, and the floor was covered with a Persian carpet, its colour duplicating the golden light that spread over every surface.

"I bought most of the pieces at estate auctions here on the island," I told Maya. "Only a few items came with me from the U.S. Jack cautions me about my overspending habits." I threw my head back and grinned dismissively.

"Doesn't look like you listen," Maya teased.

"Maybe I'll listen when there's someone here to lessen the void that spending fills, not just staying a fortnight here and there." I shrugged my shoulders. "Ready for a drink yet?"

Primrose popped her head back into the living room and asked what time we wanted dinner served. I looked at Maya for her lead; after all, she was my guest.

"I brought you a bottle of Nicolas Feuillatte, your favourite French champagne; I say we chill it for thirty minutes while I freshen up. Then, let's eat. I'm starving."

"Did you hear all that, Primrose?"

"Yes, ma'am, I did."

Primrose made a delectable penne pasta in a light rosé sauce, served with garlic bread, and a spinach and pomegranate salad with an apple cider dressing, and both Maya and I complimented her on the meal. We finished the Feuillatte over conversations about all things European, including trends in the fashion houses.

"What's the pace like living on an island, compared to a big North American or European city? You've experienced both." Maya dug into the salad first.

"Sitting on a lounger by a sun-drenched pool, swigging a classic martini, while working or relaxing? Can't be beat."

"Sounds blissful!"

"I'm keeping my business afloat while enjoying the hell out of luxury and without the constant hustle of taking taxis and attending business meetings with buyers. It's sweet!"

"That's amazing, Jem. I'll close my eyes and imagine this scenario as my reality.... No, it wouldn't work. Too many complications. So, I'll live the fantasy through your eyes for now, though it does sound enticing."

"About trends—on the Italian front, I've been following Donatella, Cavalli, and Dolce & Gabbana. Their summer and fall accessories are exquisite. But I've run across the Swaby line that comes out of Toronto and Chicago. Her avant garde creations run the gamut from basics to couture, and her accessories are edgy and wearable."

"Oh, so it's a North American brand. I must check it out."

"It is, and I believe the designer has Caribbean roots."

"How appropriate!" Maya nodded.

"I'll grab a few pieces for myself from their on-line catalogues, then, wait for the end of season clear-out to stack my business inventory. I'm considering introducing the Swaby label to some of my Italian contacts; never know where it could lead." I said, tallying up the anticipated profits in my head as I spoke.

"But isn't this island more casual? Where would you wear those fashion finds you purchase for yourself?" Maya asked, peering at me over the rim of her champagne flute.

"You're correct about the easy attire down here, generally, but you'd be surprised how gussied up folks get to attend dinner at the social club. That's where you really see the money on this little paradise."

"I can just imagine," Maya said. "And with the odd celebrity dropping in…"

"Correct. Plus, I like to look good for *me*. And, whenever Jack comes back it reminds him of the sophisticated woman waiting at home." I forced a smile and fingered the silver necklace he gave me; acknowledging that Jack wasn't around much made me sad.

"Okay, then, that's fair." Maya laughed. "Good. Now, can we chat about another subject? This one's difficult, but I've got to broach it with you."

"Sure, go ahead."

Maya crossed and uncrossed her legs and leaned back in her chair. She bit down on her bottom lip and folded her arms. I watched her fidget as I sampled my drink.

"You okay?" I asked.

She looked over at me, eyes fixed on mine, and in her lawyer's voice said, "There's no other way to say this; Jack is in another relationship."

"A relationship? Is that a joke?" A piece of pasta became lodged in my throat, and I coughed repeatedly to clear my air way.

"No, it isn't a joke," Maya replied. "I saw him with his new or old partner... however you look at it... and he introduced me."

"You're not kidding ..." I patted my lips with the linen napkin and tried to regain my composure.

"I'm not. I told him I'd planned to visit you, and he said you weren't aware, but that he had every intention of telling you."

"Telling me what?"

"He said he wasn't asking for my silence on the matter and planned to be here in two weeks to talk about it with you."

I sat stunned, my teeth sore from clenching, and a million questions crashing through my head.

Was he really having a love affair, or just sex? How did I not see this coming? How could I have...? I am here, and he is there with her. If it's an affair, does he even care about me? He said he did... What an idiot I am.

"Is this really happening," I finally croaked. "What does she look like?" I asked, hoping the answer would be "old" and "stodgy."

"He's about six feet tall. I'd say around eighty kilograms with olive complexion and slight salt and pepper hair. He was immaculate."

"Wait, wait... Did you say he?"

"I did. His name is Javier, and they share a home in Seville and Paris."

"Javier is his business par—" I began. "Shit! Some business those fuckers are up to, all those late nights … working on each other."

My chest tightened and heat filled my face. *And here I was feeling guilty for having screwed the gardener.*

"Idiot, idiot, idiot!" I dropped my head into my hands and screamed. "I satisfy him … he said so himself … so how could he have left me…?"

"He hasn't left you," Maya said calmly. "That's why he's coming to have a face-to-face with—"

"What do you mean he hasn't left me! He's with someone else right now!"

"That's where things are a bit complicated. He's working things out for himself and trying to be clear about what he wants."

"And what about what *I* want … and how come you know so much, and I don't? What am I missing?"

"You're caught up now. I know all this because I saw them kissing, and I called Jack out. We had a ten-minute conversation, and what I've shared with you is what I learnt."

Time slowed and almost stopped. I heard palm fronds rustling in the wind, the scrape of cicadas in the darkness, and the distant whisper of the sea. The walls of the room seemed to close in on me as I looked over at Maya's stoic face.

"I don't know what to say, except that I feel so fucking betrayed. No wonder he wouldn't spend more time here."

"I can see why you'd feel deceived, Jem. Maybe you need time to reflect on your relationship and how this information changes it."

"Wait, changes it? The house is in his name. Does that mean I'd have to move out? Shit, Maya, are you here to kick me out? Oh no, what's happening?"

"I'm not throwing you out. Remember, I'm your friend."

"Oh hell, I'm so confused. So, you'll be my lawyer then? Will you represent me? I have no idea what I'm talking about. Do I even have any legal rights to be here? This is so messed up." My thoughts were colliding. I held my head and squeezed my temples. I wanted to curl up and hide. *What must he think of me?*

"Chill and think it through. I'm here for a few more days, and we can chat, though I can't provide you with legal advice. It's not my area of expertise."

"I really need a stiff drink." I inhaled deeply and shook my head.

"That might help," Maya said sympathetically.

I breathe deeply to push back the walls that were constricting my space. I had to find balance. We switched to red wine, emptied a bottle of Châteauneuf-du-Pape, walked outside, and took a dip in the pool. A silvery full moon illuminated the land and seascape, but to me, the glow appeared bleak. I was bummed about Jack's affair and struggled to be the perfect host. Maya understood.

"I'm pretty wiped, so I'll hit the hay and give you some time to think," she remarked.

"Sounds good. I will too."

We left the pool and went to our rooms. I closed the door gently behind me and leaned against it. *Breathe, Jemma, breathe! How the hell had I found myself in this predicament?*

That night I lay awake, pictures of Jack and an imagined Jav in my head, the two of them having it off and laughing at me. Sleep crept up on me, but then I jerked awake with a pain in my chest and tears pricking the corners of my eyes. Back and forth for hours until I finally wore myself out and dropped off.

A brimstone dawn lit the distant clouds, and I watched it slowly cover the sky. A hollow in the pit of my stomach reminded me of my conversation with Maya the night before. Primrose brought breakfast to the conservatory, and Maya joined me after a few minutes. "How did you sleep?" I enquired of my guest.

"I must admit, the lull of the tranquil sea and cool night air is a perfect elixir for a good night's rest. I was out in less than five minutes. How about you?"

"I finally dozed off, but the first few hours were difficult. It'll take time to adjust to the news, but I'll get there." I bit into a warm buttery scone drizzled with homemade guava jam.

"We definitely need a splash now; no more of this conversation." I got up and headed for the door that led from the conservatory to the pool.

"I see you're wearing your bathing suit under your robe. I'll grab mine and be right back." She smiled and left the room.

Maya headed into the guest room, and I wandered over to the pool. A few minutes later she returned.

"I'm back! Let's get swimming ... or not," she said, her gaze landing upon Zeke's form moving among the shrubs. "Why the heck is a dreadlocked Kendrick Sampson in your garden?"

"Kendrick who? Oh, that's Zeke, my... *my* landscaper."

"You say it as though there's something more. Do I detect an undertone?"

"There isn't an implication there, Maya, and yes he's fine, but..."

"But?" She looked at me with a cheeky grin.

"Well, I..."

"You're talking to an attorney, and a woman, but okay, maybe it's my imagination, but there's definitely an undercurrent of attraction. And what's the 'but?' Is it a black butt?"

We erupted into a peal of laughter. I dove into the pool and Maya followed. She caught up with me in the deep end.

"Did you know that in the scriptures, Ezekiel was a powerful prophet and a man of great intellect? From Zeke's work, I would say he's got some know-how going on."

"I agree. And truth be told, his know-how is far reaching; it happened twice." I winked at Maya and smiled. Joy filled me up, like I'd gained some of my power back from the shock of Jack's affair.

Maya responded with a mocking reprimand. "Naughty, naughty, so you *have* gotten jiggy with the bronze Adonis. I can see why it would be hard for him to remain only eye candy."

"So, you approve?"

"I don't have to approve; you have to please yourself."

"Well, that I already do, but it's just not enough, if you know what I mean."

We looked at each other and laughed again.

"I'm not admitting to any such knowledge," Maya added with a sheepish grin.

"There's something specific I want your perspective on; you are a person I can trust."

Maya swam to the shallow end and waited.

"I'm all ears. What's up?"

I pulled my hair back into a loose ponytail and rested my elbows on the side of the pool. "Tell me if you think I'm going bonkers. I won't be offended." I told her about the sudden bout of sadness I'd experienced on the path to the sugar mill and about my dream and the bathroom visions of the sugar cane grasses.

Maya listened intently and then spoke. "I don't think you're going bonkers. You're just incredibly lonely and missing the joy you had in other parts of the world. How about taking a trip to your old haunts, seeing friends, and reconnecting with the people you know and like? Despite its beautiful setting, I think this island might be too small for you."

"So, you don't think I'm nuts then?"

Maya leaned her head back and chuckled. "I can't offer a diagnosis, but maybe a psychologist could. In fact, you might consider seeing one if your concern persists. It can't hurt and might even put you at ease."

"That's good advice, counsel," I said with a nod. "Finding someone might be tricky, as stigma may also be an issue in these parts. But I can quietly investigate."

"I'm ready for a change of scene," said Maya, evidently ready to revel in the island's beauty. "Let's go out for a drive and see a bit of this heaven you call home."

"The sunshine and the air would do us both good. I'll grab my keys and we'll go for that ride."

We spent the rest of the day sightseeing. At a few of the populated beaches on the northern and western coasts, we watched surfers and body boarders frolicking in the waves.

We stopped for lunch at the social club, and Maya marvelled at the high-end cars parked in the lot and the array of well-groomed folks entering the establishment.

On our way back, we paused and watched the late afternoon sea bathers, kite flyers, and a group of young people snorkelling. The day's exploration proved a balm for some of the earlier tension.

That evening, after a light dinner, we relaxed in the library and listened to jazz. I was unaware of Maya's love for the music, and she was delighted that my dad was an enthusiast as well and shared her love for Coltrane and Parker. As a teen Maya had learned to dance to swing and then moved on to Gillespie and Parker, the only music Ms Bea played, except for Mahalia Jackson on Sundays.

Even though Jack's affair loomed large in my head, I did my best to show my guest a good time and did genuinely enjoy Maya's company.

Later, I sat on the chaise in my room, and as I poured a night cap, I thought back to how I'd reacted to Maya's bombshell about Jack and Javier. Had I gone overboard about their affair? I didn't think I had; Jack had been sleeping with Javier for who knows how long. I'd only been with Zeke twice. Ours wasn't an affair; I'd had a fling. I was simply taking care of my needs because Jack wasn't here. Yet, I had to admit, my tryst with Zeke was powerful.

Maybe Jack would ask me to forgive him, and we could mend things. Zeke was accessible, but he could never give me the lifestyle that Jack could. I decided I'd keep Zeke for as long as I needed to. I shouldn't be deprived.

When Maya left for New York two days later, I was in a better place.

Chapter 18

Jemma

After my peculiar experience on the path leading to the mill, I'd asked Zeke to attend to that part of the property by cutting back the excess weeds and examining the innards of the mill. I ran into him in the carport one morning as I was leaving for the bank.

"How is the mill clean up coming along, Zeke?"

"Nicely. I made a few piles of de contents. You can check dem, or I can light a fire to it. You let me know."

"I'll stop by later before you leave and take a look, but I don't imagine there will be anything of value there."

"Okay, ma'am."

"Is there anything that could be salvaged? I'm happy to donate stuff."

"Is mostly trash. I don't see a lot dat people would want but is up to you."

I picked my way over to the mill shortly after 3:00 p.m. and found Zeke raking around the perimeter. I called out to him, and he joined me, pointing to what looked like mounds of rubbish. My art history degree taught me things might be other than they looked, so I began to poke around the debris.

"Dis pile got old curtains. And dis two plastic bins full of old Christmas decoration, fishing gear, golf clubs, and old tennis and polo balls. All look like rubbish, Jem."

"And what are the smaller stacks over in the corner by the door?" I asked.

"Old books and paper, broken furniture, rusted out tools, and dis seal up crate; I don't know what's in it."

"Why don't you bring the crate up to the house and we'll open it there. The other items I can look at later," I replied.

Zeke followed me back to the house, bringing the slim wooden crate with him.

"Place it on the lanai, so we don't bring dust into the house."

"Yes, ma'am. I'll get a screwdriver and open it."

Primrose was washing the inside windows of the conservatory. I passed her on my way into the living room and poured myself a drink. The heat was exhausting. I walked back out and watched Zeke pry the nails loose and lift out a frame with decorative moulding at the four corners. There was some type of wrapping covering a painting cloaked in gauze.

"I'll go back to de mill to finish up. Call me if you need anything else."

I leaned in closer to him and whispered, "I'll *always* need something from you." We both chuckled.

"Will you come over tonight?" he mouthed?

"Primrose leaves in an hour, I'll see you later," I responded quietly. Then I spoke in a normal tone. "Thanks, Zeke. I should be fine."

I carefully took the wrapper off the frame. The painting was in great shape. The image of a young Black girl who looked about seventeen years old, and with the most striking eyes, greeted me. She wore a form-fitting baby-blue dress, with long sleeves, and a bell-shaped skirt which fit her perfectly. I looked closer. There was something familiar about her face, as if she was someone I had once met in the distant past, but I couldn't pinpoint the reason at first. Then it clicked, and I realized where I had seen that face. It was in the mirror because it was me, sort of, but with dark skin.

I checked for a signature of the artist, turning the painting around. A small card stuck to the back of the frame said "Glasgow, Scotland" along with an illegible moniker. I flipped the painting around again and looked at the young girl, who gazed back at me with gentleness in her chestnut brown eyes—my eyes. Her slightly high cheekbones and full lips pursed in a half smile—my lips. I held my breath and swallowed hard. Dear God, how could this be? Then I saw her crooked baby finger: just like mine, my mother's, and her sister's. The hairs on the back of my neck rose in sync with my shoulders. And I swore I heard a voice say, "Hello, dear."

I sat and stared at the painting. What in God's name was going on? How could this Black teenager look like me? Her nose: short-bridged, with a slightly wide nasal base; soft coppery smiling eyes, and cheeks that hid a small dimple in her rounded features, it was unreal. I couldn't shift my eyes away from the image. Sweat trickled down my back and under my arms, and my cotton blouse stuck to my back. The thoughts in my head became muddled, and I pressed my fingers firmly against my forehead and searched for answers. None of it made sense.

After about thirty minutes of staring and thinking, I came up with a plan to connect with my old neighbour and friend, an employee at Oxford University's Department of Art History. She could help me solve this mystery. I hid the painting at the back of the bookshelf in the library and locked the door behind me. I couldn't let anyone see it, at least not until I could find the answers I needed.

I poured another drink, walked back to the lanai, and stared at the sea. Could this large expanse of water hold some of the answers to this unfolding mystery?

Wrapped tightly in Zeke's arms that night, I felt a comfort and a warmth never experienced with Jack. It was the first time I stayed overnight at his cottage.

Chapter 19

Jemma

Jack arrived on the red eye from New York having left Vienna a day earlier. He was coming to discuss the muddle he'd created. I had hives thinking of his visit. I was dependent on this man for the privileged lifestyle I now lived, but I had given up a lot to be with him. I'd traded a jet-setting European scene for a more relaxed way of life in the tropics. How would he explain this affair he was caught in?

The slam of a car door and the click of the key in the entrance announced his arrival. I'd given Primrose a few days off because of the uncertainty of how the face-to-face with Jack would unfold. She didn't need to witness any drama.

Jack walked straight into the bedroom.

"Hey there," he began.

"Hey."

"How about a drink? Coffee, vodka, mimosa?"

"I'm fine. Primrose is off, so you'll have to get your own drink."

"Well, if you don't want one, I won't either," he said as he lowered his body onto the chaise at the foot of the bed.

So now you're thinking about me and my wants? I waited for him to begin the conversation, but several moments went by in silence. My anxiety got the better of me, and I blurted out: "How did it go so wrong, and why didn't you tell me!?"

His response was unexpected. "Nothing went wrong. Everything went right except we… I need to work a few things out… with you."

This man has got a flaming nerve… My body trembled, and I screamed as anger fought with hurt in my chest. It felt as if sparks were flying out of my ears.

"Work a few things out? Is that how you see it? And how in God's name is this right? How could you sleeping with someone else be right?"

The room disappeared into fog with only Jack remaining, his face drooped and lined. I yelled again to gain presence as I searched desperately for empowerment.

"This is wrong Jack, all bloody wrong!"

"I know this is difficult, Jemma, but calm down for a moment, and I will explain how it happened," Jack said evenly and firmly.

I hated his composure while I sat there like a schoolgirl who had just been chided by the principal. *Control, Jemma, get control.* I took a few slow breaths, folded my arms, and looked at him squarely, being mindful not to pout as he continued.

"Javier and I were college roommates forty years ago."

Forty years. My God, he said forty years … Hell, I hadn't even been born yet. Focus, Jemma, focus…

"After a night of excessive drinking, we ended up in my bed and each other's arms."

As he peeled back the details of his affair, I pressed my thumbs into my biceps to stop my arms from shaking.

"Initially we blamed it on the tequila, but a few nights later, Jav walked in on me in the shower and something magical happened. The tequila theory went out the window, and we admitted to each other that there had been an attraction from our first encounter."

Shut up, shut up, Jack! I screamed in my head. But he was wrapped up in his memories and couldn't see the fire in my eyes, or my body twitch. So, he carried on.

"We kept it a secret and did what other freshmen in our cohort did—hang out and talk about women. I liked hanging out with the guys, but I was definitely falling for Jav. Alcohol was only the bridge that led us to the night of no return.

And here was me thinking that Bellagio was our night of 'no return.'

"For the next four years, we covertly dated. I wanted to come out about our relationship, but Javier's parents would have killed him, plus he got engaged to his childhood sweetheart, Anna, on one of his summer vacations after she'd become pregnant. I was shattered. They married after he graduated, and I was his best man. The entire situation was messed up. Instead of giving him counsel the night of his bachelor party, we made out and pledged that his marriage wasn't the end for us as a couple."

As Jack unleashed the details, I realized that what he had with Javier was true love, not just an affair, not just sex. The air around me was warm and heavy and I battled light-headedness. I willed myself to continue taking deep slow breaths.

"Broken-hearted, a few years later I married Maggie, my now-deceased wife. We'd met at college, so she knew Jav as my roommate."

So, you've deceived another woman into thinking that she was your world. You're good! The fingers of my right hand curled into a fist, and I pressed it against my quivering lips to maintain my silence.

"She was a great person, fun-loving and easygoing, championing everything I did, usually without much fanfare. I didn't want kids, and she agreed there would be none. I found a job and bought a house in the general vicinity of Jav and Anna's home. Maggie, trouper that she was, bought and managed a spa close by. There she did twelve-to-fourteen-hour days and turned it into a successful business. Our wives were acquaintances, never good friends, and their paths rarely crossed. My affair with Jav continued throughout the years and a few months ago, they divorced, and this is where we are right now."

God I hated this story. The sound of Javier's name was like an open wound bleeding pain, jealousy, and loss in hot waves. I slid my hands between my knees and squeezed them together to keep from shaking. I focused on the hem of the window curtain behind him, to avoid looking at Jack's face. Gradually my breathing and the drumbeat of my heart returned to normal, and I wondered: was it even worth a fight?

"Did they divorce because of your affair?" I don't know why I asked the question because it didn't really matter.

"Not particularly. Neither of them was happy in the marriage and agreed to go their separate ways."

"This is such a bloody mess, Jack. Why didn't you tell me about it before? You said he was your business partner."

"He *is* my business partner. And what should I have told you before? That I have a male lover, and he is my first preference? Would you have even heard that if I'd told you? Think about it."

"Oh, I would have heard it ... heard you, and I can assure you that I wouldn't have chosen *this*."

Jack had been speaking his truth in a controlled quiet tone, glancing intermittently at the ceiling and the floor.

But now he turned suddenly to face me, fists clenched, eyes ablaze, and voice loud with accusation.

"*This*? What do you mean by '*this*'? We were immediately attracted to each other on Bellagio. Maybe loneliness brought us together, but whatever did, it was good, and we both enjoyed the heck out of it. So, Jemma, '*this*' was a beautiful thing that brought us into each other's lives."

"But *it* was not built on truth, *it* was phoney, unequal. I thought it was only *us* in the relationship. You knew something I didn't."

"Truth be told, we share a stunning home with exquisite grounds on a pristine island, overlooking the sea. There's live-in help to take care of the home and a landscaper to take care of the grounds and the views. Let's be real. This is the life you've always wanted. I've even invested in your business."

My breath caught in my throat at his mention of the landscaper. I swallowed a gulp of air to gain equilibrium. Jack was correct; I loved every bit of this existence, except for the loneliness.

"Obviously I misread your cues: the flowers, jewellery, this home, I assumed that we had evolved into more than just bedmates."

"We have evolved. In my view, our relationship has progressed into a deep friendship. I do care about you, and I see this connection as satisfactory—one where we both get our needs met. You get your grand lifestyle, which I mostly pay for, and I come back, and we have fun fulfilling the other side of my world."

"But I want more Jack…." I folded my arms again, and held his eyes steadily.

"I hear you Jemma, but, I won't sacrifice Jav for you. If you force me to choose, I choose him. I love him, but I also care for you."

Those words stung despite the mention of caring. They showed me my true position: second place in his world. Better than nothing, for sure, but I had hoped for more.

"I guess I made up a scenario in my head—that we were going to be together and that this home would be ours." I stopped short of saying what I was thinking, but Jack went there.

"It's not like we have a marriage, Jemma. If I ever marry again, it will be to someone I love as passionately as I do Jav. I'm sorry we didn't have this conversation earlier, but now is as good a time as any."

"So, what does this mean for us, Jack?"

"We don't have to change what we have, Jemma. I'll continue my relationship with Jav and you can stay at the manor for as long as you wish. He knows you live at the property, and he's not threatened by you being here.

Did he say threatened? I cringed. *Now I'm endangered.* I closed my eyes and tried to blot out the image, and the words continued falling from his lips.

"In fact, we're willing to share the manor with you while he and I live together in Europe and the US. You can be our eyes and ears on Majestic. We will, however, want to spend some time together here. It's up to you if during those visits you want to stay or vacation elsewhere."

I sucked in air and held it. My stomach muscles clenched forming a barrier to absorb the verbal punches coming my way. '*Our eyes and ears*.' Did that mean that Javier owns part of the property? I was too scared to ask. I'd dropped from second place to the bottom rung, relegated to a caretaker who poses no threat, who gets out the way when the owners of the manor visit. I dropped my arms and placed my hands on my thighs, looking directly at Jack.

"I don't want to share you with Javier, here or anywhere."

"Well, you've been sharing me all along. And now you know that you can only have part of me; but it's up to you." His gaze was trained on me, the anger cooling in his eyes.

"So, what's our new arrangement?" Anger gave force to my voice, but this time I didn't yell. Guilt about Zeke fluttered briefly but then died, thank God.

"If I come to Majestic alone, I expect to sleep with you. If I come to Majestic with Jav, I'll be sleeping with only him. I cannot ask you to *only* be with me. All I ask is that you be careful were you to sleep with someone else."

It wasn't like I needed his approval, but at least his expectations were clear. I swallowed hard to keep from showing my nervous tremor.

"I find you an extremely sensuous woman, and I'm physically attracted to you. With Jav, however, we're spiritually and emotionally linked.

"So, you are bi…"

"I'm attracted to both sexes and enjoy intimacy with either one without any labels."

Still sitting on the side of the bed, I leaned forward, resting my head in my hands, palms cupping my cheeks.

"I'll need some time to let all of this sink in," I said. "When Maya told me you were in a relationship with Javier, I told myself that you were missing me and had turned to him for comfort; it was a passing need that he had filled because I wasn't there. You said that I'm the woman you want to be with, the one who turns you on, Jack, I don't like being second best, despite the trimmings that come with it." The pressure in my head was building. *What to do now?*

"Yes, Jemma, you are that woman, and there's also a man," he quietly responded. "Look, I've got some work to finish before end of day tomorrow; let me know if you've reached a decision and want to talk later. I'll be in the library."

I lay in bed for the next hour, replaying all I'd heard and pondering what the aftermath of my life would look like. Images loomed large in my head.

I cannot share him… There is nothing appealing about his proposal, except that I could still live in the style I've enjoyed these past three years. It had been that long since the night we met on Bellagio. I love this lifestyle, but do I love Jack? I'd never given that question much thought. But it didn't matter now. I must face the fact that Jack and Javier are in a loving long-term relationship, one that he has never wanted with me. My chest tightened, the room spun, and my heart slowed.

What is the hurt I feel... rejection? Now, I know the reason for Jack's prolonged absence is an affair, not work. With Zeke, it's extracurricular activities—just sex. I'm pretty clear on that front. But I don't want to give up this lifestyle. It's what I've always wanted: a prestigious home in the A zone amongst the rich and famous. Now that Jack had told me his truth, I had to figure out mine.

Jack offered to spend the night in the guest room, and I agreed that it would be easier that way. There I was in the bed we usually shared, and there he was, downstairs, by himself. It had never been like this before, awkward.

I plugged in my earphones, closed my eyes, and rode the waves of *Beethoven's symphony No. 9* on my iPad. The surging strings, occasional rumble of the tympani through the first movements, and then the glorious chorale, lifted me away from my pain and turmoil. Sleep was reluctant but eventually came.

Chapter 20

Jemma

I woke to the shower running in our bathroom. A few minutes later Jack walked into the room in his blue terry robe.

"I hope it's okay that I chose to get cleaned up here. I've put the coffee on, want some?" he asked.

I rolled over and hugged my pillow. "Suit yourself and no to coffee right now." I responded. We used to be close—now we were distant, and I wanted to hide.

"Okay, I'll spend some time at the marina today. Feel free to join me." His attempt at making conversation fell flat.

"I need some space, Jack. I'll probably take a drive around the island and see you at dinnertime."

"How about I take us out for dinner tonight?"

"Let's see how the day goes."

"See you later then," he said and left the room.

After Jack left the manor, I sat in the conservatory, sipped coffee, and ate a small, puffed pastry Primrose had made the previous morning. I was full of anxiety from the night before, and my stomach rebelled against food.

I got dressed, put the top of the Peugeot down, popped a CD in, and cranked the volume up. As I drove along the only highway, the wind whipped through my hair to Gwen Stefani's voice filling the space around me with "*The Sweet Escape*" and "*You Started It*." Soon I was tapping rhythmically on the steering wheel, belting out the lyrics, and swaying my head and shoulders to the music.

A few minutes later my sullen mood sailed off in the breeze. The drive around Majestic proved exhilarating as sun, sky, and sea spread out before me, a reminder that beauty still existed in life and nature. It contrasted with the grey sense of demotion and disappointment that lingered from Jack's announcement.

Late afternoon, mellowed by the beauty of the island, I picked up two take-out meals from a small fusion restaurant near town. The meal—Rasta pasta—was a blend of Caribbean and Italian cuisine. Jack had returned and was waiting for me when I pulled into the driveway, his eyes warm but uncertain as I walked stiffly towards him. We ate together and kept the conversation safe and about food and our likes and dislikes regarding island flavours. We agreed the meal was very flavourful, but our palates needed time to adjust to the spiciness. Primrose had found a happy medium that suited us, and her absence in the kitchen was apparent. After a few glasses of wine and snifters of cognac, our conversation died, and silence grew between us. We retired to bed: Jack to the guest room and I to the primary bedroom.

The next day we attended our businesses, me working by the pool and Jack in the library. Between texts, e-mails, browsing catalogues, and watching online runway shows, I observed Zeke moving about the garden, mixing topsoil and watering shrubs. I pondered my life. Was reality intruding and my paradise unravelling?

After a quiet supper on the lanai, Jack and I withdrew to the library, well out of Primrose's earshot. She had returned, but the strained climate in the house remained.

"I've been here three days and leave tomorrow for New York. I was hoping that by now we would've come to a decision. Where do we go from here?" Jack began.

I gulped a puff of air and let it ease out of my slightly parted lips. "I don't have an answer, Jack."

"But we can't continue like this. I know what I want, but there are two of us in this relationship."

"You mean three!" I shot out and held my breath.

"No, I mean us—you and me. How will we manage this situation?" He was slow and deliberate.

"It's difficult. I've missed lying next to you and waking up in your arms, but I know it can never be the same. How do I know you won't be imagining you're holding Javier instead of me?" My stomach lurched as the image formed in my head.

"That won't ever happen. When I am with you; I am with you—not Jav. It is different. I still like your womanly touch and feel, the smell of gardenias on your skin, the lavender in your hair, and the enjoyment we give each other. I know when I'm holding you, every inch of you. Don't make me choose. I want both."

"Jack, it would be nice to keep what we had before, but he sits on your shoulder ready to slip in between us if we come together. I don't know how to get past this."

"I'm here to be with you. Javier is in Madrid. I want you, right here, right now. Can we try this one more time?" He moved beside me, his fingers feathered my right thigh, I tensed up and moved his hand aside. I was wary.

"Jack, you are in love with Javier. It's not a fling, and I know that now. Forty years is well before I was born. I cannot compete with that kind of love. I need more time to sort out what I want. Go back to your lover while I figure this out. And, if it's still okay, I'd like to stay here for a while longer."

"It isn't a competition, and the offer still stands. You can stay as long as you need to. I'm sorry I've hurt you; I should have been open from the start. Just let me know when you've made a decision."

Chapter 21

Jemma

I drove Jack to catch the early flight to New York. Our parting was cordial, and we kissed each other on the cheek and promised to be in touch.

Roughly two weeks after he left, I'd been waiting for an end of day call from him about some financial business with the local bank, but it hadn't come. I was frustrated, so I had a couple of brandy shots, slid into bed, and soon drifted off to sleep and into a dream. I was walking down the terrace path, a riot of orange and purple blooms on both sides, on my way to speak with Zeke about doing something similar along the walkway to the sugar mill. I saw a woman dressed in a long pinafore and bonnet crouched on the ground ahead of me. As I got closer, I heard weeping sounds and noticed her shoulders shaking. I quickened my pace, and her body stiffened at the sound of my footsteps, strangely loud, on the gravel. Our eyes met, and as soon as they did, she faded away into nothingness. Two infants were lying on the same spot, their tiny arms and legs moving the way babies do. They came into focus, and I noticed that their appearance and clothing were identical; they must have been twins. I hurried over, concerned at their exposed condition lying on the earth. However, as I neared them, the ground beneath them opened like a mouth, swallowing their small bodies.

I heard screaming, but as I sat up in my bed, wet with sweat and overcome with the intention to rescue those babies, I realized that I was the one screaming. It was a nightmare.

The disturbing image of the infants on the ground played back over and over in my head, and I couldn't get back to sleep. I finally leapt out of bed and paced back and forth around the room, guzzling brandy. After an hour of striding and imbibing, my steps became unsteady, my mind calmed, despite itself, and I flopped back to bed and passed out.

I woke with pain pulsing in my head around 10:00 a.m. the next morning. After three cups of coffee and dry toast, I showered and ventured out for a short walk down to the beach. I figured that the sea breeze, sunshine, and lovely surroundings would clear the mess in my mind, as they usually did.

My walk led me down the path through the flower-bordered terrace to the water. A wash of recognition came over me as I realized I had been here in my dream. It was still alive in my memory, and I half-expected to see the crying woman again. She wasn't there, but just off the path and where the babies had lain, the earth was disturbed. It was as if, yes, as if something had happened there to disturb the soil.

I stood in my tracks and could feel individual drops of cold sweat form and then run down my back. The air pressed my head like a vice on either side and fear grew into panic. *Oh God... this is real... no, it's not real, it's your imagination.* And then before my eyes, the disturbed earth levelled out like a smooth seal in front of me.

I willed my legs to move, but it was like walking through pudding, one laboured step after the other, back up the path. Everything was in slow motion, and the skin on my back tingled with the sensation of being watched and followed. It was another hot day, but I shivered all the way to the manor.

None of it made sense. I reached into my bedroom liquor cabinet, and my hand fell on the bottle of Hine Antique brandy. I opened it and swallowed a good gulp. It was too early in the day to have a drunk relapse, so I asked Primrose to fix me one of her hearty brunches. On the sweet side: French toast with mango slices, whipped cream, and Canadian maple syrup: a touch of home to lift my spirits.

The savoury comprised freshly baked cheese rolls, a small ham and spinach quiche, and strips of candied bacon. I devoured every morsel, poured more coffee into me, then crawled back to bed.

I tried to escape being sucked back into my hallucination by turning it into another business item that needed to be addressed. So I searched the internet for a therapist on Barbados and neighbouring island nations as Maya had suggested. I needed help figuring out these bizarre and frightening episodes and what I should do about them.

Of late, I had been delaying turning into bed, for fear of interacting with some ghostly figure in my sleep. Snifters of brandy helped, but the lights stayed on in my ensuite until morning.

Chapter 22

Jemma

The mail arrived and I scanned its contents; but what I was looking for—a brown envelope, the type that delivers official information—wasn't in the pile. Disappointed that the results hadn't come back, I wondered if they would confirm my mother's claim. After finding the portrait, I needed to know more than ever.

As a child, I'd heard her say that she had Scandinavian heritage. Dad said his folks were from Belfast, though many of them lived across the channel in Dumfries, and a few were scattered in the West Midlands. Once, Ollie and I overheard her chatting on the phone with a girlfriend about bloodlines. Mother claimed that hers stemmed from a Danish monarch—a declaration new to us kids, so we pressed her for answers later that day.

She was standing in front of the bathroom mirror straightening her light-brown shoulder-length hair—a daily ritual that took at least thirty minutes. The day's heat and humidity worked against her as she brushed and flattened the same section over and over. She hated her natural curls even more than Ollie did.

"Mum, where did you learn about your Danish royal heritage?" Ollie asked.

"I believe it was told to my mother, and her mother before her. I remember learning about it from my mother's sister, who was a historian. If anyone would know, she would."

"Wow. That's cool!" Ollie remarked.

"It's not like they left us any castles and palaces as inheritance; that would have been nice," she added, rolling her eyes as she walked away.

Ollie turned to me with the widest grin. "I think that's brilliant. Now I know what I can be—a genealogist—and I'll discover facts about our Danish family history. Maybe I'll find a few palaces and a prince or two related to us … you never know." She strutted around the room, curtsying to make believe monarchs. We chuckled at the end of her performance.

As this memory came flooding back, now more than ever, I wanted to see what geneticists had discovered buried deep in my roots.

For the first time in a long while, I wondered about my mother. Had she really heard that message from her aunt, or was it one of her fairy tales to lift our family a few rungs up the social ladder? Like the time she dropped hints about us having a home in the Hamptons; being careful not to mention that it was a timeshare in one of the least expensive areas. To hear her boast, you would believe we owned one of the finer homes in the South and were the type to rub elbows with folks from Sagaponack who wore preppy pink shirts and drove Porsches. Though, my dad did drive a Benz in Toronto.

Whenever we spent our yearly, two-week time slot in Hampton Bays, mother rented a swanky sports car, let the roof down, and drove into New York City. She'd be wearing large tortoise shell sunglasses, a string of pearls, and light pink lipstick. Whatever her attire, the vintage tote and signature loafers were staples, and she never left home without them. Jackie O. was her idol, and image was important to Mother. Ollie and I learned that lesson quite quickly.

Many years later when living in Italy, memories of my sister hovered in the background of my daily life. And they did on my Copenhagen trip with Jack, on a Fall long weekend.

There were pastel-coloured buildings everywhere, leaning over canals, and tree-lined boulevards and streets bustling with Danes on bikes, a sparkling metallic horde of smiling faces, pumping legs, and motion. Tables were out on sidewalks, with people sitting and talking over glasses of beer and cups of coffee. Yet glum images of Ollie hung over me like a dark wet cloud threatening a downpour at any moment. I saw her in every doorway, on every pier, and in every restaurant.

Ollie's dream was to attend the University of Copenhagen and read History. She didn't get to live out her Danish fantasy, because she left us at fifteen; too early. How I missed her! What might she be doing had she been there? Would she have met us for lunch or dinner? Would she be married with kids of her own? And would she have realized like I had now, that her size zero figure didn't matter, and there are healthy ways to remain slim if you choose to. Most of all—fat is not ugly or a curse—mother was wrong.

I pushed these ponderings down with pints of pilsner chased with schnapps. For a split second, I imagined my mother carrying out the same ritual, maybe to drown her sorrow, and then snapped back to the present.

Hopefully it wouldn't be too long before the DNA Ancestry results showed up in the mail. It would've been good to open them with Ollie, even though she had been adopted.

The brown envelope finally arrived four days later.

Dear Ms Worley,

Thank you for trusting Core Ancestry with your mitochondrial (mtDNA) sample for analysis. To find your genetic history, we look at both genetic admixture and mitochondrial DNA markers to provide you with the most accurate results.

This letter is to acknowledge receipt of your sample. Your results will be sent to you within six weeks.

Sincerely, Cynthia J. Sommerset, President

"Oh well, more waiting!"

Chapter 23

Jemma

Although Jack and I agreed to be more open with each other, the rejection I'd harboured since he'd been candid about his and Jav's relationship had coloured everything between us. I wanted to feel that kind of love from someone. Jack wanted me, but it wasn't the way he wanted Jav and that hurt. I lay in bed at nights imagining them together, and it didn't feel good.

I'd been in a funk for over a month, sleeping with Zeke on and off to soothe the anguish of demotion, and when Jack called to say he was coming to Majestic, I had mixed emotions—until he mentioned Jav would be coming as well.

They arrived on the island ten days later on their way to Patagonia. In the meantime, I headed to New York to see a Broadway show, do some retail therapy, and gave

Primrose and Zeke a few extra days off so the men could have their privacy.

I lay in bed and listened to the street noise and chiming church bells. Oh, New York City, so full of activity. It was coming up to noon on a Sunday; time to shower and order room service. I imagined a nice hour's walk along Sixth Avenue to Central Park, becoming a part of the city and its buzz. Maya was right; I missed The Big Apple.

My phone vibrated and Jack's face lit up the screen. "Hi there," I answered.

I could hear him breathing, but he didn't respond immediately.

"Jack … is everything okay?"

"Jemma, can you come back to the island right away? Something has happened, but I can't speak about it on the telephone. How soon can you get here?" His voice was pressing.

"I can be there just after noon tomorrow if I take the 7:00 a.m. out of JFK."

"Okay, that's great. I'll see you then." *Click.* He hung up.

The conversation left a sting. I didn't know how to interpret it. I sat for a few minutes then called Maya. She answered on the second ring.

"Hey…"

"Hey back," she responded.

"I just had a strange call from Jack asking me to return to Majestic right away."

"Oh! Isn't Jav there with him? What's going on?"

"He is, or at least he was, just after I left for the US."

"Did you ask him why the urgency?"

"He told me he didn't want to speak about it on the phone, so I have absolutely no idea what's going on."

"That's peculiar. How about if I come over to hang out for a bit? Maybe we can figure it out. Plus, these files I'm working on are a bit drab. I could use the distraction."

"Sure, I'm at the SoHo Grand."

"Okay, I'll get changed, grab a cab, and be there within forty-five minutes. See you soon."

I powered up my iPad and booked the 7:00 a.m. American Airlines flight out of JFK.

I paced the floor of the hotel room, possibilities whizzing through my head like darts trying to hit a moving bull's eye. What the heck happened? Why had Jack been so guarded on the phone? I sat at the foot of the bed and stared up at the ceiling. I'm the kept woman in a complicated relationship with a man who is living a double life. What else could have topped that?

Maya's knock on the door broke into my racing thoughts.

We made our way down to the Grand Bar and ordered her favourite—Tanqueray with a lemon twist. The DJ spun a stack of old, soulful ballads. It was as if she knew the mood called for Ella Fitzgerald and the Ink Spots' rendition of "Into Each Life Some Rain Must Fall," and Mighty Mo Rodgers crooning "Picasso Blue." The music reminded me of Sunday mornings at home in Toronto.

"Do you have any fresh ideas for Jack's urgent call? I've been thinking. Maybe they broke up," Maya speculated.

"They couldn't have broken up—they came to Majestic to celebrate an anniversary, so their union should be solid. I hope Javier doesn't want me out. Maybe he fell in love with Majestic and wants it for the two of them."

"Well, who wouldn't fall in love with Majestic? But to call you back to throw you out is ridiculous. These are working professionals who live in major cities. Will they lock up the manor and keep it for vacationing? That's not being business savvy."

I was stumped and sipped slowly on my cold cloudy beverage dressed with a sprig of mint; my head churned.

"Maybe he's ill. But why ask you to come back right away? No, illness doesn't fit." Like me, Maya searched for answers.

"Well, if it's not illness, and they haven't broken up, or aren't going to throw …"

Maya interjected. "Maybe they want kids, and they're looking for a surrogate?" She peered at me over her drink.

"A surrogate?" I pondered her suggestion for a few seconds. "That would mean the kid would be theirs, not mine. No, Jack doesn't want children, and Javier already has a son."

"I meant children together." She winked at me.

"Again, doesn't sound plausible, and I'm not into surrogacy anyway. Nothing about this makes any sense." I stirred and sipped my drink. "This guessing game is giving me a headache."

"Well, you'll just have to wait and find out." Maya changed the subject.

"Did you get all your business completed for this trip?"

"Mostly, I hoped to call my parents; you know, open the lines of communication and visit them next time I'm in North America. We haven't spoken in over five years nor seen each other in over ten. I can't now, though."

We chatted and people watched for another hour. I needed the diversion. Then Maya took a cab home, and I headed upstairs and packed.

The flight seemed endless. My business class seat didn't provide a distraction from my internal turmoil. I watched two movies to take the edge off, but the touchdown of the American Airlines on Baptiste caused my stomach to tense up again.

Prying eyes were all around me on the ferry ride over. I ignored them. Even the taxi driver seemed to be staring at me in the rear-view mirror. But we exchanged no words.

Jack met me at the door, unshaven, with puffy red eyes, his silk bathrobe crumpled and sash sagging.

"Talk to me, Jack. What's happening?"

"Jemma... it's horrible... so horrible... I've lost Jav. There was a boating accident yesterday morning at sea. The boat flipped and crushed him."

My throat constricted and filled with lead. I slid down onto the sofa gasping for air, and my heart beat wildly in my chest. Then the words rushed out. "Oh my God, Jack, are you sure? How do you know this is true? Have you seen him?"

Jack paced, shaking his head. "It's true. I saw his body at the coroner's office. Jav—my sweet, my love, my everything—is gone. What can I... how will I explain it to Mateo, his son who studies oceans, that the sea has taken his beautiful Papi? I promised to love and take care of his father, and I've not kept my promise."

"That's not true. You did take care of him. And Mateo will understand. God, Jack, I'm so sorry. Tell me what you know. How did it happen?" I patted the empty space on the sofa, and he flopped down next to me. I swallowed gulps of air and struggled to concentrate.

"He was alone on the boat... I'll tell you what I think happened based on the reports and my interaction with the authorities.

"Jav woke early on Sunday. He wanted to grab a quick dive and swim before breakfast. We had talked about it the evening before, and the fact that we were at the beginning of hurricane season, so he needed to be cautious. He promised to check the weather before heading out, but the previous evening no storms had shown up on radar. He kissed me goodbye and whispered that he'd be back well before I was up and ready for breakfast. Then he left the room.

"I could see it happening in my mind's eye… the dawn approaching and the gentle waves washing against the shore… he would have checked for boating restrictions, then loaded his scuba gear, climbed aboard The Javson, and set out on a placid sea. Jav liked this time of day… quiet. He liked the feel of the fresh morning air on his face and the smell of salt water in the breeze. Maybe he was thinking that despite the challenges we'd encountered, fate had brought us back together. We were deliriously happy."

I reached over and squeezed Jack's hand, and for a few seconds, he closed his eyes and lowered his head as though saying a silent prayer to end the nightmare. Then he picked up where he'd left off.

"Jav would've scanned the open sea, and seeing no boats, would have relaxed, closed his eyes, and savoured a few moments of the dawn's solitude. He would've inhaled deeply and let the cool, salty air fill his lungs. He called it 'cleansing of mind and body.' When he exhaled, he may have sensed the starboard side of the boat tilt, then correct itself. I don't know exactly what happened, but when I close my eyes, I see the sea suddenly stormy, and building huge swells."

Jack went on to say that he believed strong winds and three-to-four-foot waves might have brought too much water on board, swamping the boat. He felt that Jav would have struggled to control it in the boisterous sea, and the force might have caused the craft to capsize. He would have been thrown overboard, perhaps pinned under the hull.

Glancing at me, eyes soft and wet, Jack continued. "All through Jav's struggle, I was tucked warmly in bed. I had no idea what he was dealing with out on the sea. I turned and looked at my phone when I woke up. It was 7:50. Had I overslept? I knew that Jav had had an early dive that morning, so I washed up, pulled my robe on, and headed into the kitchen with a peek into the conservatory. He wasn't back, so I turned on the coffee maker. We were getting low on cereal, so I waited to see what he wanted for breakfast."

As Jack spoke, it dawned on me that I hadn't checked with Primrose what groceries were needed; at the time, I couldn't have cared less. A ping of guilt nudged me, but Jack's account was more immediate, and I refocussed on him.

"I still remember so clearly standing on the lanai with a cup of coffee and checking to see if Jav had moored The Javson as yet. It was then I saw two boats approaching our small dock. I didn't recognize either of them, but then again, any vessel on the island would have been unknown to me. I watched and waited as the occupants, uniformed officers, came up the path and closer to the house.

"One guy said his name was Montgomery, with the Sierra Majestic Search and Rescue." My heart skipped a beat. "They said they were looking for me. My stomach muscles tightened as Montgomery asked if The Javson Entwined vessel was registered to me. When I said yes, he told me that the Coast Guard had located The Javson about sixty miles off Baptiste with no one on board. This was absurd. Jav was diving—of course there would be no one on board. I explained that much, giving the man an *are you crazy* look.

"Montgomery looked at the other chap and then said that the boat had capsized. And I lost it. I remember my hands shaking so hard the coffee splashed onto the floor. I heard someone say 'he's gonna pass out,' and then everything went black."

I imagined Jack falling to the floor and hoped he hadn't hurt himself. But he started speaking again. "I must have collapsed because when I opened my eyes, I saw another man and a paramedic had joined the two on the lanai. That officer confirmed that the search team had found Jav's body pinned under the craft. Everything moved in slow motion after that, like scrolling through a viewfinder."

I didn't know, or care about Javier, but Jack's pain was palpable, and soon tears prickled behind my eyelids. I listened to his raw telling, leaving nothing to my imagination.

"I answered their other questions, providing Jav's full name and other particulars for their records. I won't forget the look on Montgomery's face after I responded to his question of how Jav was related to me. To hear me say that Jav was my husband caused him great discomfort. He cleared his throat and then coughed for a few seconds.

"Husband, yes, he said husband—so they married—when was he going to tell me? Focus Jemma, focus.

Then he said, 'You did say husband, sir?'

"About fifteen minutes later, they escorted me to the morgue, and I saw my love, my joy, lying lifeless on a stainless-steel table. "I held him, and his skin was cool. I kissed his salty lips and ran my fingers through his hair for the last time."

"Jack, I'm so sorry about Javier. Tell me how I can help."

"Can you bring him back, Jemma? Tell me this is a fucking nightmare. Tell me he'll come through that door at any moment. That's how you can help."

It was awkward. Should I hug him, or just sit there? I wasn't sure, so I reached over and put my arm around his shoulders. He surprised me by hugging me quite tenderly.

"Have you eaten anything?" I asked.

"No, I don't have an appetite. I've had a few cups of coffee... I think."

"You've got to eat, Jack, if only a little." I walked into the kitchen and fixed us a quick omelette and some toast. We ate in silence, and then he stopped chewing and looked over at me.

"I have contacted his ex-wife and son. We'll bring his remains to Madrid where there's a Martinez burial vault, and he'll be interred there. The coroner will release the body tomorrow, and we should be able to leave the island in two days."

"Would you like me to come to Madrid with you?" I asked, cautiously.

"I think this is something I should do alone. But thank you for asking, I'm glad you're here." Jack's face was a mask, devoid of expression, stiffened into lifelessness by the imagined repetition of Jav's tragic accident.

"I'm going out of my mind. I should've gone out with him on the dive. He didn't know the Caribbean Sea well enough."

"But neither do you, Jack. Please don't blame yourself; accidents happen."

"Maybe if I was there, just maybe, the outcome would've been different."

We sat next to each other, and I gently rubbed his back. For a few minutes, neither of us said anything. I poured us drinks from the wet bar. Jack savoured his brandy quietly. I gripped my glass tightly, and ever so often, released my fingers in an accordion like manner, freeing the tension building in my joints.

Jack spent the rest of the afternoon making calls to friends and business associates, and I sat by the pool with my laptop, though I didn't achieve much. I ordered a meal delivery from one of the new restaurants on the island. Despite this dreadful situation, we had to eat.

Later, we picked at the meal. It was tasty, but neither of us had an appetite.

"How about if we get some rest, Jack? Tomorrow is another long day."

"Okay," he said and headed towards the bedroom door. He paused and looked over his shoulder at me. "I'll sleep in the guest room where he and I stayed. There his presence will surround me."

"And I'll go to our room," I replied, though rejection raised its ugly head again, and I fought to keep my emotions in check. This wasn't about me, dammit. Jack nodded and walked on.

I entered our room, sat on the chaise, and looked around, expecting him to follow me. I wanted to hold him close and help him through his pain, but my own anguish bubbled up, and I felt pushed aside. I called Maya.

As soon as she picked up the phone, I blurted out: "I've got bad news. There's been an accident on Majestic, and Javier was killed."

"Are you kidding? What the hell happened? How did he... is Jack okay?"

"He's alive but a mess. What a flipping fiasco. Hold on, I need a drink." I walked over to the side table and poured myself a brandy before returning my earbuds to my ears. "It's just... tragic."

"Jack must be devastated. This is catastrophic news," Maya said somberly.

"I can't imagine what Jack must be going through. He's beside himself."

"He has to be... but you, Jem. How are you coping?"

"I'm still reeling and experiencing a bundle of confused emotions. I'm sad for Jack, but apart from the death, I found out that he and Javier were married.

"Oh, that must have been a recent development."

"I assume it was. He referred to Javier as his husband, but its not the time to confront him."

"That's generous of you. It can't be easy."

"I know this is not about me, so what I'm going to say will sound selfish... but, I feel like an outsider looking in. I don't know how to help him, or if I even could."

"Don't beat yourself up. Just be there for him, Jemma, that's all you can do. Let Jack tell you what he needs. Maybe he doesn't know yet. Follow his lead."

"I hope I can be what he needs and not be a distraction. I can't help but think how lonely he must be right now. Thanks for your advice. I'll let him lead."

"Try to get some rest. You'll need it so you can support him. I'll check back with you in a day or so. Give Jack my condolences."

After she hung up, I poured myself yet another drink, cracked open the window, and let the sea breeze flood the room with its cool saltiness. I stretched out across the bed and tried to imagine what their wedding ceremony was like. But it didn't matter, with Javier gone, there was no longer a marriage.

Primrose and Zeke were due back soon, and I wondered how much they knew about Javier's misfortune. On such a small island, the accident, and the fact that Jack was spending time with his husband, would have gotten around by now. It was likely why I had received strange looks from islanders upon arriving from New York. We were caught up in this publicly unfolding story together. I just wanted to hug him, but hugged my pillow instead, and eventually drifted off to sleep.

He must have tiptoed into the room because I awoke in the middle of the night to Jack's warm breath on my neck, his arms wrapped around my body, and his right leg stretched across mine. Another unfamiliar experience was that we were both fully clothed. We slept until daybreak.

Chapter 24

Jemma

Primrose and Zeke returned the following day. I was uneasy and didn't know how to behave when I met her in the kitchen.

"Morning, Ms Jemma. I'm sorry for yours and Mr Jack's loss." She looked at me directly and must have known that I was surprised by her greeting and condolences but kept on speaking. "The coffee is on, the Blue Mountain Mr Jack likes. Should I make two omelettes, or would fruit be just fine?"

I recovered quickly and responded as normal as possible, though nothing at Seaview Manor was usual right then. "Thank you, Primrose. I think coffee and some fruit would be fine for now," I said as I tightened the sash of my silk robe.

"Would you like it on the lanai or the conservatory, ma'am?"

"Conservatory, please. I'll wash up and be there in a few minutes."

I breathed a quiet sigh of relief and walked back to the bedroom. I was grateful that Primrose had the class not to rub salt into my wound. Maybe people on the island were experiencing the tragedy as well. They didn't know Javier, but I imagined the fact that he was a visitor to their island and had met his untimely death touched their hearts. I turned my head and saw Jack sitting on the edge of the bed, his legs crossed and his left hand cradling his head.

"I'm sorry to have intruded... I couldn't..." he stuttered.

"No need for an apology, Jack. You're never an intrusion. Would you like coffee? Primrose is brewing some right now."

"Yes, please. I'll be visiting the coroner's office and then contacting the funeral home. Would you... could you... err ... I'd like it if you came, but I'll understand if you'd rather not."

I sat next to him and took his hand. "Jack, it's okay. I'll come. You shouldn't have to do this alone."

"Thank you," he whispered and squeezed my hand. I kissed him gently on his cheek and headed into the bathroom. "I'll meet you in the conservatory in a bit."

As soon as I'd agreed to accompany him, I had second thoughts. A small internal tremor began to rise in me, and nausea set in. *I'd be seen as the other woman, not Jack's partner. Javier already had that distinction.* I felt naked and wanted to cover up, shelter any self-respect I had left. But I'd already given him my word; I had to go through with it.

Primrose had laid out a platter of sliced guava, papaya, pineapple, mango, and sapodilla sprinkled with coconut shavings and flavoured with shots of Grand Marnier and orange juice before we got to the conservatory. Then she disappeared into the kitchen. Our mood reduced the meal to silence.

On our way out, we passed by Zeke tending to the peach rose bush closest to the front door. He looked up as we neared him.

"Morning to you both. Let me know if I can do anything to help." He didn't directly address the accident or offer condolences, but his offer to help was enough for me.

"Hello, Zeke, and thank you," I said, as Jack and I hopped into the Peugeot and headed into town. The fifteen-minute drive went by mostly in silence, except for Jack's mention of the state of the sea.

"Look at it. So tranquil and welcoming, yet so dangerous, and fiercely all-consuming. It can take everything away in just seconds." There was no reason to respond, so I didn't.

The sky was cloudless; a soft sun and clement breeze filled the atmosphere. The only sound was the low humming of the Peugeot's tires against the pavement. We pulled into the county parking lot and my heart immediately sank. A black hearse was parked close to the rear of the building. Jack saw it too, and bit down on his bottom lip.

"Let's get this done," he said, and we left the car.

Once inside, we were greeted by the receptionist. A large, balding, squat fellow with a soft island accent spoke from behind her.

"Good morning, Mr Generson, I'm Onesimus Thompson, Chief Coroner on the island. Thank you for coming out. Our work here is completed, and the report submitted to the proper authorities. We have a copy for you, which you will need for transport and other business. Please sign where indicated on this form. It releases the body from my care."

My care… it sounded so strange. I watched Jack sign the form.

"Would you like to inspect the body before it leaves for the funeral home? The director is here to accompany Mr Martinez," the man continued.

"Thank you, but I've…" he turned to look at me.

"I'm fine," I said. I hadn't met Javier in life and wasn't about to in death.

"Okay then, Mr Milford, the director, will take over from here."

A tall kind-looking gentleman introduced himself. "I'm Henry Milford, of Island Breeze Rest Haven. My condolences to you both."

"Thank you, Mr Milford," Jack said, nodding at the gentleman.

"We will prepare Mr Martinez's remains for transport to Madrid tomorrow. The flight is scheduled to leave Baptiste at noon, and I believe you, sir, will accompany him to Madrid. Is this correct? Do you have any questions or concerns?"

"You are correct, and I don't have any questions at this time. I've brought over some of his clothing." Jack handed Mr Milford a travel bag.

"Thank you, Mr Generson; that's all. If anything comes up or you have any further wishes, here's my card. We're located on Sea Lane, five minutes from the town centre. I bid you good day, sir."

Jack and I watched Mr Milford walk to the back of the building and we headed to the car. Soon, a young attendant wheeled Javier out in a grey body bag and placed him in the hearse. Mr Milford then got into the driver's seat and the attendant climbed into the passenger seat. They drove out of the parking lot and turned left.

I looked over at Jack and saw his tear-stained face. I interlaced my fingers with his and waited.

My heart ached for Jack and for the pain he was in. I cared less about a man who was my rival—though his loss was tragic and the cause of my lover's anguish.

"Would you like me to drive?" I asked.

"Yes," he replied. We exchanged seats, and I started the engine.

"How about getting a bite? Even if you don't have the appetite…"

Jack simply nodded, appearing too shaken to say much more.

I replayed some of the words spoken in the coroner's office: "*my care;*" "*accompany Mr Martinez;*" "*any further wishes;*" "*here's my card*" – classy – *but what kind of service did I think they would offer?* A small twinge in my stomach signalled my misjudgement. I hadn't expected their empathy and attention to detail.

I drove the car along the main road and headed west. I'd been to a restaurant and a secluded beach with Amanda in the area a few months prior. It was the perfect spot away from prying eyes. We picked up sandwiches and two light beers at the little restaurant and pulled over to the beach nearby.

We sat under a small frangipani tree and ate in silence until Jack's voice pierced the stillness. "America changed my life in many ways and taught me who I really was, what I wanted in life, and from other people. And Jav was a big part of that. Would you like to hear a bit about it, Jemma?" He looked pensive.

"Yes, I'd like that, Jack." In truth I knew I probably wouldn't like some of what was coming, but I wanted to show support, so I lied and touched his hand as he continued.

"Well, where do I begin … It was close to midnight when we arrived in Manhattan, after an almost seven-hour flight from Heathrow and an hour's taxi ride from JFK airport to the Flatiron District. I was almost fifteen.

"We'd left a beautiful row house in Kensington and moved into a penthouse my parents had purchased. The next morning, a summery Sunday, I looked out the window and saw two teenage boys around my age, sauntering along the sidewalk dressed rather colourfully: one adorned in white shorts and a bright pink shirt, its collar turned up, and the other a yellow and dark blue polka dot shirt with dungaree overalls.

"As I watched, tickled by the brave colour scheme of their attire, they paused and planted the most sensual kiss on each other's mouth. All along holding hands, and after about twenty seconds, they moved apart and continued on their journey. I kept my eyes on them until they grew smaller and smaller and disappeared from sight.

Jack's eyes had regained some of their light and sparkle as the warmth of his memory flooded back in the telling.

"I fell in love with New York right then, so open, so free, and so beautiful. It hadn't been as liberal in any of the places we'd lived in the UK.

"My older brother had remained at university in London; he wasn't a fan of the American lifestyle. I spent three fun years in high school playing on the football team and singing in the school choir. I dated widely, though no relationship lasted longer than eight to ten weeks. I was accepted and registered at Cornell, and the dice rolled in my favour again, Javier Martinez, the most beautiful creature I had ever set eyes on became my roommate, my lover, and then my husband."

Jack looked over at me softly and then away in the distance.

I wanted to hear him say that *I* was the most beautiful creature he had ever laid eyes on, but he could only say that about the man he truly loved, and it was hard to hear. A knot twisted in my stomach, and I struggled to remain stoic. I wanted to hear about *his* life not Javier's. I sat there and listened to him go on about *their* lives, not *his*.

"An extraordinary human being with an admirable concern and caring for the planet," he continued. "We visited many parts of the world so he could experience some of nature's unspoiled gems, like the kelp forest, and penguin colonies of Southern Africa. "He'd say, 'We live on a beautiful planet, and we unconsciously destroy it every day, little by little. At the end of my time here, I want to have contributed to its preservation. I want my legacy to be one of a planet carer.' I think I'll make educational endowments linked to the environment in his name."

"How very thoughtful," I replied.

"I'll need to stay in Europe for a while Jemma. There's a lot to look after. With Jav's parents no longer in the picture, Mateo or Teo and I are all the family he has. But there are multiple properties across Europe and other holdings I'll have to get quickly acquainted with. So, it could—"

"Let's not worry about Seaview at this point, Jack. I'll be here. Take the time you need to look after Javier's estate and connect with me when you can. We'll see how it evolves." I couldn't believe the words that were rolling off my tongue. I was saddened by his loss, but I still wanted him to come back to me.

Jack leaned in and hugged me. "God, Jemma, I don't know how to go on without him."

I squeezed his trembling hand. He continued to reminisce and was unceasing in his praise for Javier. From it, I got a clearer picture of Javier, the man.

"On that crisp Friday in December when Javier and I wed, there was no fanfare, just us, two witnesses, and a Justice of the Peace. It was right after I told you about us. We'd waited forty-one years, eight months, and four days for that moment. We chose Fiji for our honeymoon, and for two weeks, we swam and sunned ourselves on unspoiled beaches and snorkelled and dove with thousands of fish through the soft coral of the Rainbow Reef. It was like being nineteen again, the age I met Jav.

Jack told me that Javier was born in Madrid and spent time on Majorca, Lake Garda, and Lake Lugano, where his family owned multiple properties. He was incredibly wealthy because of the estate they left, a wealth that far outweighed Jack's own substantial portfolio.

Envy and compassion fought a duel inside me as I listened and longed for what they had together: love and money.

According to Jack, Javier was an avid water sport enthusiast, excited about his first trip to the Caribbean, to see the property, and experience the best snorkelling and scuba diving on the island. Jack gazed out into the distance and shared how Javier researched Majestic to uncover its treasury of coral reefs, with their colourful schools of fish and hidden crustaceans. He investigated to find where spray and blue crabs could be found, and especially looked forward to swimming with the dolphins. But he was nervous about sharks.

"The Patagonia trip would have taken us from this warm island to fields of ice and snow. Jav had vowed to experience, up close, the blinding whites and blues of Perito Moreno's glacier. He'd seen a documentary where blocks of ice broke off from the mother shelf and fell into the water, becoming icebergs in the process. I could never have imagined that a trip to the end of the world would become a different kind of end, an end of Jav and our world together.

I kissed Jack on the cheek. "Javier was the perfect human being—and like you said—an extraordinary one. Know that I'm here if you need me," I whispered.

"Thanks for understanding," he replied. "It is getting harder by the hour. I'm not sure how I'll cope in the days and months ahead, but knowing that you're in my corner will be a great help."

We made our way back to the house and found a note from the Whittle family: "Sorry for your loss, Amanda and Sebastian."

Jack went into the guest room to pack; he needed time to sort the extra luggage.

After a light supper, we turned into bed early, only this time Jack came directly to our room. There was touching and tenderness between us during the day, but I wasn't expecting the intense desire that ignited. It was like our first night all over again. There were no conversations; we just clung to each other.

Jack needed me, and without any guilt, we found comfort in each other. There was something sad, yet beautiful about that night. But in the morning his face again sagged with grief, and his attempt to smile didn't reach his eyes.

I drove him to the marina to take the private hire yacht to the airport on Baptiste. We shared a tender kiss, and I watched him walk off with the porter. I headed back to Seaview, a feeling that he would be gone for a very long time, swirling in my belly.

Chapter 25

Jack

I watched the silver hearse parked on the tarmac, and the sight hurt my eyes and fed the dull pain in my chest. I'd purchased two seats and booked them right next to each other, so you could ride up in business class with me. The travel agent was confused when I purchased your seat. And here I am sitting in comfort, and you are in cargo. Just the thought of that aggrieves me.

"Sir, I need the name of the passenger sitting in 2B. You have requested and paid for seats 2A and 2B, but you have only provided one name."

"Javier Martinez, that's his name, the passenger in 2B."

She asked for our passport numbers, and I gave her both.

Now I'm walking slowly towards the aircraft, and I want to make a detour, rush over to the hearse, pound loudly on the window, and wake you up. I want to leave this terrible nightmare we're floating through, while some five hundred yards down the tarmac, our beautiful Lady Daniela sits, her engines cold, awaiting your warm hands to throttle up and fly us to Patagonia. You named her Daniela as a tribute to your mother, Daniela Martinez, the only woman you loved. We purchased and named the Mastercraft 300 The Javson Entwined, and you said it was in celebration of our love, and rightfully named for both of us, although you never called me Jackson.

You told me that you never loved Anna, though you stayed with her for almost forty years. You said she was the blanket that shielded you from the disdain that could come your way, should members of your family ever find out your true identity—the one that you and I and those closest to us know.

You asked me if I had ever loved a woman, my wife and Jemma included, and like you, I'd answered, 'only my mother.' I told you that with Maggie, it began as a casual friendship and deepened, but never grew into love... and that with Jemma, it began as a sexual attraction and morphed into an easy friendship. I told you that you were my prize, my special prince, and that no woman could ever dethrone you. I told you that Maggie, and now Jemma, were simply my company until you were free. We chose not to label our love, because labels complicate things. We were just two human beings blissfully in love with each other.

And all these years, dear Jav, I've kept my promise, even though temptation hovered, I've been faithful in my heart, if not my body. I've slept with multiple women, but none of them penetrated the powerful emotional connection I have with you. Death cannot either.

After Maggie died and I met Jemma, I told you she was my new filler. You pouted and told me that you didn't need filler, that Anna never served that purpose. You reminded me that sleeping with Anna was a duty you were expected to fulfil by your parents and her parents, because of Teo's birth. You added that you were never content. And when both her parents ended up in care six months apart from each other, and two years later you lost your parents, you knew it was time to walk away from the marriage and so did she. You told me that except for Anna, and very early experimental sex with other boys, well before you met me, there had been no one else.

I loved you then, I love you now, I'll love you always. Can you hear me? I promise that you will live on in my heart, and no one, woman or man, will ever take your place.

Now I'm buckled in my seat, your favourite grey cardigan lying next to me in 2B. Passengers are flooding the aisle, making their way to the belly of the aircraft.

I see the hearse slowly drive away… seems you've boarded before I did, despite being in cargo. I wonder now if you are right beneath me. I can picture you in my arms, your warm breath on my neck, your nose against my cheek, and your slender, but firm hands seek and interlace with mine. I swear I hear your heart beating, the slow, gentle rise and fall of your chest on mine.

"Sir, Mr Generson, sir?" I opened my eyes to see the KLM flight attendant peering down at me.

"Sir, I'll have to ask you to remove your cardigan from the seat, it belongs to another passenger who hasn't boarded yet."

Her words were jolting. I swallowed hard, then replied: "Thank you. Yes, I know, he's already here."

She smiled, glanced at her passenger manifest, and walked away.

Chapter 26

Primrose

Ms Jemma is not a bad person; she nothing like Ms Amanda. Come to think 'bout it, she only a li'l mix up. Cause how she can come to Majestic posing with a man who marry another man? She should know there ain't no hope in that situation. The way she roll up in bed with him, you think he sweeter than honey, and all this time he got a husband pon the side, or maybe she is the woman pon the side. Poor thing!

Lawd, if GG ever hear 'bout that, I wonder what she would say? First, I think she would say, 'Is none of your business, but she should look for a man who like ooman, it sure make things easier that way.'

When word get out that the visitor who had the accident was Mr Jack husband, it really confuse people, even me, and without much information, the island lips slap without cease. At the bus stop I overhear two women from the village chatting 'bout it.

"Wait … he married he … but is what you saying?" Cilla, the shorter of the two step back, arms akimbo, mouth ajar, and eyes narrowly squinted.

"Dat is what I seh. Dat is what everybady seh," Minty, the taller of the two responds.

"But if he marry he… then she kinky. Let we ask Primrose. She sure to know."

"Go waste you time. You never get nutten outta she. Dat one lip as tight as a size thirty-eight bubby stuff in a size thirty-two brassier! So tight, the wearer can hardly breathe."

"You right you know. 'Is none of my business' is what she gon seh."

Neither one of them come over to question me, because they already know the answer. As long as Ms Jemma and Mr Jack pay my wages, I don't care what they do with their lives.

One day I watch from the kitchen window at how Ms Jemma eye Zeke in the garden. She look like she was riding a seesaw; he bend left, she bend left, he lean right, she lean right. Poor thing must have been lonely, 'cause while Mr Jack was busy in faraway places, and Zeke might be free, he ain't got that kinda money she accustom to. There in the big bed all by herself, while Mr Jack climbing his bean stalk somewhere in Europe or America.

I really hope Ms Jemma and Mr Jack find a way to stay together so she don't up and return to America like Madame F up and go back to France. I can't be left high and dry again without a job! Maybe Mr Jack will settle down now and move to the island, seeing how his sweet man husband gone.

I wonder if the husband did know 'bout Ms Jemma. After all, we both left the manor house before Mr Jack and he visit. *Primrose is none of your business.* Yes, GG, I can hear you all up there in heaven, but I was just wondering.

Chapter 27

Jemma

A few weeks after Jack left for Madrid, I was thrilled to receive mail from the esteemed Bodleian Library of Oxford University. The letter read:

Dear Ms Worley,

Our Department of Art History reviewed the painting submitted to us for evaluation. Below are comments based on our preliminary findings:

The portrait was produced in 1834 in Glasgow and a copy is housed at the Kelvingrove Art Gallery & Museum, Glasgow, United Kingdom.

Painted by Franklin D Ebberhausen, a Belgian artist, the likeness is of Antonia Kathleen McNally, born on October 23, 1816, on the island of Sierra Majestic, British West Indies.

The last known location of Antonia K Creag (née McNally) was the colony of Upper Canada, now Ontario, Canada. She married Rory Creag, a Scotsman from the Highlands and moved with him to Upper Canada where they raised a family.

Cordially,

Hansen B McGregor,

Senior Art Historian

I read the document at least three times before it sunk in. The woman in the painting, Antonia McNally, was born on this island and ended up in Ontario, Canada. This was becoming more fascinating by the minute.

My initial reaction was to reconnect with my friend Annabel at Oxford to expand the search with the Ontario government. But who better to do this than a Canadian: I would do it. How exciting it would be to locate the whereabouts of Antonia's family. I would use the information I had received from the Bodleian as background to continue my research in Ontario.

One evening, about a week later, my phone dinged. I rolled over and looked at it; Maya's profile showed up. "Good time to call?" the message read. "Perfect time" I responded. Five seconds later, my phone rang.

"How are you holding up?"

"Not sure," I said. "I'm a bit lost and don't know what my plan is. I'm sensing Jack won't come back to the island, and if he doesn't, I'm not sure what will happen to Seaview. So, I'm rather stressed and depressed. I vacillate between being a caretaker and a part owner. Things are very confusing, Maya."

"You've got a lot going on. And what are you doing to take care of yourself?" Maya probed.

"Drinking a lot, that's what," I said my voice thick with sarcasm. "Thank God Zeke is here to take the edge off.

"You need a heck more than drinks to get a handle on your troubles. I'm glad you're still seeing Zeke. How is that going?

"He realizes I'm struggling, and he supports me—without judgement. We spend a lot of time together, in and out of bed." I chuckled.

"And have you considered seeing a therapist on the island, like we discussed?"

"I plan to but haven't done anything yet. There's so much going on."

The truth was that I'd felt a bit ashamed about seeking out a therapist in the region. I believed Maya sensed my apprehension.

"Why don't you come back to New York for a few weeks and get sorted, or at least begin the process. I get the sadness and depression, but what's causing the confusion?"

"Remember the odd visions and sudden mood swings I'd experienced? Well now I've found a portrait of a Black woman in the old sugar mill on our property. She has a peculiarly strong resemblance to me."

"Did you say a Black woman? Okay, JW, what the hell have you been smoking? It must have been some really potent stuff. Wow!"

"The thing is, I wasn't smoking or drinking at the time of any of these occurrences. That's why I'm bewildered."

I filled Maya in on my findings about Antonia and how she ended up in Ontario, Canada.

For a moment, she was silent. I wasn't sure she heard me or knew the significance of the information I'd shared. "Are you with me?"

"Yes, I am … and you're from Ontario, correct?"

"I am. Toronto is the city and Ontario is the province. It's my birthplace."

Maya was quiet again, then very slowly she said, "Don't tell me the two of you are related."

"How could that be? I'm White. But when I first saw the portrait and the resemblance, I searched her face for other characteristics. I looked deep into her eyes, and swear I heard her say, 'Hello, dear.'"

"You're freaking me out, Jemma. Now you're talking to dead people? This is some weird shit. You must see somebody—ensure you're not delusional. Promise me?" she asked, disquiet in her voice.

"I can try to see someone, maybe on one of the neighbouring islands."

"Good. That's a start, right?"

"Yes, but there's one last freaky point; I noticed that the right pinkie finger of the woman in the portrait was slightly bent, a trait shared by female members of my family… my mother, my aunt and me. My sister Ollie didn't have it and I found out why later."

Maya reminded me that I had been experiencing a lot of stress and again encouraged me to seek psychological help. She shared that her therapist had helped her tremendously through difficult times.

"Okay, okay. I'll inquire about seeing someone on Baptiste or on Barbados, and if I don't find the right fit, I'll come to New York."

"Also, maybe your DNA ancestry test results will confirm that you are every inch a White woman of Danish and Irish heritage, just like your mother said. You did do it, correct?"

"I did, and am awaiting the results."

"Great. Do take care of yourself. I'll connect soon."

Was Maya right? What if it was stress causing me to hallucinate? Checking out a mental health professional online couldn't hurt, but I didn't know much about psychotherapy. So, I surfed the internet for local psychologists and psychiatrists and connected with a Dr Jonathan Breckenridge, a therapist practising on both Jamaica and Barbados, and a native of Baptiste who knew Majestic well. His website described his approach, which was based on Jungian psychology. Fascinating but kind of scary too. I called him and liked his empathic voice right away.

He explained that Jungian therapy is based on the principle that our unconscious is full of ideas and symbols rooted in our culture and history, going back to the remote past. He lost me at a couple of points, but the gist was that this 'collective' unconscious comes out in our dreams and fantasies and causes symptoms if the conscious mind can't handle it. I wondered what he might make of my recent experiences.

We did sessions via Skype and telephone. I told him about Javier's accident and my relationship with Jack, and he seemed genuinely moved. But the freaky events were what really got his attention. I talked about the very sudden mood shift I had experienced on my way to the sugar mill: the vision in the bathroom mirror and the dream about babies being sucked into the earth. He didn't seem surprised or shocked, which relaxed me right away. However, as I got into my experience of the portrait and what I had discovered, Dr Breckenridge began throwing out questions.

"What do you know about the house in which you live, and the earlier inhabitants?"

"Not much, except for what we've been told by the previous owners. The house was in their family around two hundred years. Her ancestors were plantation owners who employed many of the people on the island." I felt good being able to answer his question.

"To the best of my knowledge, that description is partially correct," said Dr Breckenridge in his calm, reassuring tone. "There were plantation owners that held hundreds of enslaved Africans on Majestic. To call the work they did 'employment' is a stretch."

It suddenly hit me that what Zeke had told me made sense. We had purchased an old sugar plantation with all its history that I knew nothing of and had to research on my own. Amanda must have known about this history and carried on the tale that her family spun.

"Do you think the manifestations I'm experiencing could be linked to the manor's history?" I asked, as a cold shiver ran down my spine.

"Ms Worley, I think that your unconscious is trying to get your attention. But part of you is fighting it. Seaview Manor must have deep roots; roots you don't yet know or understand. You are tapping into old memories and events and family connections you have to this place, and they are pushing into your awareness. The question I have for you is, are you willing to accept what the past has to say? It may change your life if you have the courage to let it happen."

I sat in the library after our session and stared out the window at the sea and a shaded slice of the garden. *What was Dr Breckenridge getting at? How could I possibly have a connection with Seaview Manor? Besides, only the sugarcane sighting took place in the house itself, through the bathroom mirror. The other strange events happened outside.*

The idea that secrets from the history of this place were not only connected to me but 'wanted in' somehow, was frightening. However, the doctor's attitude had been so matter-of-fact, I was comforted. Still, chills ran through my body and my tightly fisted hands shook. Just then Primrose knocked on the door and I let out a gasp.

"Dinner is almost ready ma'am, when would you like it served?"

It took me a moment to come to. "Err, six thirty would be good. Thank you. I'll eat in the conservatory and watch the sun go down."

Primrose left for the kitchen, and I pulled a bottle of unoaked Chardonnay from the fridge. I had a few glasses with dinner, and stared out to sea, as a dying sun burned itself out on the edge of the horizon.

My DNA results from Core Ancestry arrived in the mail the next day. I opened it hesitantly, nervous about its findings.

Dear Ms Worley,

I am pleased to report that based on admixture mapping we have determined that you share genetic ancestry with peoples of the British Isles and West Africa: 87.5% British and Irish and 12.5% West African. The DNA sequence patterns are explained in the attached document...

West African... West AFRICAN? Oh God!

The rest of the words in the letter collided and blurred into each other. *West African means that Black blood runs through my veins. Holy shit! Twelve point five percentage would mean that the African ancestor is a recent relative, not that far removed. But how recent? And whose side are they on? My mother's side, three or maybe four generations removed? Oh God... it could be mother's mother, my grandmother... no, that's too close... maybe it was my mother's grandmother... the crooked little finger... Antonia is related... no, I'm related to Antonia. Oh shit, oh shit, this is flipping real.*

It was time to have a honest conversation with mother. If I was 12.5 percent, she must be even higher. The straightening of her hair, the bleaching of her skin—she must know—dear God!

Images whizzed through my head like flying saucers in another galaxy. What to do, who to tell? Uncertainties came with this new awareness. Could the DNA results change my life? And, what would Jack think if he knew that the girl with the porcelain skin was really a mix of black and white. Maybe he didn't have to find out yet. Like an unknown relative, appearing suddenly and uncertain of welcome, my Blackness waited for acceptance.

Chapter 28

Jemma

Jack had been gone six weeks. He was steeped in the probate process of Javier's estate and becoming better acquainted with Teo, who he'd only met a couple of times over the years. He soon learned that settling an estate valued at some eighty-five million Euros, while managing his own assets of twenty-five million USD, was intense and time consuming.

While Jack remained immersed in new learning, I continued my weekly sessions with Dr Breckinridge. They were unlike anything I had ever experienced. They always began with him asking me about my dreams from the night before, which I was supposed to have written down in a journal. He would focus on some aspect of the dream and ask me the first thing that came to mind. I found this hard because sometimes those thoughts were sexual. At other times, he would ask how I felt inside. If I said I was feeling down and bad about myself, he would ask me the same thing: "What do you associate with being a bad person?" All sorts of old family stuff I'd forgotten came out, but also odd images of people I didn't know and had never met. Some of them were Black, which made no sense. But, as always, he didn't seem surprised by anything. Even more remarkable was how brave I was talking about the strange experiences and visions I'd had.

Dr B said it would be a good idea to learn more about the culture of the island, as it was clearly triggering something in my unconscious. He put me in touch with Professor Mavis Abassa, an historian and genealogist at the University of the West Indies, Cave Hill, whose field of study was the Afro-Caribbean diaspora. A month later, I received an e-mail from Professor Abassa, who confirmed that Emerald Hill had indeed been a sugar plantation with some two hundred and twenty-three enslaved Africans, owned by a man named Corinus Othello McNally, who went by the name Othello. She and I had a follow-up telephone conversation which shed more clarity on her findings.

"I was able to extract some historical information, including birth and baptismal records from registries and churches, and I can say that McNally and his sons behaved like many other plantation owners of their time. He fathered eleven children—three with his wife and eight with his house slave Octavia."

"That's bizarre. Are you telling me that McNally impregnated Octavia multiple times while he lived with his wife in the same house? Where was his wife during this ongoing assaults on a powerless woman? It all sounds unreal." I shook my head in disbelief.

"Yes. Mrs McNally lived at the home, and these situations were quite common. In Mr McNally's case, he was enjoying his spoils. He owned Octavia, so her body belonged to him. At least that's how the law viewed it back then. As you know, now it would be seen as rape."

"Oh my! So, what happened to the rest of McNally's children by Octavia?"

"Five of the babies were sold off to other plantations by McNally's wife, Amelia. And after she died, Octavia gave birth to Antonia. A few years later she birthed twin boys."

"Great, so even after Antonia there were more?" I inhaled deeply. It was difficult to find hope in this story.

"Unfortunately, the twin boys were found strangled on their mats before their second birthday. Island folklore suggested that McNally's deceased wife was displeased and took out her displeasure on the babies." I listened in disgust. "Note I used the word 'folklore,'" Abassa emphasised.

"How sad that must have been for poor Octavia... wait, twins... you said twins, and the babies... that I saw in my dream

...they were dressed in similar outfits, and I assumed they were..." I closed my eyes and held my head tightly to squeeze the vision free. My stomach churned; my chest tightened. "Oh, I can't... my God! The trauma she would've endured!

"Sad and traumatic would be good adjectives to describe the situation. It was rumoured Octavia suffered from melancholia and died of a broken heart some years later."

"The poor woman. I don't have kids, but I could imagine the ongoing heartbreak she lived with. Death must have been her greatest escape."

"You mentioned his sons... how were they implicated in this drama?"

"His eldest son died of malaria. But after receiving their European education, McNally's other two sons fathered three children each with young enslaved girls on the estate."

"I'll send you the report by mail, and I encourage you to be in touch if I can be of further help."

I thanked Professor Abassa and ended our call.

I pressed on my temples with the tips of my fingers and breathed in deeply and slowly to release the tension.

The story of Octavia and her children disturbed me greatly. I lay in bed for several nights thinking about her, and how it must have been to lose all except one. And then to lose even that child when she was sent away for an education. I'd sought books on slavery in the Caribbean from both Professor Abassa and Dr Breckenridge. With their recommendations, I read about the history of the region and the reality of daily life on a sugar plantation. I also read novels by Caribbean women writers, including Jamaica Kincaid and Merle Hodge. I began to understand the less obvious but truer nature of this supposed paradise. Paradise for some, and a hell hole for others.

My school memories of Canadian history were vague, but I had pride in the birth of our nation, which happened at a difficult time when people were afraid of being taken over by the United States. However, in trying to find out more about my background I was learning things about Canada that I never knew. And some of it wasn't pretty, like the way we treated Indigenous people. We had starved and forced them off their land and onto reserves with unsafe drinking water. We removed their children from their homes and placed them in prison-like schools, where we abused them and didn't allow them to speak their own language. This was a blot on our humanitarian reputation.

When it came to Black people and slavery though, I had always thought we were the good guys, offering refuge and freedom to the enslaved escaping from south of the border. Reading articles and viewing website interviews online shifted my perception. That idea was only partly true, as there had been enslaved people held in the colonies that eventually became Canada. So, we weren't perfect; and those enslaved Africans who escaped the U.S. weren't welcomed to our country with open arms. White Canadians made their lives difficult and still mistreat their descendants today. We were better than the Americans, which we love to say, but it was a low bar. That's the part we leave out.

How to wrap my head around this – that my family included both the holders of the enslaved, and the people they enslaved, criminals and their victims. I needed some time away from Majestic to clear out my colliding thoughts. I needed New York.

Chapter 29

Jemma

My flight into JFK to meet Jack was on time. He'd suggested we get together and discuss how things were going at Seaview. Since I was the only one living at the property, I'd mentioned the idea of turning the manor into a holiday let or bed-and-breakfast. It would bring in money to help with the bills. He asked for a business plan, and I came prepared.

I was happy to see Jack and wondered how he felt about seeing me. Would my betrayal with Zeke be written all over my face? Was it even really betrayal? I never promised monogamy, and he hadn't been at Seaview in ages. I was seeing Zeke and enjoyed having him in my life.

I arrived at the Manhattan penthouse, and Jack met me at the suite's elevator door. My breath caught in my throat, and I forced my lips into a smile. *How could a person age ten years in six months?* He reached out and hugged me, but the hug was half-hearted. I assumed from his light embrace that this was going to be platonic, as he had indicated—business.

We sat next to each other on the sofa to toast our meeting. I pressed my insteps into the rug to keep my legs from shaking, reached over, and accepted the gin and tonic from his trembling outstretched hand. He had made reservations at our favourite Italian restaurant, which was within walking distance, and we arrived on time after I'd freshened up. Our small table was neatly tucked into a window bay, and we people watched while waiting for our meals. For the first time since my arrival, we looked directly into each other's eyes. I could still see his pain, but I could also sense his tiredness. Jack now lived in an envelope of sadness, which both held and hid the love and desire he had lost.

"You look absolutely lovely, Jemma. Your complexion, your eyes, your skin is so radiant. The Caribbean has been good to you," he said, reaching for my hand.

He'd noticed and he was correct. I'd been rejuvenated over the months since he'd left, but I wasn't ready to admit to him just how thoroughly I was enjoying my time; I definitely couldn't mention Zeke.

"Aww, thanks, Jack. I've been keeping busy but finding time to relax as well. And Primrose has kept up with her exquisite cooking. No complaints in that department. How have you been?"

"I've had better days. To say I'm tired is an understatement. But I'm happy to see you," he said, tucking both of my hands in his.

"Same here," I replied with a smile.

"It's been an uphill battle. Our short six months of marriage meant that much of the paperwork to include me as co-owner of our holdings had been in preparation but not yet filed. So, it's been demanding on some fronts. We made our wills before we were married—a wise decision."

"Excellent planning on your parts, I'd say. None of us could have imagined this outcome. How is your relationship with Teo coming along?"

"Nicely, and I have some news to share. Teo and I have created the *Javier Martinez Chairs in Ocean Conservation Science* in honour of this man who meant so much to us. The goal is to protect and preserve the world's oceans through research and education. And, to this end, we will fund universities in Africa, Europe, North America, South America, and the Caribbean to implement these programs."

Jack's eyes lit up, and I saw glimmers of the man I'd met years before, sitting across from me.

"Now that's a legacy! Bravo, Jack." I released my hands from his and lifted my cocktail in a toast.

"I think he would be pleased. Teo did most of the work for the initiative. It couldn't have happened this quickly without him. He's a polite, introverted fellow. Our conversations are usually short, but I like him. Working together has given us something to cheer for—something Jav would approve."

"Marvellous, Jack. It sounds like your relationship building is off to a good start." I watched a smile fill his tired face.

"Now, let's hear about you …"

"I wish you and Teo well in your efforts. I mean that," I said as I gently squeezed his hands.

"Thank you. I appreciate you. Now tell me more about this bed-and-breakfast idea. Does this mean you plan to move back to Europe or North America?" Jack leaned forward in anticipation of my response.

"I love living in the Caribbean, but it is costly. I have this notion of keeping two rooms— the primary bedroom and Primrose's room, because she needs some place on site to live—and renting out the other five rooms."

Jack tilted his head and cupped his chin. "Will that arrangement yield a profit?"

"In high season, at minimum, it could bring in between a hundred thousand and a hundred and twenty-five thousand U.S dollars each year, based on occupancy. Here is the draft business plan that you requested." I reached into my leather binder and presented him with a hard copy.

Jack took about ten minutes to study the plan, while I sat tapping my toes in my warm ankle boots, scanning the room, and sipping my cocktail. I had worked hard on the proposal and hoped he would notice.

He looked up at me. "You seem to have addressed everything. That's remarkable, and I like it very much. Let me think on it some more, and I'll let you know my thoughts before you leave. How long will you be staying?"

"I'm in the US for two weeks and hoping to fly to Toronto to see my folks. That way I can get some business done and have some family time." Jack was excellent at spotting deals, and I figured he'd see the value in my plan and let me proceed.

"I hope to see you for some of that time as well," Jack said.

"Well, I'm staying with you. It'll be hard not to spend time together," I teased.

Dinner came and we continued our conversation between bites of pappardelle pasta and chunks of lobster, mine smothered in the nutty flavour of fresh parmesan. We shared a bottle of dry Riesling from Alsace, one of my favourites. In the background Louis Armstrong growled and blew his trumpet to some of my dad's favourites, including,

"A Kiss to Build a Dream On," while people scurried by outside and light snow dusted the sidewalks.

A chilly evening breeze swept us along the slushy sidewalk amidst the blaring horns of yellow cabs, cutting in and out of clogged lanes of traffic. The city was alive and hopping. Back at the penthouse, Jack lit a fire while I poured two nightcaps into brandy snifters. We sat close to each other on the loveseat, enjoying the elevated view of the snow converging on Manhattan, while the fire warmed the winter's chill.

I offered to stay in the guest room, but Jack insisted that I share his. The air was thick with discomfort, and his love for Javier hung like a barrier between us. Not to mention the months I'd spent with Zeke. We tried to rekindle the old pleasure. He lingered over foreplay in the old way, but the urgency once held in check was now missing. Jack had changed and so had I, and we watched ourselves going through the motions.

The next ten days were challenging. I was sleeping with a man I'd desperately wanted in my life at one time. Now he lacked any allure. Still, I needed to be agreeable because my lifestyle on Majestic depended on it. As I awaited his response to my proposal, I shopped and reacquainted myself with New York City's boutiques. But thoughts of Zeke crept into my mind. I was hit with twinges of guilt and reminded myself that sleeping with Jack was an insurance policy. I hoped Zeke would forgive me if he ever found out.

We lay in bed cuddling around 4:00 a.m. the day I would be travelling to Toronto, and Jack asked if I would like to make the New York trip a quarterly occasion.

"We could meet here at the holidays, you know, in December, at the beginning of April, again in summer, and then once in early Fall. It would be a great way to remain connected as well as keep your business fresh. I'll cover the cost of your trips. What do you say?"

My mind raced. I liked the offer of a paid New York City trip four times a year but wondered if Jack wanted more than I was now willing to give. Was he asking to pick up where we'd left off? Or was this something new? I needed him to be clear; I swallowed hard.

"What are you saying, Jack? Are you proposing a new arrangement?" I had to be sure. I liked my current life with Zeke, and the control I had over it, but I needed Jack's money and all its trimmings. I waited for his response.

"I don't know. You know how much I like being with you, but no one could ever replace what I had with Jav. Maybe we could continue to enjoy each other as long as it works for both of us." His eyes penetrated mine as he waited for my reply. This was going the way I liked.

"Sure, we can try it and see how it goes. And, if all goes well, we can extend it. Is that the idea?"

"It's exactly what I'm proposing. And about your business idea, I've come to a decision. How about I sign Seaview over to you, and you put your plan in place. All I'll ask for are updates here and there on how the business is progressing. Your proposal is sound, and I know it'll be a success. I won't be visiting Majestic anymore; the memories are too painful."

I heard him but wasn't expecting this news. "Are you... is this a joke?" I looked at him wide-eyed and with a natural amount of skepticism.

"No, Jemma, it's not a joke. I want you to run your new business and become a success. We've been together almost five years, and you've been many things to me. When I told you about Jav, which couldn't have been easy for you, you gave me my space and the respect I desired. When I needed to be comforted, you were there right beside me. Losing Jav was the most traumatic event of my life, and you stood by and supported me throughout the ordeal. You've proven to be a friend, ally, and a phenomenal lover. It's one of the ways in which I'm saying thank you. If you accept, I will call Daniel, my attorney, tomorrow and have him do the paperwork. Do you accept?"

My head was spinning, and it took a few minutes to fully comprehend what the gift meant. "Yes, yes... of course I accept. Now this is... well, very generous of you, Jack. Your gift will change my world. In fact, you've changed my world since the day we met. I'll make this a successful business venture, Jack. I promise."

I could soon call myself a millionaire; I could have my Caribbean dream just like I'd imagined. I could have it all; Oh God! This was too good to be true. But it is … Yes, Jemma, Yes!

I rolled over and began kissing him slowly. He responded in kind. I ran my tongue in gentle circles around the whole warm landscape of his body, beginning with his neck and chest. Our bodies found the old tempo again, and for the next while, I showed Jack gratitude, the best way I knew how.

I managed to get up with enough time to catch the 9:00 a.m. flight from JFK to Pearson International. I had a perfect seat in business class that allowed me to recline and get comfortable, despite the quick flight. As the jet pierced the clouds, I recalled the life we'd lived in the city of Toronto. Things had been so different then.

Dad's income in Canada had been good, but his surgical skills brought in the big bucks from around the world. A storied ophthalmologist with a retina specialty, and credentialed in many jurisdictions, his expertise took him across Asia, the Middle East and Europe where, on some vacations, he performed difficult procedures like repairing large retinal tears as well as the simpler corneal transplants. He chose to attend the most challenging surgeries in faraway places. He was a complex man, drunk on power in his work world, but sweet and gentle in his private life.

We lived in a 4,500-square-foot house, set back on just under an acre of manicured lawn. There was a horseshoe-shaped driveway and a mammoth deck off the rear which led to a large in-ground pool shaded by huge sugar maples: the dream home of many people.

Gardens in our neighbourhood were exquisite, with each household spending copious amounts of money to outdo the other. My mother lived for this competition, and during our trips to South Africa and various points across Europe, she visited specialty garden shops and purchased what she called 'showstoppers.' The plants often weren't cultivated for our hardiness zone, but she bought them anyway. Her refrain was always, *"How would you know if you don't try it?"* It drove dad up a wall, but he indulged her. His thinking was that if she's busy pressuring Alejandro, our gardener, to "try something new," she wouldn't notice the female staff providing more than just professional services in his examination room.

My dad was brilliant and a philanderer; mother knew but chose to look the other way. She was satisfied to shop in Yorkville for the finest clothes and shoes, take expensive vacations, and keep her various properties in order—a home in The Kingsway, a cottage in the Muskokas, property in Cape Town, and timeshare in the Hamptons. She'd purchased the timeshare with a girlfriend in one of her drunken stupors and without dad's knowledge. He was furious.

After Ollie died, our lives changed significantly. Dad's antics ramped up. He chased anything in a skirt, and mother dealt with it by drinking until it became noticeable. I went off to school in Genoa and never returned. No one cared.

I watched the flight circle the mostly frozen lake, then heard and felt the wheels release from the well in preparation for landing.

I reflected on my departure from this city and how empty, hurt, and angry I had been back then. Things were considerably different this time. Hopefully, seeing my parents would be healing for all of us. I couldn't tell them about the DNA findings just yet. It made sense to reengage with them first, to heal the hurt that had separated us. The findings could wait.

The festive Christmas and Chanukah lights twinkled behind windows covered with freshly fallen snow as the airport limousine turned off Royal York Road. We pulled into our driveway and my stomach tensed. Was I ready for this?

Chapter 30

Jemma

I hadn't seen my parents in over twelve years and had no idea what to expect. I'd only communicated with my dad a few times, and never with my mother. When I called from New York, he was overjoyed to hear from me and even happier that I planned to visit Toronto.

My mother, on the other hand, was restrained in her enthusiasm. Her only comment: "Where were you, and why now?"

I ignored her sarcasm. "Busy creating a life, Mother. See you in a few days," was my retort." Now this all seemed like a big mistake, but I needed to go through with it.

Not much had changed. Only Dad came out to greet me. He looked the same except a bit greyer at the temples.

"Jemma! I'm so very pleased to see you. Come give your old dad a hug," he said, arms spread wide. I worried that he might lose his balance and fall on his back.

"It's great to see you too, Dad. It's been a while."

"Your mother is in the kitchen. The caterers just delivered a light brunch, but we can go out to the Old Mill if you'd rather," he said as he led the way into the house.

I entered and noticed that things had indeed changed.

The furniture, the rug... even the old artwork in the living room had been updated from Bateman's wildlife to other Canadian pieces including Tom Thomson's sketches for *The Jack Pine* and Dad's favourite, *Northern River*. These images took me back at least sixteen years. As teenagers, we had visited the McMichael and the National Gallery, and Ollie and I had mocked our dad's speech on these prints … 'Something about these two works evoke dear memories of my teenage summers in Algonquin Park,' he had said.

The framed sketch of a vintage saxophone purchased at auction still graced the spot above the fireplace—another of dad's treasured collection.

All dividing walls between the living and dining rooms had been taken down and exposed a new kitchen with a large island and white Carrera marble countertop, new glass front cabinets, a coffee bar, and new shiny appliances. My mother's obsession with having the newest and the best was still evident. Yet, images of my growing up, especially my last days in this home, remained seared in my memory, coming alive like a soaring flame.

I closed my eyes for a moment and among the visions and redolence that attacked my senses were the oaky and dark roast aroma of my dad's Cuban cigars, the sweet cinnamon flavours of long stem red roses cradled in a large handblown crystal vase in the centre of the living room. And, to the right, I could see Ollie's slender legs skipping up the rambling staircase leading to the upper floor. So vivid though close to twenty years ago.

I blinked, shook my head, and returned to the present. As though he'd been a part of my reverie and read my thoughts, Dad's eyes locked onto mine, and he waited for me to speak.

I smiled widely. "Wow, is Mother still keeping up with the Joneses?"

Dad's face relaxed into a gentle smile. "Your mother has always liked nice things, and shopping is still one of her hobbies."

At the sound of footsteps, I turned around. A well-dressed blonde woman with my mother's features entered the room.

"You've gained some weight over the years," was all she said, as she leaned in and gave me a pseudo embrace.

"I'm pleased to see you too, Mother, you've gained a new hair colour. And, I've learned to love my curves, thank you very much. They're seen as healthy in my circle. How have you been?" Butterflies swirled in my stomach, and I immediately felt cheapened as her eyes roved up and down my body. I struggled to stay grounded.

"And what circle is so forgiving, pray tell?"

I observed her slender five-foot, eight-inch frame clad in winter-white slacks and a matching cable-knit cashmere sweater. Her short string of cultured pearls and diamond studs below a shaped bob was appropriate attire for the ice queen she was. My confidence slowly returned.

"Oh, you know, people with money and estates overlooking the sea, either the Mediterranean or Caribbean," I recited as casually as I could, watching curiosity replace smugness on her face.

"Well, well," she said.

I had her full attention but wanted to keep the suspense going, so I changed the subject. "How have the two of you been?" I asked, looking at one, then the other. Dad responded, while my mother looked puzzled, as if figuring out the next question to ask.

"I'm approaching retirement and very happy about it. It would be nice to resume travelling again… we haven't really since Ollie." My dad looked over at my mother.

"That's great, Dad. Maybe you'll come visit me on one of those trips."

"It's coming up on fourteen years since she passed. Time does fly," I said still watching them, though neither responded.

A few minutes after eleven, we were all sitting at the dining table in front of pasta, seven-grain and cabbage salads, bierwurst, and an assortment of prosciutto, roast beef, black forest ham, and a variety of breads to complete the spread. Dad poured a *Hacker-Pschorr* lager into his half-litre beer stein, while mother fussed around with various whites from the wine fridge, pulled out a Riesling and added it to the Zinfandel and Merlot already on the table.

The meal suggested that she still catered from her favourite delicatessen on Eglinton West for preferred cuts of meat and Rahier Patisserie for brioche, focaccia, and croquembouche.

"Are you still in Northern Italy?" he asked.

They looked at me, awaiting my reply, and I took my time pouring my Zinfandel and selecting perfect slices of prosciutto. The anticipation was palpable. The only sound that echoed in the space came from the crackling fire in the living room. I dipped my focaccia into a fusion of balsamic and olive oil and looked up. "I'm based mostly on Majestic, in a beautiful manor house overlooking the sea."

"Majestic?" My mother squinted at me and then cast a puzzled look at my dad.

"Yes, Sierra Majestic. It's an island in the Caribbean. I spend most of my time there now," I said casually.

"Yes, If I recall, it's where quite a few celebrities' own homes, correct? "Dad asked.

"Celebrities do own many Caribbean properties, but I can't say we move in the same circles. At least not yet," I responded with a smirk.

"Well haven't you moved up in the world!" my mother drawled with a crooked smile. "Are you going to tell us how you're affording this type of luxury?" she continued.

"Well, that was direct. But let's just say it's legal," I responded.

They glanced at each other, and then back at me.

"We're waiting…" my mother said. She surprised me as I watched her tuck into the charcuterie. Usually, she stuck to the salads.

"It's a gift from Jack."

"Jack?"

"Yes, Jack. My lover and friend," I said in a perfunctory tone. "Dad, pass the gherkins, please."

"Did you say lover? Who the hell are you sleeping with, a multi-millionaire?" My mother's eyes bugged out of her head, and her mouth opened wide enough to fit a tight fist.

I kept up my nonchalance and watched what I hoped was her disbelief build.

"Yes, Mother. You should know that they're out there and not really that difficult to find—no disrespect, Dad." Were wheels turning in my mother's head? I couldn't tell, but her eyes were locked on me and didn't blink.

"None taken my dear," he replied.

"Is Jack North American or European?" she cocked her head and supported her chin with her fist. It was her favourite posture to adopt when she believed she'd caught you out.

"What if I say he's Caribbean?" I said with the widest of grins.

"Caribbean? A White Caribbean man?"

"Yes, mother. Jack Generson is White, of British ancestry. His parents brought him to the US as a teenager. And what if he were Black?"

"I refuse to answer that," my mother replied, a smirk on her face. "But it's good that he's not. So how old is Jack and what does he do for—"

"He's old enough, and he's an architectural engineer."

"So, are there wedding plans in the works? Is that why you're here? A manor is a bloody expensive engagement gift if I can say so myself."

"Mother don't run away with false ideas. Jack and I have no plans to marry now, or in the future."

"Why, is he already married?"

"No, he's not married and I—"

"Eileen, Eileen," my dad jumped in. "Let the girl have her privacy. She deserves to have some, you know." My dear, sweet dad; leaping to my rescue.

"Mother, you're not the only one with the ability to find the right kind of partner. Some of us younger girls can be just as lucky and find ourselves in the right place, at the right time. I met Jack at a party on Bellagio some years ago, and we've been together since."

"I wouldn't think the Caribbean an ideal place for an architectural engineer to drum up business?" My dad was clearly listening, his interest now piqued.

"It can be, but it's not where Jack runs his company from or negotiates his deals. We've used the Caribbean, mostly me, for relaxation and running my online enterprise. Jack spends much of his time in Europe and the US."

We spent the next few hours chatting about how things had changed over the years for them, and for me: dad's new roles at the hospital, and mother's new foray into professional design and staging. I shared about my business and the connections I'd made in the Los Angeles, New York, and Montreal markets. My mother showed great interest in my merchandise and asked for samples. I suspected she'd wear and showcase them to her friends at the Granite Club.

"Maybe I can drum up some business for you. Have you considered a foray into the Toronto fashion scene? People here have money and expensive tastes, you know." She looked down at her outfit to demonstrate a clear example.

"I will consider it, Mother. Can't promise anything yet but, I will pass by the Yorkville shops, gauge their merchandise, and pick up some of my favourite champagne truffles at William Ashley's."

"Will you be spending the night?" Dad asked.

"No, I'm headed back to New York City this afternoon. I've a meeting and dinner date, and my flight to the Caribbean leaves tomorrow."

"A short but lovely visit, Jemma," my dad said with a beaming smile. "I hope your mother will join me on a visit to Sierra Majestic. We have a lot of catching up to do."

"It was for me too. And one other detail... Mother? You know how we both have crooked little fingers? I've found a painting in the Caribbean that might intrigue you. That's all I'll say for now. You and Dad should come and visit me."

My mother, though guarded in her response, replied positively. "I'm intrigued, so I'll definitely come along, if only to see it for myself."

My parents were headed to a midafternoon event at The King Edward Hotel, so I hitched a ride with them to Yorkville. As we drove through the different neighbourhoods, the brown faces were more familiar than I remembered and no longer background, but front and centre – at least to me. My heart skipped a beat when I saw a beautiful man with shoulder-length dreadlocks standing on the corner of Ossington and Bloor, waiting to cross the street. I missed Zeke and couldn't wait to get back in his arms and the warmth and comfort of his little cottage.

On the corners of Bloor and Avenue Road, I bid my folks goodbye and spent the next fruitful hour in Yorkville enjoying some flavours and aromas of Toronto's affluence.

I felt some peace knowing that I'd reconnected with my parents. I sensed Ollie's presence throughout the visit, and once the initial discomfort between mother and I had subsided, the rest of our time together was enjoyable. I had to accept that she and I would always see things differently. Being both strong-minded, we had to make room for the other's perspective, with one exception, there was no room for her racism.

I got back to New York in time for my meeting with two suppliers. Then Maya texted me that her flight was delayed, and she would have to miss dinner. So, Jack got lucky. We had a great dinner, and an exhilarating rendezvous. His zest had returned.

We parted at JFK around noon the next day: me for Majestic, he for Rome. I wondered if Jack knew that Zeke had been keeping me fulfilled during the months he was in Europe. I suspected that he did and smiled at the thought.

Chapter 31

Jemma

There is something wonderful about waking up to sunbeams across your face, and the sound of birds singing in nearby trees. The sea's tide washed up to the shore as though choreographed to "O' Happy Day," and I gradually remembered why. I had gone to New York for two weeks, and my entire world had changed.

Everything appeared brighter; the trees were greener, the birdsong sweeter, the sea even a deeper cobalt. I had decluttered my mind, reconnected with my parents, and the contract between Jack and me was clear. Best of all, I'd become the owner of Seaview Manor. And I could continue with Zeke or whomsoever I chose, as long as I showed up for Jack a few times a year. How lucky could a girl get?

After checking in with Primrose the next morning, I donned the new bikini I'd picked up on Fifth Avenue, threw on my lacy cover-up, and went over to the pool. I watched Zeke working and telepathically dared him to look my way. Seconds later, he did, and we waved at each other.

Later that afternoon, I walked over to the cottage and entered to the most mouth-watering aroma. Zeke had cooked a fresh pot of callaloo soup, steam rising from the bowl.

"Welcome back," he said, a giant grin on his face. "I can't compete wid Primrose, but it will hold you til you get back for dinner," he smiled as he offered me the tray.

"Oh, thank you. It smells amazing. Where's yours, and where did you learn to cook like this?"

"My cooking lessons began with Asabi and grow from dere.

"This is delicious; is callaloo the same as kale?" I asked.

"No, is not. Dis is spinach wid a bit of okra, bell pepper, pumpkin, coconut milk and lots of seasonings … dat sort of ting." he replied with a smile.

"And who is Asabi?"

"She was … how you say … mi soul mate twenty plus years ago. De first woman who help me find miself. Mi first love." His voice trailed off, and his mind seemed to follow.

We ate in silence for a while, then Zeke looked over at me. "Did your trip to America go well?" He asked quietly.

"Yes, it did. Thanks for asking."

He pulled out a spliff, lit it, and inhaled. When he exhaled, the room filled with a smoky blue hue. I nearly expected to hear Alberta Hunter belt out "Nobody Knows You When You're Down and Out"—one of my dad's favourite blues recordings that he'd listen to while reading the Sunday *New York Times*, a cigar smouldering in his mouth.

I sensed that there was more Zeke wanted to know about my trip but wasn't sure if he should ask. So, I helped him out. "I got some business done, saw family, and did a bit of shopping. It's cold and wintry, so I stayed mostly..." I'd almost given away that I'd shared a bed with Jack and made a segue. "...indoors, with my friend, Maya. You remember her. She visited about a year ago."

"Yes, yes. Ms Maya. I rememba."

I glanced over, and he seemed content with that answer. If he wasn't, I couldn't tell.

"What did you do while I was gone?"

"I filter a new batch of fertiliser for de plants. It does wonders for de overall blooming and especially de foliage. I also worked at de manor a lot."

"Was Primrose there as well?"

"I guess for some of de time. I didn't go up to de house," he replied. *Phew, good answer, Zeke.* Was that my jealousy creeping in? Was I beginning to have feelings for this man?

"Are you still working on cleaning up the old sugar mill? I'm thinking about creating a small museum with a gift shop."

"I mostly finish … but a museum?" he said, with a quizzical look.

"Yes, a sugar museum, with a gift shop. Of course, we'll have to put a roof on top, so the artefacts are protected."

"Artefacts? What type of artefacts … and what will you sell in de gift shop?" Zeke seemed to be, as the British say, 'taking a mickey.' But my idea wasn't over the top, so I replied.

"It'll be island-specific items. I haven't quite figured out all the pieces, yet. I'm still thinking it through."

"Who will run it? Or you haven't figured dat part out yet," he added with a mischievous wink.

I looked over at him and stuck out my tongue. A sudden warmth flooded my being. I liked being with him and laughing with him, and instinctively reached over and kissed him, a sweet and tender kiss. He responded in kind, and we fell into each other's arms.

Before we knew it, the lightening of the blackness out over the sea gradually turned pink and orange, sending ribbons of gold across the awakening sky.

I got dressed and started my walk back to the manor. Bathers were out for their morning swim, and swallows were chirping in the trees. I entered the back door, and Primrose greeted me in the hallway.

"Would you like breakfast now or later, ma'am?" she asked, and I couldn't help but notice the subtle sweet smell of frangipani in the air, and it wasn't coming from me.

"Yes, soon Primrose. I'll have a quick dip before I eat, so how about in thirty minutes on the lanai."

"Okay, ma'am." I wanted to ask her about the fragrance in the room but chose not to.

I reflected on the wealth, not only material, but in intimacy and emotional experience, that had entered my life. Joy filled my heart, and the world was delightful. Giddy with happiness, I changed into my favourite red swimsuit and dove into the pool.

The mill began to take shape as a museum, and my relationship with Zeke progressed. We were meeting at least twice a week at his place or on the beach nearby. Only once, when Primrose went home to her cottage for a few days, did we sleep together at the manor. Zeke was uncomfortable; something about separation of work and play. So, we took our meetings back to his place.

About eight weeks later, my dad messaged that he and my mother would be visiting the island for a short stay. I was pleased and shared the news with Primrose and Zeke. Both asked if they could help in any way. I confided in Zeke that my mother could make insensitive comments about race, though I didn't outright call her racist. Zeke raised his eyebrows in response but didn't question me further.

I was eager, perhaps too eager, to see my mother's reaction to my discoveries about our family history. Sierra Majestic might well be the reckoning we feared but needed. For the first time I realised that I was doing what Ollie had promised to do; Denmark though, had been replaced by Sierra Majestic.

Chapter 32

Primrose

With the rich plant life that Zeke grow at Seaview, I'm in my own little heaven, trying a 'pinch of this and a pinch of that,' just like GG teach me, and discovering new fragrances. I make scrubs by mixing sea moss and mint and adding sweet oils and white powdery sand to the brew. If I massage it into my instep, heels, elbows, and knees, I notice it lift up the rough dry skin. And, when the sea surf wash over my tired feet after a good scrub, it's like crush ice sliding down a parch throat. I had to bottle this blend. Maybe one day if Clarence come back, he'll be surprise how good I still look and smell. It was my own little fantasy. Sometimes I had dreams of the two of us on the beach on Baptiste, some of the best days of my life.

At nearly fifty years old, I look thirty-five, but my heart still wear the padlock I place on it the day Clarence Brandt walked out of my life and trade Baptiste for New York. I did have a secret crush on him.

I wasn't surprise when Ms Jemma ask me about the "exquisite scent that linger in the kitchen." Them her words, not mine. I been mixing new potions right under her nose in the manor kitchen the two years I live here, but she was too occupied with other matters to notice.

"That fragrance is from the bright pink frangipani, ma'am," I told her. "I add a few hints of nutmeg oil to encourage the sweetness."

"You create your own oils?" she asked, looking at me with squinted eyes.

"Yes, ma'am, been doing it for many years. I even got small containers Madame Fournier sent me from France to package them, but I only use them as gifts which I don't do much of since GG and my mama died."

Then she look at me and say, "How sad, Primrose. You do have many hidden talents. Did you ever consider marketing—I mean selling—your oils?"

"For money, ma'am?" I wasn't sure I hear her right.

"Of course," she continued, "for money. I could help if you'd let me. I'm actually thinking about opening a museum and shop in the old sugar mill at the back of the property. Maybe you can create a product line for sale there. The proceeds from that line would be all yours. Would you like that?"

I couldn't believe my ears, but she was standing in front of me chattering on like she been the past little while, since she come back from New York. Something was different. She look at me different, spend more time around me, and even ask me how I getting on. Whatever it was, I hope it continue. And now she want to help me sell me oils. *Lord have mercy! Primrose died and gone to heaven.*

"Of course, ma'am, of course," I managed to say before she change her mind.

"Okay, then. Leave it with me, and I'll let you know." With that, she walk out of the kitchen.

My head was spinning. I could have my own business… oh, what would GG think about this and Madame F… she would be happy for me. Primrose Sapphire Mortley, owner, proprietor, just like Madame F. *Okay, Primrose, relax. One step at a time.*

I walk into my room, close the door, and sit down on my bed. I cast my mind back to my life at the manor from the time I come to work with this woman—and now she offering me the dream I always want.

Come to think of it, I wonder if Ms Jemma know that I know she and Zeke making merry? I use to think she was only window shopping when I catch her watching Zeke from under the pergola. The poor woman head bouncing back and forth peeping at him from behind them dark glasses and swallowing big gulps of whatever clear drink was in her glass. And I know it wasn't water.

Then I see her come home at daybreak with the same clothes she left wearing the evening before. I remember she did slip through the front door right after Zeke left and head down the path and something tell me that she had walk into the shop, and now, she trying on the merchandise instead of just looking! She couldn't have gone too far; her car engine cold in the driveway all night, so I add one and one and get two. I did. But like GG used to say...

Ms Jemma did tell me that she liked her coffee "black and strong." Maybe she was sending me two messages. Madame F use to call that kind of talk "*subconscient.*" Oh dear, them hidden or buried messages.

I don't blame Ms. Jemma for wanting a companion. Even me, I sometimes wonder if Clarence really did like me and if we would have been together now if I had let him kiss me. Although GG would not have approve of any kissing, and Lord knows what she would have done if she found out what Maynard did to me... my heartbeat speed up just thinking 'bout it.

I wonder if Clarence ever marry. Till day like today, I can't trust a man. It's just how it is. But Zeke and Ms Jemma seem content with each other. She look much more relax these days, and he got 'pep in his step.' From what I see,

Zeke is a man that keep his business to himself, and she ain't chatty-chatty.

Now, because I keep my mouth shut and mind my own business, it look like Ms Jemma gon reward me. Too bad GG and Mama ain't here to see me become a businesswoman. GG was right all along. *Hope for the best, Primrose, hope for the best.*

Chapter 33

Jemma

My parents arrived from Toronto at precisely 4:00 p.m. on the Thursday before Easter. I picked them up at the marina, having booked a private boat to bring them over from Baptiste. I imagined that my mother would especially enjoy the ride across the billowing blue Caribbean.

As suspected, mother was thrilled with her boat ride to the marina.

"I can't believe you're living like this, Jemma! Waking up to such a beautiful vista every morning; it must be heavenly." She grinned, hugged me, and climbed into the back of the red Range Rover—Jack's newest toy, purchased just before the horrible accident. I drove it a few times each month to keep the battery charged.

"It is fantastic," I responded.

"How far away is the house? Can you see the sea from the windows?" Dad asked.

"Well, it's called Seaview, Jasper," my mother jabbed. "So, I would think you can."

"Yes, Dad, you can see it. We'll be there in about twelve minutes."

He smiled. "Honey, I'm so pleased for you."

My mother was quiet in the backseat; her eyes hidden behind her sunglasses with their dark blue lenses and gold clasped hinges. She wore a crisp white linen shirt, a single strand of pearls, and a pair of beige linen slacks. Camel loafers, matching handbag, and a patterned silk scarf sashed around its handles, completed her look.

As we headed out of town, the lush green foliage all around us was alive with the darting movements of birds that I knew would catch my mother's eye. The vegetation started to clear, and we felt the salt breeze of the sea once more as we neared the coast and took the turn off onto the property.

I pulled into the driveway and made the announcement. "We're here."

"You said it's a gift from Jack, Jemma. Did you mean the gift of a rental property?" My mother asked, finally removing her sunglasses.

"No, Mother, I meant the gift of ownership. I own it, I really do." I loved how that declaration sounded and saw no reason to include the business aspect of the arrangement.

"This is phenomenal! The garden is amazing, the variation in colours, and the greenery so rich. Someone knows what they're up to—this could win a City of Toronto Garden prize. Maybe you should have your father's lawyer, or your own lawyer check the deed for this place, you can't be too careful … and when do we meet Jack?"

"In time; if he wants to meet you, that is," I said, snickering.

"Why wouldn't he? What have you told him about us?" she growled.

"Eileen, there you go again," my dad said, rolling his eyes." It's not always about you, you know."

I looked up and saw Zeke heading toward the garden and waved him over.

"Who is that?" mother asked, her eyes bugging out of her head.

"That's Zeke, my exceptional gardener. He's the one who has transformed this landscape into a thing of beauty." I felt warmth in my chest and flutters in my stomach as I spoke about him.

"Mother and Dad, this is Zeke, landscaper extraordinaire." I grinned as he joined us.

"Thank you," he said, and nodded to both my parents.

"My mother is a gardening enthusiast and—"

"She's in awe of the beauty you've created ... we both are," my dad interjected.

My mother was silent throughout the interchange but smiled politely.

"Glad you both like it, and I hope you enjoy your visit," was all he said and returned a beaming smile.

"Alright you two, let's get you and your luggage inside," I said.

Primrose waited for us by the door to show them the guest suite. I smiled as I made the introductions. "And this is Primrose. She looks after the house and feeds me well."

Primrose said her lilting "hello" and showed them to their room. I went upstairs, sat on the bed, and took a few deep breaths. I'd been nervous about them meeting Zeke, but relaxed, as things had gone well, for now.

At dinner that night, I watched my mother try every type of drink. She complained about the heat, how even a swim in the pool hadn't cooled her down. But she did seem to be enjoying herself immensely with all the different mixes, settling on the twenty-five-year-old El Dorado rum as her aperitif. Primrose served beef bourguignon with carrots and mashed potatoes; I'd told her that it was dad's favourite, and he loved the meal.

"Primrose is a *wonderful* cook," said Dad. "She should be called a chef! Everything was nicely proportioned," he continued, patting his belly in approval.

"Well, Dad, you can tell her yourself when she brings in the dessert. We're having crème caramel with rum sauce."

"I definitely will! Oh, and here she is already." He beamed in her direction. "Primrose, this meal was most excellent, and I look forward to dessert."

"Thank you, sir," Primrose replied politely, as she served dessert before moving back to the kitchen.

"Mother, can we have a chat about family? I would love to learn a bit more from you about our ancestry," I began.

"That's an odd request. You already know about our family," she responded with a blank stare.

"I don't think it is. You've told Ollie and me that your heritage is Danish—Danish royalty, to be exact—and that Dad's is Irish. What is the source of these facts, and do you have any proof? Ollie and I were both convinced we were royalty, and then I found out that she wasn't."

"Like I told you girls then, I learned about my background from my aunt. Why would she lie about such a thing? With Ollie, fine, she wasn't royalty, but you still don't know the real story." She swallowed her Amarone and left her dessert untouched.

"I don't? Go ahead, then, I'm listening."

"Well, Ollie was your half-sister—your father's daughter by his secretary."

I heard the words leave my mother's tongue and aim for my gut. The punch precise; my breath suddenly cut. I watched her smirk and stick her spoon into her dessert. My dad's fork fell from his hand; mortified at how callous mother was in delivering the news and attributed it to her consumption of drinks.

"Eileen? Maybe it's time for just *Perrier* now."

I looked at him squarely. "Dad, is this true?"

With slumped shoulders and lowered eyes, he responded in the softest voice: "Yes, it's true. I had an affair."

My mother butted in. "Try a couple dozen of them! And that's not counting the one-night stands. The other bimbos were smart, this one wasn't. Your father has a zipper problem. He can't keep his up," she added with a laugh, and finished her drink.

I swigged my wine, swallowed hard, then looked up at my mother. "I'm going to come back to this, this... bombshell, and as shocking as it is, you still didn't answer my earlier question. What other proof do you have about your ancestry, Mother?"

"I don't have written proof or a scroll or any such thing, but I do believe my aunt. And hold on—why is this so important now?" she said, sounding annoyed.

"It's important because I recently did a DNA ancestry test, and the findings are mind-boggling. Not only is there no Danish in my bloodline, but I'm also linked to people in West Africa. Nigeria, in fact."

I looked over at my parents and saw two slack-jawed faces, eyebrows crawling up their foreheads, stares fixed on me. I'd thrown my own sucker punch and caught my mother right between her eyes.

"We can't be African, you silly girl! Unless we're South African Boers, at least, they're white."

"No, Mother, the genetic markers are clear. I'm 12.5% West African, the rest came up as 87.5% English and Irish."

"Jemma, maybe your mother had an affair with a Black man. Did you Eileen? You talk about my indiscretions, but how about yours?" My father gave a half smile, furrowed his brow, and peered over at my mother mockingly.

"What are you saying, Jasper Worley? Let's not go down that path. You know I'd never touch a coon much less sleep with one!"

"Please refrain from using that word in this house Mother. It has a horrible history for people of African descent."

She gulped her drink and rolled her eyes at me.

She had sent another punch to my gut. I wanted to scream my truth about Zeke, but no, not yet I wasn't quite ready.

I handed them both copies of the Certificate of Ancestry I'd received with the explanation of the findings. Both stared at it; my dad reading in earnest while my mother scanned rapidly, head jerking in small movements, mouth a tight line of disapproval.

"I'll leave you with these copies to digest. We can talk more later," I said. "But you might need another stiff drink after this further exposition. Come into the library with me."

I had hung Antonia's portrait on the only free wall in the library, making sure the lighting was good. There she was in her dark and inescapably African beauty, with a partial smile, but also a hint of sadness in her eyes... or was it pain? I steered my mother by the elbow into the room to stand right in front of the painting.

"What is that, and why are you showing it to me?"

"What do you see, Mother?"

"I see a dressed-up Black girl. I didn't think they were allowed to wear clothes like that back then."

"Well, Mother..." I began, and she started up again.

"What kind of sick joke is this, Jemma? Who produced this silly likeness? Have you gone mad?" My mother stared at the portrait, her mouth slackened, and she backed up, as if distancing herself from it.

"It's not a sick joke, Mother; it's a true portrait of a woman who might be related to us... to you and me. It was done in 1834 by a Belgian artist. Look at her baby finger: crooked, like ours."

"Or maybe created recently by one of these island coons trying to sell you a bag of goods, claim relations, and take this house!" she rambled on, but I persisted.

"Mother, it's real. The sitter was Antonia Kathleen McNally, born October 23, 1816, to an enslaved woman and white sugar plantation owner. I have the documentation to support what you call a sick joke."

"It makes no sense," she screamed and continued her retreat to the library door.

"Maybe the reason I look so much like her is the creator's way of reminding you that you can't run or hide from who you are."

I watched my mother's face turn green, her body begin to jerk forward, and her knees buckle. I rushed her into the bathroom across the hall.

"Sit down, Mother. Sit down," I urged.

My father eventually appeared with a brown paper bag, as my mother's breathing had become short and shallow. Beads of perspiration pooled on her forehead where wisps of blond hair began to stick to her face.

"Breathe into the bag, Eileen; you're hyperventilating."

She reached for the bag, barely got it to her face, and started retching. I stood back and observed what I envisioned as a dramatic performance, but it soon became too real for an act.

"Mother, Mother! Are you okay?" I peered at her in disbelief.

She didn't answer but sat on the toilet holding her head and gasping for air. My mother liked to say that she was "above" Blacks, but this reaction was bizarre. I looked at my dad. He fixed his appraising medical gaze on her and slowly shook his head.

"Eileen, why is it such a big deal that this woman's portrait resembles Jemma somewhat? It's what she's been telling us all along. You appear to have African ancestry somewhere, and both the documentation and the portrait shed light on these facts. You're making a big deal about something you can't change."

"And the finger, Dad, the finger! It's a dead giveaway. It's called clinodactyly. Mother, you told me that you, your sister, your mother, and I believe even your grandmother, had this abnormally bent finger; so it's inherited."

"You're correct, Jemma. That's the medical term, and Ollie didn't have it," he added.

"Maybe it began with Antonia, or even before her. Did I mention that I distinctly heard her whisper 'Hello, dear' when I first discovered the portrait?"

My mother found her tongue again, and her breathing normalised. "My daughter is having conversations with ghosts! Don't you see how ridiculous this all is? It's a hoax, Jemma! Someone's messing with you."

"Mother, no one's messing with me. It sounds more to me like the ancestors reaching out to us. I find it all intriguing." I was pleased she appeared to have gotten over the initial shock of seeing the portrait and hoped she'd at least share in my curiosity.

"Ancestors?" she barked. "I have no Black ancestors. And what's so intriguing about discovering you're the descendant of a slave, anyway? Haven't I taught you anything?"

"I'm not saying I'm Black, but I do have partial Black bloodline, and all along I believed I was Scandinavian-Irish. It's fascinating!"

"There's nothing, absolutely nothing, fascinating about those findings. Do you hear me. It's scandalous to have any trace of their species in your DNA. I'd rather be the descendant of a donkey."

"Like I said, you can't change it, Eileen. Just accept it and move on." My dad was evidently enjoying this revelation. His voice was matter-of-fact, but I could see a smile tugging at the corners of his mouth.

"Jasper, stop saying that! Of course, I can change it, and I will! I won't accept this bullshit, and in fact I think Jemma should get rid of this bloody portrait and all that phony certificate shit. Because that's what it is—*shit*." She screamed at us and stomped out the room.

I looked over at my dad with raised eyebrows and shrugged my shoulders.

"Jemma, your mother is overly dramatic. It's who she is. Can I tell you a story about how this behaviour almost cost us your life?"

"My life? Go ahead, tell me."

"Your mother takes things too far sometimes. At four months pregnant with you, she was out shopping with a friend when she started spotting. Her friend took her to the hospital, but she refused treatment because the attending physician was Black. Can you imagine? She wouldn't let him touch her. By the time I reached the hospital she was rolling around in pain. She agreed to his care only if I stayed in the room. Thank God you weren't harmed."

I sat speechless staring at my dad. "What in God's name did Black people do to her? Why is she so racist? It's insane to think she put her health, and my life at risk. I could have died because of her insanity. Dad, this is beyond dramatic—it is sick. Mother needs psychiatric help." I was incensed. I closed my eyes and took a few deep breaths to calm myself down.

"I'll go find her," Dad said. "I'll talk to her and hopefully reason with her."

"Dad, I'm so sorry. I didn't want to ruin your vacation."

"Who said anything about ruining a vacation? Your DNA findings may have uncovered a secret meant to be kept hidden. No one will know about this unless she tells them." He looked at me with a twinkle in his eye and a silly grin before walking out of the room.

I sat quietly and replayed my mother's outburst. Granted, she wasn't fond of Black people, but the force of her indignation, and her visceral response surprised me. What was it about being Black that she found so intrinsically repulsive?

Maybe she'd known about her Black genes, and wanted to deny, deny, and wish them away. She raged against Black people to hide her own Blackness. It all made sense. Her frantic denunciation made the truth more apparent.

And then, it suddenly hit me: she could never find out about Zeke. A blood-curdling sensation filled my chest, and for the first time, I wanted to protect him, protect us. I heard alarm bells ringing. My mother would try to destroy my relationship with him; probably say something ghastly to his face. I couldn't have him anywhere near her venom, couldn't risk him seeing her ugliness.

That night, I lay in bed for hours, reflecting on the evening. On my visit to Toronto, I'd told myself that I had to make space for my mother's perspective, but this was about our lives, our history. I felt an obligation to correct a distortion and get to the truth of who we were.

I also thought further about Zeke. If there was a choice to be made between my mother and Zeke, my lover would win. I wasn't sure, though, that if he were faced with the same choice, I would be his pick.

My mind went back to my conversation with Jack about Javier. They chose each other because they loved each other. Zeke and I enjoy each other, but given the option, would he choose me?

The next day, Mother was in a better mood; she and Dad sat beside each other at breakfast, touching and making googly eyes. The ocean breeze could be blamed, but some lovemaking must have taken place.

Afterwards, my parents donned their masks, snorkels, and fins and spent part of the morning in the Caribbean Sea. I passed on the adventure and observed from a lounger on the beach. After all these years my mother's pinched look of disapproval as she scanned my body could still make me feel ashamed. And I didn't want to feel ashamed this morning here in the glory of my stunning property and good fortune.

We spent the afternoon sightseeing. At one of the secluded beach bars, we ran into a couple of Italian movie stars mother recognised. She was thrilled. At dinnertime, Primrose served a coq-au-vin on the lanai; my parents had seconds.

Mother continued to surprise me with how much she ate, but then, I hadn't been around for years. Maybe she'd had a change of heart after losing my sister.

A multi-layered Hummingbird cake with cream cheese frosting was served for dessert. Each of us tucked into the banana, pineapple, and pecan layers arrayed on the dessert plate. My mother broke the silence.

"That woman knows her way around the kitchen. Her knowledge of haute cuisine is commendable." She didn't look up but continued to savour the sweet course on her plate.

"So glad you're enjoying it mother, it's one of my favourites. Primrose is known for her local cakes and pastries which have won accolades from the island elites. The woman never consults a recipe book—she's that good. We're lucky to have her expertise at Seaview."

"I guess it's what they do best, serve their betters. Remember how well Zanele, our maid in Cape Town cooked, before she got ill and had to leave? Your dad hoped for her potjiekos for dinner and malva pudding for dessert every night. For me it was the miso roasted brinjals. I'd never had eggplant that good and was impressed how succulent her dishes were."

Here she goes with her bloody bigotry again; this woman is exasperating. I racked my brain to find a way to bring the topic back to our ancestry. We savoured dessert for a few more minutes, and then I voiced my thoughts.

"So, Mother, was anyone in your family of a darker complexion … like your mum or her mum?"

"No, darkies, it's a mistake," she replied, her eyes piercing and cold.

"But the DNA …" I prompted.

"DNA tests can be wrong, and they were this time. Our family is not tainted with those people; perish the thought!"

"You're not going to get a different answer from her, Jemma; it's what she believes," my father interjected. "Give it up." He claimed to be exhausted from the sun and day's outing and left the room for an early night. Mother followed him.

I finished my drink and went up to my room. I couldn't get the things I'd learned about my mother that day out of my head. I'd given her many opportunities to come clean about her deceit and bigotry, and I'd had enough. After thinking about it some more, I came up with the perfect plan. I smiled, rolled over, and fell asleep.

The following day my parents prepared to take a local flight to Barbados and transfer to an international flight to Johannesburg enroute to Cape Town.

"I'm looking forward to relaxing in the Cape and watching the penguins sun themselves and fish in the ocean surf. It'll be my first birding trip on the continent since Ollie left us." Mother bit down on her lower lip as though forcing back the pain that came with the memory.

"I remember how much you enjoyed those outings. Ollie and I knew that when you returned from one of them, we could hit you up for anything, because you would be so mellow." I smiled at the memory of my sister and me plotting for some big clothing purchase at the Victoria and Alfred Shopping Centre. Mother smiled.

"The first time I went to rescue wounded birds in the city with Alexandra, my university roommate, I figured I'd go just for the excursion in her Saab. It beat sitting in our dorm reading boring history notes. But when the baby Blue Jay with the broken foot and wing looked up at me with its sad black eyes, my farm girl instincts kicked in, and I had to save it. I've been a sucker ever since."

"Lucky birds," Dad chimed in from the hallway.

"Maybe we'll make it up to Durban this trip to see the endangered cranes—you know, the blue, the grey crowned, and the wattled crane. My favourite of these is the wattled. Touted as the largest crane on the African continent, and the second tallest in the world, she's a magnificent creature. It would be a thrill to spot one of these feathered friends through the lenses of my binoculars."

We headed outside, and as I started the Range Rover, I saw Zeke making his way up to the house.

He stepped aside, gave the car clearance, and waved as we went by. I slowed down and exclaimed: "My parents are leaving; we're off to the marina."

Zeke nodded and smiled, and my parents reciprocated. As we drove out, my mother piped up from the back seat.

"God, Jemma, how could you stand being around all that filthy, matted hair? I bet you insects have made a home in that mess."

I pressed my lips together, controlling the scream that was trying to escape from my gut. Instead, I calmly replied.

"They're called dreadlocks, Mother, and, they're not filthy. People from many cultures, including people on the islands, wear their hair this way. Zeke said that wearing them means different things to different people. For him, it's about connecting to his African ancestry, spirituality, and oneness with nature."

"You're that close to him, that you have those kinds of conversations?"

"He's easy to talk to and full of wisdom. In fact, Zeke has been keeping me company and he has taught me a lot."

"Be careful, Jemma, he can come between you and Jack."

"Well, he might already have ..." I looked at her in the rear-view mirror, and she glared back at me. We drove in silence for the next five minutes, and then I broke the stillness.

"There is something I must tell you both, and mother, I've had to listen to you, especially on this trip—it's now your turn to listen to me, just for a moment." I pulled into the parking lot of the private boat dock and locked the vehicle doors. My mother would have no escape from my truth-telling. I needed their uninterrupted attention.

"Mother, when you were a child, you let people tell you who you were, and you believed them. You lived your life under a cloak, trying to hide your true identity. To some degree you succeeded. But you've lived a lie and brought me up to live the same lie. I've felt ashamed of what I looked like, and I've also held contempt for the blood that runs through my veins—the black blood. That's wrong mother, terribly wrong. The shame and contempt end here. You no longer hold the power to define what my life is or will be.

I'm unsure of how this is going to turn out, but know that the man in my life now is Zeke, not Jack. Yes, Jack is a very, very dear friend, and we were at one time, in what I thought had been a committed relationship. But that has changed. It is now Zeke who fills me up. So, know that you are both welcome to remain a part of my life and visit whenever you can, but it's important to me that you know the truth.

I looked in the rear-view mirror at my mother. I was expecting drama but found none. She stared outside the window and appeared detached from the information I had shared. Dad reached over, touched my hand, and spoke firmly, with warmth.

"You're grown. If he makes you happy, you won't hear me complain." He smiled softly at me."

I smiled back, released the locks on the vehicle's doors and climbed out. As the porter stacked their luggage on the trolley, Dad reached over and hugged me. Mother stood a few feet away, her sunglasses resting on her head. For a moment, I thought I saw tears in her eyes, but she quickly pulled the glasses down and covered any evidence. She didn't hug me, or wave, as they silently walked away.

I sat and watched the water taxi pull out of the harbour.

As it skimmed across the sea, I felt an ease that I hadn't in a long time. I'd stood up to my mother, spoke my truth, and rejected her bullying.

Mother's main activity in life was dispensing judgements and criticisms about other people, thereby elevating herself, or maybe it was deflection, so that the focus was on others and not on her. I recalled all those years growing up and listening to her diatribes about race and class and physical ideals. I realized, not for the first time, that I did not like my mother very much. Did she have any real tenderness for Dad, for anyone? The only soft side to her character was a love of birds.

Over the years she had become one of the most knowledgeable amateur ornithologists in her birding group. She talked about her passion in an engaging way, and if you knew nothing about birds, she could make you want to learn about them. It was fascinating to listen to her expounding facts about the different types and their migration patterns in the spring or fall, or their mating styles, the colours of their plumage, the length and shape of their beaks, or their tails.

She could also speak about what certain birds did for the environment. She could go on and on about the types she loved to watch for at Point Pele National Park in Ontario, like the Glossy Ibis with their iridescent green and reddish tones, or the Peregrine Falcon, with their slate and blue-grey wings and bright yellow feet.

On one of our trips to the Hamptons, mother raved that the male Scarlet Tanagers with their blood-red bodies and jet-black wings sang sweeter in Ontario than they did in The Hamptons. After a good laugh, my dad piped up.

"That's such a ridiculous statement, Eileen. There aren't Canadian and American tanagers, they're the same bird."

"I know," she answered, "but for some reason the birdsong is more pleasing there."

Upon reflection now, there were two birds that mother didn't particularly care for—the double-crested cormorant and the American crow. Incidentally, both of these birds are black.

The afternoon after my parents left Majestic, I missed them, despite the clashes I'd had with my mother. To ease my loneliness, I went right back to work and invited Zeke in for a cold drink and to talk to him about plans I'd been ruminating on. Primrose had gone to her cottage for a few days, and I wanted a local viewpoint before inviting Maya to the island to discuss things.

Zeke joined me on the lanai. I wasted no time on niceties and got straight to the point. "Zeke, I need your perspective on an idea that's been swirling around in my head, and I'd like your honest opinion."

"Okay," he said.

"I'd also like you to keep it between us, at least until I've decided whether I'll move forward with it or not."

"Alright."

"I'm thinking about turning this manor into a holiday let. The plan would be to rent five of the seven double en-suites to tourists. What do you think?"

"Will you still live at the manor or somewhere else?" he asked in a quiet, steady voice.

"I'll be here most of the time and travel for some. Sort of like Jack used to do, but Seaview will remain my home base." I looked at him squarely to read how he was receiving my information.

"It sound... well, it sound like a good idea, but will you still need me... around?" His voice trailed off, and I promptly interrupted.

"Of course, I will, Zeke. Are you still okay with staying on?"

"I might be able to," he replied.

"I'm also considering a major-minor partnership strategy. I'll ask my friend Maya, who's a real estate lawyer, for her advice on that later. So, everything still has to be worked out, but what it will mean is—"

"Dat you and Mr Jack will own de majority shares, and you sell smaller parcels to other folks," he softly said, his smile widening. "I get it."

"The property is mine, Zeke. Jack won't be coming back to Seaview, at least not in the near future. I'm willing to look at accepting service for part ownership, but Maya will have to advise me on this, if it's even feasible. By service I mean... taking care of the property, as you already do, but for part ownership."

He was still smiling, but his response surprised me. "I would have to think 'bout it. Not sure I want to be tied down in Majestic. I already have de family property, you know. But we can talk again."

I had expected him to jump at the chance, but he didn't, and got up to leave. I walked with him to the door. "I've missed you," I said.

"I missed you too," he responded.

"Would you like to stay for a while?"

He didn't speak but turned around, reached out, and pulled me gently into a deep kiss. I preferred that answer. We then held hands and walked up the stairs to the bedroom where we stayed until the next morning.

Chapter 34

Jemma

I messaged Maya and found out she was in Abu Dhabi. My proposed business idea was new territory for me, and I needed the right person to help me navigate the landscape. I promised to pay for her advice, and she agreed to call when she returned to the U.S.

Maya called two days later. "Hey! What's up?"

"Before we chat about me, was Abu Dhabi business or pleasure?" I dragged out the word pleasure and laughed.

"A bit of both! And yes, he's as fine as can be, smart and respectful too." I could hear the joy in her voice.

"Does 'respectful' mean you didn't push the needle? Like nothing happened?"

"I didn't say that. He's just a calm and easygoing type of guy who wants to take things slow, and I like that. But enough about me, what's up with you?"

We chatted about my acquisition of the property, and the plans I had dreamed up to make it successful. I let her know of Zeke's position on part ownership and my intention to approach Primrose.

"Well, well! You have been thinking a lot. How about I investigate the legalities of the partnership and come back to you in a few weeks so we can discuss the possibilities?"

"That would be great, Maya. Thank you."

"And are you still on track with Zeke? How's it going?"

"Still pretty good. Zeke is a proud Caribbean man, and the more I learn about him, the more I want to be around him."

"Sounds promising, Jemma."

"He's opened up a lot about himself. I learned about his only love, who he lost tragically many years ago, and I think he's shielded his heart since then. He might even be dealing with some post-traumatic stress as a result of that loss."

"Wow! Are the barriers around his heart coming down?"

"Can't say for sure, but something is going right. Maybe it's because I don't ask for love, just companionship, it's a safe place for him. There's no hope in hell that I can replace her. I'm a drinker and an increasingly hopeless carnivore who can't cook! Zeke lives a clean lifestyle where neither of those vices reside."

"Well, it looks like the two of you have found a groove. I hope it continues to work out. Gotta run! Will connect soon. Ciao!"

Chapter 35

Jemma

Zeke had worked tirelessly on the museum project: sometimes up to six partial days most weeks, after tending to the landscape. He'd cleaned out the mill's contents and washed down the insides. We left the stone natural instead of painting it. Professor Abassa connected us to a curator from the Department of History and Anthropology at the university, who visited and discussed the museum's layout and contents. I was ecstatic.

With Zeke's input, we agreed the museum would showcase the true history of the sugar plantation system on Majestic. It was important that visitors got the full story and not just a curated account. The gallery would include dioramas that told narratives of the island, and not just of those who ran the plantations, but the

Indigenous population, the enslaved and freed Africans, and their descendants. The shop would sell only products manufactured on Majestic, by its people.

A few weeks earlier, we had approached the Whittles for any old photographs they might have kept in their library; they provided the curator with a treasure trove of documents, including photos of Amanda's fourth great-grandfather—the man who'd initially purchased the property from the McNally's. Amanda indicated she'd never gone through the pile and hoped we could find worthwhile historical content.

Within the stack were pictures of a three-roller grinder which was housed in the mill and used to extract cane juice. Similar prints showed grinders powered by the enslaved walking around in circles, while another fed the cane through the chopper.

The artefacts were coming together, and Primrose was producing her fragrances, so I approached Zeke about contributing as well.

"Hey, Zeke! How do you feel about selling your environmentally-safe seaweed in—"

He spun around and shook his head, startling me. "I can't sell my fertiliser, Jem, dat would make me... well, it would be like selling part of me for a profit. Dat's what de slave catchers did, sell our people for profit."

"Zeke you've lost me. It's seaweed; what does it have to do with slave catchers?" Stumped, I waited for his response.

"De fertilizer come from de sea where so many of our fore parents lose dey lives—so it sacred to me."

"Fore parents? You mean the Africans who perished off *Nearly There Cay*?"

"You rememba ... yes, dem and many, many more on de journey from de African coast."

Zeke's eyes had a tender glow as he looked towards the sea.

"Well, I don't fully understand your logic, but I respect it." Confused, I shrugged my shoulders and walked back to the house.

Over three months, I'd worked with our contact at the university and collected a rich combination of narratives, photographs, artwork, period utensils, and equipment that together would tell the story of the island and its heritage. Zeke and I had rescued some of these items from the sugar mill's trash heap and others were on loan from the university. Artefacts included narratives of the earliest inhabitants of the island, the Taino of the Arawak people, followed by the Caribs, and eventually the Europeans, who introduced enslaved Africans to work the land—hardly the picture of employment outlined in Amanda's tale.

A large, corroded ladle and two grossly tarnished and punctured cauldrons were in the mounds of trash Zeke had gutted from the mill. It turns out that these items were part of a series of containers used in the boiling house to extract sugar crystals from cane syrup; information confirmed by the curator.

After the discovery of Antonia's portrait, I made several trips to the mill site. On one of these visits, a rusted, sealed tin box about six-by-twelve inches caught my eye. It sat on a small pile of refuse. I picked it up, pried it open, and released a subtle whiff of tobacco. A neat stack of letters addressed to "C.O. McNally" still in Glasgow postmarked envelopes, lay inside. There was also correspondence from Billingsgate Private Convent School and some personal letters from Antonia. I thumbed through the first few and got a sense of young Antonia's life in Scotland those many years ago. I brought the stack back to the house.

As I made my way toward the path, I noticed a mottled brown rectangle lying on a smaller trash pile. It must have been in one of the overturned boxes Zeke had emptied. Looking more closely, I saw that the brown rectangle was a cover and there were page edges, perhaps once white, now yellow, protruding from the sides. I picked up the heavy, damp book and examined the faint markings that may once have been flowers drawn in a child's hand. Could the child have been Antonia? I added it to my earlier finds and continued up to the manor.

I resumed reading the letters on the lanai.

Tuesday September 18, 1832

Dear Mr McNally,
I trust these lines do find you well sir. You asked that I
write to let you know how I am settling into Billingsgate.
The nuns at the school treat me well but my classmates
are unkind. They speak ill of me and make faces at me
behind the teacher's back.
No one here has my colour or hair like mine.
I long for my mother and my home.
I remain dear sir,
Your obedient servant, Antonia

~

Tuesday November 6, 1832

Dear Mr McNally,
I trust these lines find you and your household well.
Snow fell today in Glasgow.
The houses are made of stone and are damp and cold.
I miss seeing the sun and the sea, and I long for home.
I remain dear sir,
Your obedient servant, Antonia

~

Tuesday December 4th, 1832

Dear Mr McNally,
It rains or snows every day in Glasgow and becomes dark quickly in the afternoon. I complete my homework and turn into bed well before 8.
I received a turkey red hankie as a gift from a nun. Anna a classmate said her father works in the dye factory and produces them for darkies.
I miss my mother and my home dearly.
I remain dear sir,
Your obedient servant, Antonia
~

Tuesday March 12, 1833

Dear Mr McNally,
The school term will be over soon and literature is still my favourite subject.
My favourite poets are James MacPherson and Robert Burns.
Although English is the language of instruction, I am now learning Gaelic in my spare time to help me understand the Scottish culture.
I continue to miss home and my mother dearly.
I remain dear sir,
Your obedient servant, Antonia

The brown tattered book contained several undated diary entries, written by a much younger Antonia. I began to read from the first several entries:

Tuesday
I can write. I will write when I can. I will use my drawing pad to write.
Today Miss Rochefort say it is Tuesday. I will write on Tuesdays.
Mama look sad today.
Massa McNally want mama to fix his room again.
Mama don't talk for a long time after she fix his room.
Every night mama like me to rub her foot and hands. It make her happy when I tell her what I read.

~

Tuesday
I must dust and tidy Master Aaran and Master Dunstan room and the dining room every day.
Master Aaran hide in his room and touch me. I don't like it.
Master Dunstan read a lot. Master Arran does not read that much.
I like to listen to Master Dunstan play the piano. Sometimes I keep the music in my head a long time. I do my homework every day. I like to read before Miss Rochefort tell me to.

~

Tuesday
Mama said it is my birthday today. I turn ten years old.
Massa McNally said that to Mama yesterday. Mama make
a pudding just like every year, and we eat it in our room
after Massa McNally go to bed. Today my mama smile.
~

Tuesday
Master Aaran come up behind and push me down today. I
hit my head and cry. He say don't matter what father said
you not brighter than me. You're a nig nog and you less
than me, not even real people. Nig nogs just like horses.
Why he think I less than he?
I don't understand mama.
~

Tuesday
Today I hear Master Dunstan song in my head. Massa
McNally say Master Aaran will go far away to school
soon. He will travel on a big ship. I was happy when he
say no more Master Aaran here.
~

Tuesday
Massa McNally come in early yesterday. I was helping
Mama fold the washing. He tell mama to go to his room.
Mama was gone a long time and when she come back; she
eyes was red from crying. When I ask mama why she cry,

she said so you not have to baby.

I didn't know how much more of this I could absorb. Conversations with Dr B and Professor Abassa had confirmed that Octavia had been raped at the hands of her owner, C.O. McNally, and now I know the minor child Antonia was aware of the abuse her mother faced at the hands of this louse. After hundreds of years, I was discovering these writings… the past *was* coming alive and reaching into my life.

It reminded me of what Dr Breckenridge had said about the unconscious breaking into the daylight of awareness. I wasn't sure if I was expected to do anything with the letters, whether it was my destiny to have found them or just chance. Of course, Dr B said there was no chance or luck and that everything was related to everything else. At the same time, I was sad and confused. I had a drink and calmed my nerves before reaching out to Dr Breckenridge and discussing my findings with him. There had to be an explanation, and he would help me understand.

Chapter 36

Jemma

A red truck pulled up the driveway of the manor, blocking the Peugeot. A short stocky man hopped out and began waving.

"Morning, ma'am! I'm looking for Mr Browning."

"Morning! But there's no Mr Browning here. Do you mean Mr Generson?"

"No, ma'am, is Mr Browning it say it right here pon de delivery slip."

I walked over to the truck and the wind brought a strong stench of manure, which I realized later was covered under the green tarp on the trailer. I asked to look at the slip and sure enough it said "Mr Browning, Seaview Manor, Majestic."

I was baffled, but before I could ask another question, Primrose, who had been dusting in the front hallway and heard the exchange, chimed in. "Might be Zeke he looking for, ma'am."

"Zeke? Oh, right." Suddenly my cheeks burned with embarrassment. The manure made sense, then. I turned to see Zeke heading over to the truck from the back of the property; he'd been working in the mill.

I excused myself and scurried into my bedroom. How could I want to be with this man and not know his last name? And then I remembered that on one of the early days, he had welcomed me to the 'Browning homestead.' And in a later conversation he had said something about the Brownings being "solid people of the earth," so I did know but must have forgotten. Either way, it was embarrassing. I'd been sleeping with him close to two years; his full name should have been more prominent. *Get your act together, Jemma!*

My thoughts remained on Zeke. Of late, he'd been foremost on my mind—when I opened my eyes each morning, his face was the first image that swept into my head, and the last image that lulled me to sleep each night.

I couldn't recall anyone's likeness being so salient before, not even Jack's. For those many months he was away, I realized that just having a warm body in my bed was what I missed most. I needed to be with someone, not just have sex, although that was important too. And the many gifts he gave were proof that someone cared about me. As I looked back on my life and other men I'd known, the theme was recurrent. Sex wasn't just for fun or to manipulate men into getting what I wanted, it was my way of having and keeping someone in my life. It was my solution to loneliness. It worked with Jack, but with Zeke, I got more than I had bargained for. I got love.

During Jack's stay in Spain working through Javier's probate, I got to know Zeke much better. Sometimes we had discussions about culture; his versus mine, and I'd share highlights gathered in my readings, especially historical facts about Caribbean life. He asked questions about Canada; Toronto in particular and showed keen interest in our weather patterns. On those weekends when Primrose went home, I stayed at his cottage the entire time. There had been so much drama at Seaview, that I sought refuge and built a nest in Zeke's world.

We held each other for hours, and I wore my expensive fragrances and best makeup when I visited him. I dressed in different outfits on each visit and checked myself in the mirror before I left the house. And I often skipped along the beach to his place. Sometimes he'd meet me part way and greet me with a kiss after his lilting 'hello.' He routinely complimented my figure and my attire. At times we'd race each other to the cottage, like kids. Once I feigned a leg injury, and when he stopped to help me, I pulled him down onto the sand, jumped up, and ran as hard as I could—and, of course, won the race. When he reached the cottage, we both giggled hysterically because I'd outsmarted him.

Lying on the beach, we played a made-up game of spot the cloud and name the stars. I had looked up cloud types on the internet, but he was ahead of me.

"I like de nimbostratus; de one commonly called de rain cloud. When I see it in de sky, I tink bout de promise dat Mother Earth will soon be able to drink and quench her thirst."

"That's cool, Zeke. You see it as a promise, and I see it as a threat. When I see a rain cloud overhead, I either grab my umbrella and raincoat or stay indoors and watch the drops trickle down my windowpane."

"Is just two different sides of de same coin," he said, chuckling.

"Well, my favourite clouds are the altocumulus—the fluffy ones, almost cotton ball-like. They reminded me of flocks of sheep grazing in a meadow."

"And dat cloud remind me of you, soft and cuddly," he said as he reached over and hugged me.

One night, as we were stargazing, I told him about Ollie. Tears tracked down my cheeks, and I couldn't keep my voice steady when speaking about her passing. Zeke pulled me close, wiped my tears, and moved his comforting hands along my back. Then he kissed my cheek. I pressed my head against his chest, loving the closeness, and he ran his fingers through my hair. I wanted to remain on the beach tucked snuggly in his arms for the rest of that night while the cicadas buzzed and the sea lapped against the shore. I began to see this caring gentle man in a new light.

Before my last trip to New York to see Jack, I had spent twenty intense weeks with Zeke. He filled me up completely. Why settle for less with Jack?

I want Zeke to want me. I want him to always hold me, and comfort me, to be playful and silly with me, to make love with me, and to miss me like I miss him when we're apart. I know it in my heart and in my gut. These feelings are real.

But I'm terrified to let him know what I feel; I couldn't handle a rejection by a man I'd finally let into my heart. So, I'm choosing to shield myself and continue life as usual, pretending with Jack Generson, but quietly loving Zeke Browning. Maybe if I don't force a solution, the universe will work it out. In the meantime, I'll wait.

Chapter 37

Jemma

I'd approached Jack for his input on restoring and transforming the mill into the museum and shop. He not only had the expertise, but a whole team behind him to pull the design together in record time. His team used photographs to create a new blueprint that rejigged parts of the interior but kept the integrity of the original structure: new wooden cyan doors on the front and rear sections, and solar panels on the roof. Contractors from Baptiste worked on the building, and Zeke's expert application of flowers and shrubs softened the hard-stone face of the building.

He cleaned up the path leading to the mill and laid down river rock as far as its front door. Yellow and green banana croton shrubs dotted each side of the walkway, white and lilac wisteria framed the small trellis around the entrance. At night, star-shaped solar bulbs lit the path.

Raul, my assistant in New York, set up a website for the Inn, just like he had for my online merchandizing business. The site went live on my birthday, May 1, and by May 31, four rooms had been reserved and paid for; I was delighted.

Despite all the additional work he put in, Zeke refused any extra pay. I slipped money into secret places in his bedroom, but he always returned it. He only accepted money for products he'd purchased for Seaview at the hardware store on Baptiste. One evening as we lay in bed, I asked why he rejected compensation for the additional responsibilities he had undertaken.

"Cause we together, and you need dem tings done. You know how de rich men give roses, chocolates, and perfumes? Well, dem tings disappear, while de tings you require and I do, last."

"I see, but aren't roses and chocolates meant to express love?"

"If dat is your understanding, you been watching too much movies," he joked.

"So are you saying you don't believe in love?" I teased.

"I never say such a thing. I just saying dat's not my understanding."

"Well, should we be defining our relationship?" I held my breath. I should have left well enough alone.

"I don't need definitions, Jem. I know what I like, and dat's all I need."

I had to shut this conversation down; I'd started on a path that might have a difficult end. "Well, I guess I don't need definitions either. I like our relationship, and I appreciate all you do for me. If I can reciprocate, I hope you will let me know."

I didn't know if reciprocate was the appropriate word, but it'd just popped out. After a moment, I felt his breath on my neck, and his arms enveloped me in a warm embrace. "Here is how you can reciprocate..." he whispered, and with touch and movement building our excitement, we proceeded to enjoy each other.

The next day after the mail arrived, I made my way into the conservatory with the stack in hand. An official-looking brown envelope with a Canadian Postmark caught my attention. I threw the rest of the mail on the teak table and ripped the large envelope open. The letterhead read The Archives of Ontario.

A short note addressed to me indicated that at the request of colleagues from The University of the West Indies, the following letter had been pulled from their archives. It was part of their current holdings and a gift from the estate of Antonia K. McNally Creag. It listed the full south-western Ontario address of the donor in Wallaceburg. I sat down to read its contents.

July 10, 1838

Dear Sir,

This letter that I must write, will remain in my private papers until such time that it is appropriate to greet daylight. I received your letter of Wednesday June 25, in which you advised of the untimely death of my mother. Please accept my thanks for this notice although it was received with a heavy heart and occasioned great unhappiness as well as a sad relief. It has also inspired, indeed compelled, a resolution on my part to declare sentiments which I shall risk exposing. I have a vast deal to say and have given allowance to my pen to address you in this way.

My dear sweet mother, who gave me love, comforted me always, even when life for her was an endless trial of suffering and oppressive cruelty, has left this prison of earthly life. It is a tearful blessing as much as a loss. I have memories of tears pouring down my mother's dear face as she hid and took refuge in a dark corner of your kitchen pantry, a place full of sweets in jars but also overflowing with bitter and painful experience. You may ask "refuge from what?" but from you Sir! Your vile imposition of physical desire and violent disregard in the service of your own pleasure. I must think back again and again to the many nights you savagely had your way with my gentle, sweet mama. My naïve presence in the very room with pretence to sleep occasioning no hesitation or uncertainty in your urgent animal lust that knew no decency or sympathy.

My mama told me that many brothers and sisters of mine were sad fruits of your vicious mastery, not deserving the respected word of "father," I will never have their acquaintance or opportunity to hold them precious in my arms as family. They were sold away in thoughtless brutal transaction, their cries for mother unheeded, their prospects hopeless in endless servitude.

Now my pen leads me on to the most terrible truth. I was seven years old when mama gave birth to my twin brothers, and I loved them as a sister should and witnessed the love in her face whenever opportunity or indulgence granted her their presence. I was given allowance to be their little mother after mama fed and dressed them. Oh, but dread connivance stalked those hallways in the bodily forms of your other sons Masters Aaran and Dunstan. They gave voice to evil intents and made horrid and threatening remarks about the little ones who lay innocent on their mats. The Masters vowed that they would be your only sons. And then that morning of infamy when kindness died and sin triumphed while I slept, as mama left the babies alone in the room to oblige her burden of work for your family, the twins met their deaths. Suddenly, but not unseen as I woke to note the coattails of your murdering Masters and sons, slink out of our room, their evil smiles an image that has haunted me ever since and ever will.

The grief and anger that makes my hand tremble in guiding the pen as it fills these lines, prompts a question to arise in my mind. Why could you see my mama only as some part human to be kept chained to your home, degraded, and treated beneath even your large brown horse, who was at least allowed to leave the paddock to graze and enjoy the liberty and free air of the countryside? Did never a thought of any simple mercy cross your proud mind?

Mr McNally, I was taught that all white men were gentlemen and the most exalted beings walking the earth. But through your wicked example and that of your sons, I came to believe that all were evil. In Scotland, I have renewed my education to discover that some do have hearts and souls, like young Mr Rory Creag. He is indeed a fine young man, who makes a lie of your example, and we intend to marry and venture a life in Upper Canada.

I have expressed my sorrow at my mother's death, which was a release from the weight of the relentless suffering you caused. I have been given a life of comfort and privilege at your command. It does not escape my attention that it could have been otherwise as it was for my dear mother. However, the knowledge justifies no gratitude on my part. Sir, you have sinned greatly and if you have a conscience at all, then I leave you to its stings.

Your daughter,

Antonia

I looked down at my hands and wondered whether hands like mine had ever held a whip or slapped a dark face cringing in fear. For the first time in my life, I could hear the distant voices of my Black ancestors.

For the next hour, I sat mortified in the conservatory, swigging snifters of brandy and staring out to sea. Octavia was McNally's pick, and he ravished her body whenever it pleased him. She had no choice. And this enslaved woman was my ancestor. My God!

My heart ached for Octavia and Antonia and the brutality that filled their lives. There was a time when a Black woman's life could be controlled completely by White men. From birth to death: no escape, no mercy, no refuge, and no safety. And some of those White men were my ancestors. I get it Maya; I get it!

Later that day, I looked up the Wallaceburg address and learned about the occupants over the years. I began my research online, and in less than a week started plotting our family tree. I found out that Antonia and Rory had five children, all married with families of their own. An article in a local newspaper mentioned that the Creag twin girls married men from Dresden, a nearby town, one a boat builder, the other a doctor. Both sisters moved with their husbands to Dresden, once a terminus of the Underground Railroad between the US and Canada.

Based on a faded photograph accompanying the newspaper article, one of the husbands appeared to be Black. I wondered if that twin was my great grandmother, then it could mean more Black ancestry was introduced into my bloodline.

I had more digging to do.

Chapter 38

Jemma

Maya arrived on an afternoon flight from Miami. Her trip to Majestic would be a quick stopover to help me sort through details of the partnership. Dressed in skinny white jeans, a white tank top, and baby blue Chanel blazer, her off-white leather sling backs and matching knapsack were perfect for travel. I greeted her and asked about her trip to the UAE.

"I will follow the business where it leads," she replied.

"And is he Arab?" I probed with a mischievous wink.

"Huh?"

"You know the *business*… Mr Abu Dhabi?"

"Ahh! No, he's American, and things are just fine." She laughed. "I don't have to ask you about Zeke, he's written all over you!" We cackled like schoolgirls.

"Is it that evident? Am I really glowing that brightly, or is it because, you know?"

"Brighter than a three-hundred-watt bulb without a dimmer!" She cast a sly smile at me.

A thought of Zeke started a wave of warmth in my chest. "I've got to find a dimmer switch, and soon. Thanks for the tip."

"You're most welcome."

Primrose was off, so we decided to pick up a bite at the social club and relax with dinner at home. We both opted for eggplant parmesan and continued our drive to the manor.

"So, about my idea, the thing is... I'm running out of funds to keep this place going. I can't continue to pay salaries and upkeep for much longer," I said.

"Have you considered asking Jack for a loan until you can go it on your own? I'm sure he'd pitch in if you did."

"The business plan I gave Jack didn't include any financial backing on his part for my projects. Are you saying my idea isn't feasible?"

"I'm not; your proposal is compliant. You can offer shares of the property in lieu of a salary. They'd no longer be your staff though, but your business partners."

Maya's advice delighted me, and I filled her in about Primrose's interest, but Zeke's apprehension.

"I see. That's unfortunate. So, what's your back-up plan?" she asked.

"Get tourists into the rooms as soon as possible. I suppose I could apply for a small bank loan and use the property as collateral."

"Sensible move. Why wasn't that your first option?"

"I've learnt much about this island's history ... about how much Black people gave to this region, and how much they lost. I guess it was my way of giving Zeke and Primrose a piece of the wealth their ancestors toiled for but never enjoyed."

Maya stared ahead, quite fixedly. "I really don't know what to say, Jemma. This doesn't seem like a decision you're making lightly. But what brought this on?"

Previous missteps with Maya had taught me to select my words carefully, so I was gathering my thoughts before responding. And she was becoming impatient.

"Please tell me you're not trying to buy Zeke, I don't get this gesture?"

I glanced over at her, trying to avoid a heated exchange while driving. She read my mind, and quickly added: "Don't answer. Let's have a drink before we continue this conversation."

I pulled the car into the carport and turned the engine off. I looked over at Maya, and her cheerful mood had vanished. In fact, I couldn't read her mood.

"I am not buying Zeke or giving either of them reparations. This is about acknowledging that a part of my roots is buried here."

For a moment, Maya's dark velvety eyes penetrated mine in silence. Then she blinked, shook her head, and began to speak. "What? ... What are you talking about, what roots?

"I found out that I have Black ancestors, from the DNA test I did a few months ago."

"Okay, but that happens all the time, and it still doesn't explain—"

"So let me explain! I feel like the wealth I have, and will amass, should be shared with those whose bloodline also runs through this soil. My ancestor Octavia and her stolen offspring poured their essence into this soil, but so did Zeke's and Primrose's ancestors. Maybe one day we'll learn their names."

We pulled her luggage through the doorway, dished up our meal, and took it into the conservatory. I poured glasses of cabernet sauvignon, and we continued our conversation.

"I believe the portrait I found is an ancestor of mine, Antonia, and she was born on this island, on this very property. Her mother's name was Octavia."

Maya sat speechless, staring out to sea; then she slowly looked over at me. "But how? If there's any truth to your claim, maybe the ancestors brought you here to communicate with you."

"You think?" I nodded to the open library door and a clear view of Antonia's portrait hanging on the wall.

Maya's head swivelled to follow my gaze, and her jaw dropped. "Crap! It's you, all bloody you. Jem, I don't know what to say except... you're home!"

"Looks like it, doesn't it?"

"Ms Bea, my foster mother used to say, 'God will tap you on the shoulder a few times, and if you continue to ignore him, he will knock you over on your backside to get your attention.' You might have responded to the shoulder tap, but from the ancestors. Who else knows?"

"Knows what?"

"About your Black ancestry?

"Very few people. Let's see… my parents, and of course the DNA lab folks."

"Are you telling me I'm the only one outside that circle who knows?"

"I am."

"You haven't told Jack? Or Zeke? These are the men in your life. Why haven't you told them? What am I missing?"

Maya's eyes narrowed and penetrated mine, as if I were a defendant under cross examination. I looked away for a moment, before slowly turning back to face her.

"I haven't told either of them because I'm not quite ready to embrace this new part of my reality."

"But you told me." Maya cocked her head and squinted.

"Yes, because you asked about the thought process behind a decision I'd made. But I'm not ready to reveal this discovery. Both of these men formed a relationship with a White woman."

"And your point is?"

"Well, if there's any chance my new identity will change how Jack sees me; I'm not willing to risk it. It might not matter to Zeke, but I'm not ready to talk about it publicly… that's just me.

"Maybe you suspect that Jack might have hesitations if he learns that you are mixed race. Could that knowledge threaten your lavish lifestyle?"

"Jack has given me the property; it's mine—I'm not threatened."

I was secretly questioning whether that possibility existed, though not openly admitting it. I was beginning to feel pressure from Maya, but then she relented.

"Jemma, you have a choice of keeping it to yourself or disclosing it. There's no rule book for this; it is up to you."

"I don't believe there's much Jack can do, unless he can take it back, claiming I received it under false identity." There I said it.

"That's not a legal argument." Maya's gaze was focused, her voice steady with confidence. "You're Canadian, and it's a known fact that twenty percent of your White American neighbours have a Black ancestor. The whole human species originated in Africa; everyone was most certainly Black at one point."

"So, it's not a big deal—unless I make it one—I suppose."

"Correct! Blackness is not a kind of make up that can be applied and removed at will. It lies deep in the bone and it's final. You can pretend it isn't there, but the truth comes out. But, it's your life; your choice."

"That's correct, Maya, and right now I choose to carry on living the way I always have. Maybe a time will come when I am fully able to embrace the part of me that is Black, African… just not now."

An uncomfortable silence sat between us for a few minutes. To break the impasse, I refilled our glasses and spoke. "If this secret makes me a coward, then so be it. Can I ask you to keep this to yourself?"

"Like I said before, it's your life. You get to share your news with whomever you wish. I won't breathe a word."

"Thanks." *Well, there it was, out in the open, but with only one person.* Still, something heavy that had been pressing on me shifted and lightened.

"Just imagine that this ancestor was born and lived here on Majestic, and possibly on this very spot… talk about spine-chilling! It's as if the ancestors are connecting with you because there's unfinished work. Fascinating!" Maya added.

I poured two nightcaps and handed her one. "Here's to fascination, my friend." We swallowed and said our goodnights. I stared at my face in the bathroom mirror, a place I'd received one of the many signs from the ancestors. Maya's comment about unfinished work floated through my head…what an eerie prospect!

The following morning Maya worked with me to complete and file papers for Primrose's partnership. She left on a British Airways flight for Heathrow that evening and promised to return to Majestic soon for a longer stay.

Chapter 39

Primrose

Madame F's birthday was in three weeks. Since she return to Kaysersberg, I been sending her birthday wishes by letter every year. This year, I was excited to tell her about the business opportunity Ms Jemma offer me. I didn't ask for her help directly, but I said that I will have to find a way to showcase my goods in the museum shop, just like she did at the bakery.

Patisserie Paradis had the best pastry and cake window on the island. Even the shops on Baptiste couldn't compete. People would come by to look in, especially when Madame would display her opera cakes, croissants, éclairs or mille-fueille. She would say, "La présentation est importante." And it was important to present the product well.

About six weeks after I send my letter to her, the mailman come by with a brown cardboard box covered in blue and white 'par avion' stickers and some other international labels. I thought it was for Ms Jemma but soon realise it was for me, from Madame Fournier.

When I open it, under the foam and other packaging material were fancy wrappers with gold lettering, made, I believe, from ivory linen paper. The print stand out boldly and said Sapphire Rose Eco-friendly Toiletries in English and French. Included also were rolls of clear wrapping sheets, strips of sheer lilac ribbons with tiny rose twists to add a further touch of style to the packaging.

I was beside myself and start to clap my hands with joy. I suspect she would send me some packaging, but nothing this fancy. Right away, I bundled three items: hibiscus and rose oil, mint scrub, and frangipani skin balm, in clear wrap and tie a perfect bow to each batch. I repeat the cycle and mix in different fragrances; some for the guest rooms and others for the shop. The sale items I package in the linen paper, sure look expensive in the display case. I step back and admire the presentation—pretty!

It was the beginning of school vacation, and Ms Jemma hire, and I train, two young people to assist me now that I was Head Chef. They work morning shifts in housekeeping and take turns in the museum and gift shop in the afternoons.

The gallery was open to visitors at noon, five days a week, Tuesdays through Saturdays.

According to Ms Jemma's reservation list, the first set of guests arrive on July 20 at Seaview Inn—our new name. There was to be three couples from Wiesbaden, Germany, and a retired gentleman named Claremont Matthews III, from Connecticut. Ms Jemma said that Mr Matthews is Caribbean-born, but he emigrated to the US some thirty-five years ago. He plan to move back to the Caribbean, and this trip was one of exploration. My mind immediately run on Clarence.

One morning at breakfast, I catch Mr Matthews admiring me from his wicker lounger. I was accustom to Ms Jemma carrying out the same action with Zeke from behind her sunglasses in that very spot, so I know the moves well. And GG lessons in *broughtupsy* kicked in; 'you know de man watching but pretend you don't see he.' I must admit, though, that my face was like a hot plate: you could fry egg on it. And, while I continue to ignore him, he wait patiently until it was his turn to be serve.

"Good morning, Ms Primrose!" The accent was clearly Dominican—yes!

"A very sunny Caribbean morning to you, Mr Matthews. Could I get you another cup of coffee or an island fruit salad? The papaya and pineapple are in season and quite sweet." I had rehearse these types of lines at the bakery, so I was smooth.

"I would welcome another cup of coffee, and I'll consider the fruit a bit later on. I hope I'm not being too forward, but are you from Majestic, Ms Primrose?"

"Yes, I am, Mr Matthews."

"So, this island… it does produce other sweet stuff then, other than fruit? Am I permitted to make that observation?" His eyes moved from my feet and travelled to my face, then he winked at me and smiled.

I struggle to come back with a response, and that surprise me. I hadn't heard a compliment in years, maybe not since Clarence. The man making me blush too much, and this time I have no place to hide.

"Well, thank you, Mr Matthews. That's very kind of you."

I had to get out of this situation before embarrassing myself. It was all I could think at that moment. One of the German couples beckon me over, and I hurriedly leave Claremont Matthews company.

I return to the kitchen and check how many days this sweet talker was going to be staying at the Inn. I let out a loud sigh that cause my two helpers to break from their chores and ask if I was okay.

"I'm okay, I'm okay," I reassure them. I was thankful that Claremont Matthews would only be here for two days. I wasn't comfortable with his flirting, but he was a paying guest, so I had to be polite.

At dinner time, Mr Matthews persist with his charm; I smile back at him and did not encourage conversation, but he call me over.

"Ms Primrose, I was wondering if you would mind spending some time with me later, on the lanai, and telling me about the island. I'm a night owl so I get to bed in the early morning hours. And you can call me Claremont. Mr Matthews is so formal."

"Mr Matthews, I'm happy to get you information about the island. Have you visited the museum? We have a lot of material there that you can read at your leisure." I smiled, continuing my formal tone.

"But it's just not the same as hearing directly from a local person."

"Unfortunately, I can't Mr Matthews. As executive chef, I spend my evenings preparing for the next day's meals." *I like how the title roll off my tonge with such importance.* "I'd be pleased to ask one of our young staff to chat with you and answer any questions that arise from the brochures before you leave tomorrow. I hope you have a pleasant night." I smile at him as widely as I could, gave a nod and walk off. I could feel Claremont Matthews' eyes on my backside as I move away from him. *Lawd, today is the day I shoulda been wearing that new panty girdle. Backside, please stay in place, and don't roll too much.*

As soon as I was out of his sight, I let out another sigh; this time, quieter. My legs were unsteady, so I nip into my room, shut the door, and sat on the edge of my bed. I look down at my sweaty palms, and instinctively begin to rub them together. Immediately, GG's voice was like a boomerang in my head… '*Girl you gon rub them hands together till you see bone.*' In response, I shake my hands loose and open my fingers wide, but my feet continue to bounce so I breathe in and out to help myself relax. A few minutes later, I return to the kitchen to resume my evening chores.

In bed that night, a sense of pride come over me at the way I handle Claremont Matthews III. If he really like me, he would have to come back and try harder to win me. Then I roll over with a big smile and went right to sleep.

The following morning during breakfast, Mr Matthews wait and watch, drinking his coffee slowly. I greet him and he respond politely, then gave me a small brown envelope, before leaving the conservatory.

I open it that evening in my room. A business card said, Claremont J Matthews, Vice-President, Sales, Bank of America, New York, NY. A note was enclosed that read: "Thank you for your kind service. I hope to see you on my next trip" and two $100 bills.

I chuckle and sit down on the bed. *We'll see, Mr Matthews. We'll see.*

Chapter 40

Zeke

I sit down pon mi favourite boulder and watch a leisure boat go by in de distance. Mi mind run pon Jem. She is a decent woman, and though not a Caribbean woman, she sure is willing to learn and fit in. I like dat she open to new tings, including de way I live. She never turn up her lip pon me or mi house. I wonda if she really digging me or if is only de romping she like. I okay with dat, but I tink she really like me.

Sule, my brother, I pour dis libation to you ... I need answers to why dis woman roam through mi head when I in de garden and should be tinking 'bout spacing for mi plants. She even float through mi head when she not in mi bed and sleep should come to me. Sometimes I reach over, rub de sheet, touch de extra pillow, and wish I could mek she appear—just like a magician mek a dove appear out of a hat. Sule, why I tink bout dis woman so? Someting tell me she belong here wid me, but dat someting can just be Yappy.

Yes, she's Babylon, and maybe she just lonely, but I like dat she turn to me for comfort, and I enjoy every bit of it. I must admit dat when she first reach out, mi ego say: "Zeke, you have to give her a tryout, she giving it to you pon a platta." At least dat is what I tell miself. But, now, I can't bring miself to stop wanting her.

Right now she in America, and I longing for her to come back; a strange feeling I nevah had before. She growing pon me like long beans climbing pon trellis, and I don't know if I should cut it back or let it sprout. If I let dis situation continue to sprout, it can choke off de rest of de plants and overtake de garden. Maybe I trim it back just a little; see what happen. But how? Mi head full of her smooth curvy body, full buxom breasts, and firm backside. De only negative is dat de woman can't cook, even if her life depend pon it! But maybe I can teach her how, like Sabi teach me.

I wait at de edge of de water close to one hour, but Sule nevah come up to meet me. And I wait and watch de fading sun, sit down red and outa shape, burn itself out pon de edge of de horizon. And real slow, I start to walk back to mi cottage, glancing over mi shoulder once in a while to see if he surface.

Just before I round de corner, a big wave crash gainst de shoreline, and I turn 'round and hurry back to de brink of de sea—and Sule— son of Chief Samba and man of wisdom appear.

"My brother, life's usually not just black and white; but there is grey, many shades of grey. And what your eyes alone see is the outside of things which hides a different interior, like the prickly pineapple skin covers the sweet juicy fruit. Or like the manchineel apple, the outside may be smooth and look tasty, but the inside hides a poison that will kill you. You must look at this woman with more than your eyes; you must look with your heart. Has she come to the island as an outsider to squeeze out its beauty, or is she finding her way home? That is the question you must answer. Remember I told you; the past is coming back to connect with the future."

Before I could ask him a question, Sule disappear into de weeds. I play back over and over in mi head what de brother say, 'outsider or coming home' but how?

Lying in bed dat night, Sule words float in mi head: 'what your eyes alone see, is the outside of things.' So, I close mine and try to welcome sleep. I never did get de chance to tell Sule how Jemma body fill out nice, just like Sabi own did. But I will tell him next time.

Chapter 41

Jemma

Jack had to cancel our early fall meet-up, as he and Teo had multiple meetings with university administrators. This Christmas it was New York, and the trip would be a short one—five days, instead of the usual two or three weeks.

As the time drew close, I lacked energy. Zeke gave me gentle massages and was very relaxed about the fact that I wasn't in a romantic mood.

I arrived in New York, and it was a struggle to be with Jack, as I was unwell. I told him that I might have been overworking at the Inn, as we'd received quite a few bookings since the launch of the new website. Jack told me not to worry since he was slowing down himself, and we agreed to a gentle pace, at least for this trip.

Initially, our time together wasn't as taxing on me, since he was caught up with business dealings, and for an entire day and night we were not intimate. I slept much of that time while he spoke with associates in Vienna, Zurich, Barcelona, and Seville. He did, however, make up for it the following day.

I lay in bed and Jack stroked and fondled my ass. A few minutes later he shifted to my breasts. My nipples were quite sensitive, as though I was about to have my period. Come to think of it, I couldn't recall the date of my last period; my heart skipped a beat.

Throughout foreplay, questions coursed through my head. I was present in body but not in mind. *Did I have it a month ago, six weeks ago, or two months ago?* I couldn't remember. His voice jolted me out of my meandering.

"Jemma, your body is glowing more than usual."

My brain fired off dates, and I struggled to pinpoint one.

"Firm and silky to the touch, is how I would describe it. Maybe it's been too long." He clasped both breasts with gentle pressure and looked me in the eyes. "Should we consider moving these meetings up—make them more often. Would you like that?"

"Dear, Jack, your flattery works every time," I said, gently squeezing his butt cheek. "It's busy for both of us. It'll soon settle down." I'd become a politician, giving a charming response, but not answering the question.

By the time we got to intercourse, my breasts were hot and painfully sore, and I bore the discomfort quietly. Later, as Jack slept, I went to the bathroom and examined them. They were definitely larger, which confirmed why I had to loosen my bra hook earlier that day. I returned to bed and stared at the ceiling. I knew.

The following day, Jack and I walked to our favourite coffee shop for breakfast. He gazed at me across the table for a few seconds and then spoke.

"Jemma, are you still enjoying the times we spend together? I ask because it seems like you're not fully here with me. If this arrangement isn't working for you, you would tell me, wouldn't you?"

I hadn't seen that question coming. I gulped my coffee and swallowed hard to deflect from the tight fist swelling at the pit of my stomach. "I'm a bit under the weather, that's what you're sensing. I do look forward to our meetups and spending time with you."

I said this, knowing that things were different. I knew it within the depths of my soul. I was attending to his needs and enjoying all the spoils that came along with it, but something had shifted.

We went back to the apartment and spent the rest of the day in bed. He fell asleep twice with my breast locked between his lips, and I had to gently pry myself away both times. Jack had picked up steam, while I was drifting away. My body still responded to him, but it was a faint echo of what we once had, so I played it up and pretended. I had just over thirty-six hours left in New York and saw it through.

Jack left for Seville early the next morning, and I prepared to leave for Majestic the following afternoon. As Maya was in Europe, the only other connection I made was with Raul to pay some invoices from my European suppliers.

I had to know for sure what was happening inside me, and practically ran to the nearest CVS Pharmacy, barged my way between two teenage girls who probably had the same idea, and grabbed a test kit from the shelf. Standing in line was agony; a woman with an almost full shopping cart was redeeming coupons for almost every item. Finally, I was out and flying down the sidewalk back to the penthouse. The elevator seemed to crawl up to our suite. Inside, I fumbled with the box but managed to do the test. More torture waiting and then, despite my best attempt at willing a different result, I saw the double lines appear. The room closed around me. *Shit, I'm pregnant! What am I going to do now?*

I rubbed my temples to ease the explosions in my head.

I've taken my birth control pills. Is this possible? Maybe it's a false positive. And am I ready to be a mother? I want to be a mother… but to a Black child? Could I handle it? Will the father want this child? And will he continue to want to be with me as the mother of his child? This will put an end to my relationship with Jack. I'll be pregnant, then someone's mother. I'll no longer have the freedom to travel, to be with him. My life will change.

Another image sailed into my head... Oh hell ... my mother! It will blow her mind when she finds out her unmarried daughter is pregnant by a Black Man!

My heart raced; my body quivered. I was overwhelmed and needed a drink.

Before I could stop myself, I leaned a bottle of Barolo to my head and swallowed two large mouthfuls. Slowly my nerves settled, and I drank some more. It was comforting and soon, the bottle was empty, and sleep found me.

I spent a few hours under the covers, trying to figure out how far along I was. I had soup at a nearby café and went for a walk to clear my head, then I returned to bed.

I woke with the renewed knowledge that I had a child growing inside my belly. I considered messaging Maya but decided against it. I needed to figure this one out myself.

I turned in Jack's keys to the concierge, and I gave him a very generous tip. He looked surprised but smiled and thanked me. It could be my last visit to the penthouse.

My flight to the Caribbean was full and had a few firsts: the first time that crying sounds of children on board didn't annoy me; the first time I refused alcohol in business class. The crying reminded me that alcohol was prohibited during pregnancy. I wasn't sure what the outcome of the pregnancy would be, but I didn't want to cause the foetus harm.

The usual five-and-a-half-hour flight was excruciatingly long. I swallowed an anti-emetic mid-flight to keep the nausea from aircraft turbulence at bay.

I promptly fell asleep and woke to the first officer's announcement of our descent into Baptiste. My stomach had settled, and I freshened up with a hot towel before gathering my in-flight belongings. That evening I took a private boat to Majestic and a taxi ride to Seaview. I arrived home to a vase of pink and white roses and a note from Zeke that said: "Welcome Home."

I remembered our conversation about roses and chocolates and tears flooded my eyes. What did this mean? Did he love me, or was he just being welcoming? I'd heard stories about hormonal pregnant women; was I becoming one of them?

Whichever it was, cutting and leaving the flowers was still a sweet gesture. I smelled each bud with a tear-stained face, and then spent the next few minutes showering and settling down. I made myself a cup of tea and retired to my room.

A date of conception was impossible to pinpoint, as was a timeframe for my last period. So much had taken place setting up the Inn that my days had warped into each other. But slowly, very slowly, it dawned on me that at least ten weeks had elapsed, which meant I was at least two months with child. I still hadn't made up my mind what to do, or who to tell, so I went to bed and did nothing.

I woke to the last two guests chatting loudly in the conservatory, getting ready to leave for the airport. I quickly dressed and joined them for breakfast and asked about their stay. They had arrived while I was in New York but had been cared for by our very competent staff. They intended to be back every year for an extended time; I was delighted to learn about the success of their visit.

As the taxi took the visitors away, I looked over and saw Zeke working in the garden. He waved at me with the sunniest smile. I waved back and walked over to thank him for the flowers.

"How was your trip?" he asked.

"It was good, but tiring," I responded.

"And Ms Maya, how is she?"

"I didn't see her this time. She's currently in Europe. I did some work with my assistant in New York, but I was too lacklustre to go shopping or do much."

"You still not well?" His voice portrayed slight worry.

"Let's say I'm a bit… under the weather," I replied with a coy smile.

"Maybe you should see a doctor."

"Maybe I just need some good rest," I fibbed.

"Will you still come over tonight?" Zeke asked, holding still in expectation.

"If you make me some soup, I might. I need to be pampered."

"Okay, soup is at six," Zeke said with a smile, before continuing to trim the peach bougainvillea bush.

"Just promise me you'll hold back some of the spice. Not sure my stomach can handle it tonight." I laughed but meant every word.

"A light broth, coming your way," he announced over his shoulder.

I walked away, my head still exploding with wild imaginings, mostly of Zeke. *He's a kind soul, but will his kindness continue if he finds out his child is in my belly?*

Doubts and fears, my familiar enemies sprung up and began their work.

Maybe if I tell him, he might leave the island and then where will I be? I may never see him again. He'd said he didn't want something to tie him to Majestic. I'd have to start all over... but start what, though? I know he cares about me, but is that enough to stick around me and a kid? Am I prepared to be a single mother? My God, this is flipping scary...

I walked into the kitchen and had a good catch up with Primrose. She had a knack for numbers and coordination and brought me up to speed on how things had progressed during my time away.

We first discussed guest impressions; next, the food items. She flagged the bills that needed to be paid, including the toiletries. The guests loved her balms and oils, especially the fragrant oils she burned at night in their rooms. The extra help had been working out well, and Primrose was overjoyed to be executive chef and supervisor of all. I only stepped in if she needed me. She was doing well as a shareholder, and I was thankful for her. Now, I needed her more than ever. I informed her that I'd be working in my room and then walked up the stairs, through my bedroom door, turned the lock, and crawled into bed. I was exhausted and nauseous. I took another pill and went right to sleep.

Shortly before noon, I awoke, washed my face, changed my shirt, and poured myself some Perrier with a twist of lemon. Primrose would be serving lunch soon, so I went into the conservatory.

I bit into a slice of warm spinach quiche, the buttery pastry melting in my mouth. A fruit salad of juicy pineapple, shards of golden Julie mango, sprinkled with passion fruit, burst in my mouth, as I flipped through the latest trend magazine. But, the nausea returned, and I sipped my sparkling water slowly to keep from heaving. *How could I go over to Zeke's place in this state? I had to find a way, or he would figure it out.*

After another nap, I took two more nausea pills and made my way along the beach to our love nook. By the time I arrived, I was yawning continuously. Zeke greeted me at the door. The kitchen air was redolent with the smell of fresh herbs, as various pots boiled on the stove top. He was ready to fall into our usual pattern, and I smiled and went through the motions. It was wonderful to be with him, but what was happening inside me kept getting in the way. We'd been in bed for about thirty minutes, and he rolled over and looked me in the eyes.

"You not enjoying it… you here with me?" He was cautious in his questioning.

"I'm here with you, and I'm enjoying you." It was the truth, though skewed. "Maybe I need that wonderful smelling soup for some energy. I'm wiped."

"I'll get it now."

He returned with the most delicious seaweed broth, seasoned with sprigs of thyme and shadow beni, aromatic herbs, common in Caribbean cooking. I devoured it. Zeke had said that this soup was a good source of energy and was rich in iron, calcium, iodine, and vitamin B. And I needed energy.

The next few hours were pleasant. We lay in each other's arms, snuggling and making out.

"I miss you a lot dis time, and I can't figure out why," Zeke said, cupping my face with his hand.

"Oh, Zeke, that's so sweet. And those flowers were the nicest treat. Thank you."

"I like being with you, Jem… it's easy … not too much fuss, and I like dat. De flowers… well, it was my way of showing you…" He squeezed and kissed me.

Those bloody speculations started to course through my head again. *Tell him! Tell him now! No, wait… he said he likes that being with you is easy, and no fuss. Telling him will change everything. It's good right now, so why not keep it that way? But my belly will continue to grow so how can I… Stop it, Jemma! Stop!*

"I like being with you too, Zeke, let's keep it this way." I don't know why I said those words, but it felt like the right sentiment at the time.

"You staying over, right?" Zeke asked as he stroked my hair.

"I should go back. I'm expected to be on an international call very early, and I need my sleep…. lover." I kissed him on his right cheek.

"Okay, one more snuggle before you go." He reached for my breasts, and a replay of my last night with Jack took place. As he buried his head in my chest and locked his lips around my nipples, I squinted and squirmed. The soreness was unbearable; I gently kissed his locks and eased myself free.

"Come on… let's get dressed and go. I've got to be in bed before midnight."

As we walked back along the beach, a silvery moon shone brightly across the water, and rolling foamy waves gently swept the shoreline and slid back into the sea. Zeke held my hand most of the way, stopping once to playfully pat my ass.

"We nevah did it in a moonlit sea," he said slyly.

"When's the next moonlight night?" I teased.

"Maybe tomorrow?"

"Maybe tomorrow, then," I responded with a smile.

He walked with me to the kitchen door and kissed me as he had done a few times lately. I figured he was much surer of himself and our relationship, and I didn't object. I wasn't certain Primrose knew or cared that we were sleeping together. I didn't flaunt it nor purposefully try to keep it a secret anymore.

I walked by Primrose's room; her door was closed. I surmised that she must have turned in early. If guests were at the manor, she often stayed up well past midnight to ensure everyone was having a full Seaview experience.

I sat on the chaise in my room and tried to put my life in perspective. Zeke was one of the kindest men I'd ever known. He'd never taken advantage of me in any way, though I was here on the island, single and alone. The only gift he'd ever wanted from me was me. I was enough. As I grew to know this man, my feelings had changed. Jack gave me all the material things I wanted, but Zeke has shown me that simple things are equally valuable: like caring, joy, kindness, walking along moonlit beaches and having tea on quiet evenings.

My shower and bed were a welcome treat. Increasingly, it would become a challenge to be with Zeke. I'd jumped through many hoops with him tonight to keep my secret, but it weighed me down.

As the cool shower droplets washed over my tender and engorged breasts, I decided that I needed to begin a new relationship with Zeke. I wanted him to choose me for me, and not because he felt obliged to, as the father of my child, a child he might not want. So, the following day I made an appointment with an obstetrician. Two days later, I travelled to Baptiste to see Dr Channing, a sixty-something year-old female physician. An examination and ultrasound soon confirmed my eleven-and-a-half-week pregnancy.

"There are two foetuses; you're carrying twins Ms Worley," Dr Channing said in a matter-of-fact tone.

I swallowed hard. "Twins?"

"Yes, twins. And before you ask, it's too early to tell the sex of the babies," she said and smiled at me.

She must have seen the terror in my eyes because she immediately asked if I was prepared for this pregnancy.

"I'm not ready for one, let alone two ..." I replied. My head was spinning, and my heart raced. It all sounded surreal.

I had shared two lovers across the globe; savoured an

upscale home on a charming Caribbean Island overlooking the sea, travelled the world with a man who catered to my desires in New York, Bellagio, Copenhagen, Berlin, Alsace, and Rome. Even just the freedom of sleeping in or splashing in the grand pool at Seaview; these babies would change all of it. And a deeper doubt and fear welled up from somewhere. I had always wanted children, still wanted them. But could I be the kind of mother I'd never had myself? I was my mother's daughter. Was she lurking inside me, waiting to come out, to belittle, reject, and meet only her own needs? I couldn't be sure, wasn't ready, might never be and took a deep breath and exhaled slowly. *I'll have to return these children ... maybe I can bring them back another time.*

Dr Channing must have recognised that I was overwhelmed as we talked further about my readiness for motherhood. We discussed my apprehension about the timing of the pregnancy, and I admitted that I wasn't ready. We explored options.

Twenty minutes later, I'd completed my paperwork for termination. The procedure would be done at the clinic in a week's time. I purchased some anti-nausea medicine and headed back to Majestic.

That night, Zeke and I had our moonlight rendezvous. We began on the beach near his cottage with a small picnic. He had prepared a lemon babaganoush, made with eggplant, and served with strips of red, yellow, and orange sweet peppers, all from his vegetable garden. The roasted yuca sticks were smoky and flavourful, and the mint iced tea was a perfect balm that settled my uneasy stomach. Later we smoked some weed and basked in the sea. It was one of the best beach forays I'd experienced in a while, and also my secret celebration. I'd made a decision and would soon be able to continue this chosen lifestyle without being bogged down with the uncertainties that came with single motherhood.

I rolled over on the sand and looked at him. "I was thinking, Zeke, do you still feel the same way about the partnership deal I offered you earlier? It's just that you work so hard... Primrose has taken me up on it, and she's been doing well financially. I'd love for you to have the same opportunity."

"She might have more money, but that ain't everyting. Peace of mind is worth a lot more to me. I like simple tings, like working de land, enjoying de sea, a bit of ganja, some meditation, and a good woman. And I have all dem tings right here, right now. A lil bit a money can't change dat!" Zeke closed his eyes, threw his head back, and laughed.

"But you'll let me know if you change your mind, won't you? I'm so lucky to have found you." I meant every word.

"No worries. Here, take anodda hit." He passed me the spliff, and I sucked slowly and deeply, then I stretched out on my back across the sand.

"These girls seem fuller tonight." He kissed my left

breast and stroked me gently.

"Could be they're just happy to be with you." Now I'd become a proficient liar and didn't like it one bit.

"See? Dat right dere is worth more dan money," he said with a hearty laugh.

"I'm going to Barbados for business, soon. I might only be gone two days." Another lie!

"You want me to come with you? De next guests arrive late next week; I have some time to kill."

If I hadn't been lying down, I would have collapsed at his choice of words. *Kill.* My stomach tightened, as though the children had heard and were responding. I struggled to recover quickly.

"I'd love for you to come, but I'm meeting a few of my American buyers at a conference. I won't have any time." I felt like a fraud. Lies and more lies.

"Alright, just come back home as soon as you can."

"Yes, I will. How about one for the road?" I was exhausted but wanted to compensate for the pack of lies I'd just told.

"Yes, ma'am...sea or land?" he giggled.

"Sea, please." The cool salt water was soothing on my weary body. Being intimate was much, much more pleasurable and comfortable this way, the water's buoyancy a bonus.

We kissed, swam, and made love some more. Zeke showered me with massages and salty kisses and every inch of it was wonderful.

"I probably won't see you until after I'm back. Will you

take time away or stay around the manor while I'm gone?"

"Mi garden need some care, so I might spend de time home. Baptiste might be a nice getaway too. You need anyting doing here?"

"No, please have a few days off, Zeke. I'll see you when I'm back."

Later that night, I packed a small overnight bag and placed it in my closet. Two days till 'T-day.'

The only thing I wanted was to have this situation resolved. I'd spent the night tossing and turning. Dawn broke, and I hadn't slept a wink.

I worried and questioned whether I had made the right choice. In one sense, I was low-spirited knowing motherhood would have to wait… but joyful that I'd be able to resume life as I loved it. I was a mess.

I arrived at the clinic at 10:00 a.m., as required for the scheduled noon procedure, and I could leave around 5:00 p.m., barring any complications. The receptionist escorted me to a shaded room with a twin bed, a tiny locker to store my belongings, and a white wicker chair similar to the one in Zeke's living room. She mentioned that Dr Channing was attending an emergency C-section, so my procedure would be a bit delayed. I thanked her and sat on the bed. She stepped back into the hallway and encouraged me to buzz for her if I needed anything, then walked down the hallway.

I closed the door. Overcome with exhaustion, I crawled into the bed and fell asleep faster than I could count to ten. I must have been asleep for less than fifteen minutes when a sudden gust of wind blew in, the blinds separating.

There was Antonia, dressed in a blue silk brocade dress and bodice embroidered with gold metal thread, and a drop front skirt. On her head she wore a pale blue bonnet trimmed with white lace and tied with a silk sash.

She sat down in the chair at the foot of the bed. I noticed that she had two tiny bundles—one in each arm. She set them down on her lap and slowly unwrapped them; two infants cooed softly up at her. One baby raised its little arm to touch Antonia's face, and the crooked little finger came into view.

A gasp escaped my lips and a sharp pain shot through me when I saw the tiny hand. It wasn't until then that I realised fully where I was and why. I was there to kill my beautiful babies and maintain my cushy lifestyle.

Antonia rose from the chair and walked over to the bed, laying one baby on her left shoulder, she held the little girl out to me. I froze looking up into Antonia's eyes, which were like pools reflecting all the ancient sadness of Seaview Manor: from the sugar mill to the mounds of earth covering the remains of precious children… those children, murdered with casual disregard, out of an act of petty jealousy. But I also saw a love for me and the generations that followed her. I held my head in my hands and covered my eyes in shame at what I was about to do.

Suddenly I woke up with a start. Clear-headed and determined, I launched myself to the door with one thought in mind: *I have to speak to Zeke!* Then the thought became a scream: *Zeke! Zeke!*

Acknowledgements

"It takes a village" is an appropriate adage for the creation of this work, and I am indebted to the 'villagers' who stepped up to bring this narrative to life. Franz Kafka wrote, "A book must be the axe for the frozen sea within us." I hope this book causes readers to pause and reflect on how life on the beautiful Caribbean Sea could have unfolded over the centuries.

Our world has changed so much since I began writing this novel four years ago, but in some ways it is still the same. Many of the difficult themes I've broached continue to haunt us. I owe my deepest gratitude to family and friends who read and provided comments on multiple drafts. Rosemarie Wright-Alese, and Wendy Blain were two of my early readers and believed in my vision. Ladies, your input helped shape the development of the story line. Thank you.

As the pandemic roared on, and multiple revisions were made, avid readers Christina McLaurine, Sher Bovay, and Carla Blackmore provided excellent feedback. I thank each of you for bringing your keen focus to the writing, and helping me navigate some of the difficult topics.

Grace Wynter, editor at The Writer's Station, did a fabulous job editing this work, expertly flagging sections that needed attention. Grace, your input was invaluable.

Heartfelt thanks to Waubgeshig Rice. Your mentorship and encouragement as I struggled through challenging sections of the manuscript were insightful. Your constructive criticism improved the narrative considerably.

Teya Hollier, I greatly appreciate you taking time out of writing your novel to read and comment on mine. Thank you for providing such encouraging feedback.

Doris Heinrichs, Maurice Glaude, Yolanda T. Marshall, Glen Synowicki and Maria Vespa, are some of the family and friends who rooted for me throughout this journey. Thanks for believing in the worlds I've created. My dear friend Ann Clark, our many neighbourhood walks and joyful laughs we shared along the way sustained me during the evolution of this story. Our friendship is special.

I am grateful to my siblings Sylvia, Marilyn, Norbert, Leslyn, and my niece Carole for their unwavering support. They helped me choose the perfect logo that honours two gutsy women—our grandmothers, and Carole's great grandmothers: Isabel and Leah.

To my life partner Walter Heinrichs, you've been the keenest champion, supporting me in innumerable ways: from the many editorial suggestions, to our vigorous debates on perspectives. We agreed to disagree many times, yet you never gave up on me. Although focused on your second work of nonfiction, you made time to console me when rejections or critiques sometimes came my way. You reminded me that I had an important story to tell. Thank you for your enduring love and for always being in my corner.

About the Author

Eleanor P Sam is the author of *The Wisdom of Rain*, Isalea Publishing, 2022. Born in Guyana, South America, she received her bachelor's degree from York University and her master's degree from University of Toronto. She lives in Toronto, Canada with her husband.